The Power of Sight

Book 1

Contact Information: evolutionofvision.com
Development Editing ⸱ Becky Wallace, Kristin Errico
Copy and In-Line Editing ⸱ Becky Wallace, Kristin Errico
Proofreading ⸱ Kristin Errico
Beta Readers ⸱ Sugandh, Kelly, Kristina

ISBN: 979-8-9914925-0-8

First Edition: August 2024
10 9 8 7 6 5 4 3 2 1

E⊙lution
of
Vision

The
Power
of
Sight

Robert Andrew Sturm

Dedication

To the three angelic figures in our midst and the heavenly protector keeping watch from above.

Contents

World
of
Change

1

Past

Nicolaus focused on the blood trickling from his hands instead of the dead child cradled in his arms. Every time he glanced at the small, round face, his sister's ghost appeared before him, blurred by the tears that streamed down his cheeks.

He had witnessed the carnage and the atrocities in Yemen, Sudan, Ukraine, Syria, and more. He'd seen the true evil of drug lords, human traffickers, and tyrants. The worst humankind offered ricocheted through his memories, a reminder of the four years he spent engaged in secret missions and covert operations. Yet, the weight of this child's body cooling in his arms triggered more horror and heartache in him than all those memories combined.

Nicolaus wanted to make a difference. He wanted to save the innocent from the crusades of warmongers, who terrorized and threatened to rain hell upon the earth. But everyone had a limit. And he feared that, after four long years in these trenches, he may have finally reached his.

María, another in their elite squad, ran up to him, still carrying her assault rifle, and put her left hand on Nicolaus's shoulder. "We did the best that we could."

He nodded and took in the surrounding scene. The acrid smell of chemicals and decomposing bodies overwhelmed his senses, burned his nose, and stung his throat. Their "best" freed over forty human trafficking victims and brought down a notorious methamphetamine drug lord, so the mission was a success by most measures.

Nicolaus focused on Akari as she strode out of the Myanmar compound, silhouetted against the flames shooting out of the building. Her famous swagger and powerful posture dissolved his worries and reaffirmed his resolve.

Akari stopped in front of them, took in the young child, and recognized the pain in Nicolaus's eyes. She scanned around the landscape, her eyes narrowing against the smoke.

"María, grab some of those lotus flowers in the ornamental pond." As María hurried off, Akari lifted the little girl out of Nicolaus's arms and laid her on the ground.

Across the driveway, an injured assailant pleaded, but Veton, otherwise known as Dodge, the fourth crew member, shot two rounds into the man's skull. "Fuck you and your synthetic drugs."

María returned, placed the lotuses on the little girl's chest, and called Dodge over. Akari hugged Nicolaus tight before they all locked hands, closed their eyes, and said a prayer. "Amen."

"Yo, we have to go lickety-split," Dodge said, even as they moved out. "The dirtbag we exterminated has another facility like an hour away, and his brother will want retribution. We either face another sixty cockroaches or bug out and let the Federation clean them up."

Nicolaus reloaded his gun while Akari unmuted her microphone to speak with the command center. "Four Shadows of Light, ready to roll out. Targets eliminated. Are all the friendlies safe and evacuated?"

"Affirmative," replied the command center. "Everyone is aboard trucks, and air support is on standby for coverage. Follow the yellow brick road and get your asses to the extraction point now!"

Each member jogged to the field, their guns held tight against their ribcage, ready for any unexpected surprises. Nicolaus's hands tingled, and he peeked over his shoulder just as the last adversary prepared to shoot him from a tree.

A rapid succession of gunfire erupted, followed by the sound of a body thudding onto the ground. Akari winked at Nicolaus as she sauntered by him, a silent recognition passing between them. All four of them sensed an instinctive and Divine power in the air, as if an ethereal voice whispered in their minds, helping them to save the innocent or showing them a precise back door route to surprise and eliminate their draconian enemies.

When they reached a safe distance, Nicolaus pointed his finger at María. "Do your thing and blow it back to hell."

She pulled out the detonator. "With fucking pleasure, cousin." The compound lit up the night sky as if the sun were hosting a surprise birthday party.

"Another asshole bites the dust." María fist-bumped Dodge.

Akari gripped Nicolaus's right hand, leaning close to him as she whispered, "I love you, and your tears only make you more irresistible to me."

Dodge smirked at María and turned on his microphone. "Dude, a live mic. Don't want to hear your cute little hormonal thing."

Akari flicked him off.

"Queen Teuta over here," Dodge said, referring to María, "She doesn't kiss during battle because she's loaded with head-ripping estrogen. You two are, like, so the opposite. Let me kill a guy, and then let's kiss."

Akari glared back at Dodge, raising an eyebrow. "Please confirm you have the trade documents and flash drive?"

"Yes, I do, mother dearest."

"Good," she grumbled, her tone sharp. "Now, zip it."

María smirked. Dodge had always been the class clown of the bunch. "You're lucky she doesn't kick you in the nuts right now."

In the distance, the military chopper sliced through the air, its powerful rotors creating a deafening roar and stirred up the musty scent of the swamp.

"Job well done," said Veda Devi, the CEO of the United Federation of Enforcement over the microphone. "Your efforts and impact on both the country and the world have far exceeded our expectations. Mr. Zhao from the Coalition also extends his congratulations. Enjoy your retirement from special operations."

Akari responded as she entered the helicopter. "It's been an honor for all of us, and we're happy to start our civilian lives."

María climbed into the helicopter as her skin encountered the heat emanating from the powerful engines and tossed her gun onto the floor. After Dodge and Nicolaus jumped in the chopper, the pilot gave a thumbs up and the Four Shadows of Light felt the rush of wind and the sensation of weightlessness as they rose into the night sky. They peered down upon the last battlefield they had conquered as Green Berets.

Nicolaus stroked his goatee on their promise to unravel the mystery surrounding the true essence of their Divine power. With her eyes closed, Akari concentrated on her breathing and mapped out an approach to their own investigation into the Federation and the Global Reform Establishment Coalition or referred to as GREC.

Dodge strummed his hands on the gun in his lap, and he realized that was the last time they would use their super trooper abilities in the military. Dodge smacked his lips. "So that was it. No more doing our saving the world of military things."

"Let's not think of it that way." Akari took a slow and steady breath. "It's the start of the next chapter in our lives. That was only the beginning. We have so much to learn."

Nicolaus moved his hand over Akari's. "Now the fun begins—finding out the who, what, when, where, and why." He winked at María.

María gritted her teeth, desperate for answers about her mom's and Nicolaus's families' deaths. Although her mother, Julieta, played a pivotal role in starting the UFE, she couldn't help but sense the ten year-long investigation was an orchestrated coverup. Suspicion coursed through her veins, directed towards Veda, the UFE, and the Coalition.

Birthday
of
María

2

Present

María bursts into laughter and snorts at Dodge as they exit his jacked up, heavy-duty pickup truck. They survey the vibrant green front yard plastered with colorful birthday lawn decorations. The festive display of a HAPPY BIRTHDAY, MARÍA VALKYRIE! sign with enormous letters, streamers hanging in the trees, and a big 26 sign dangling from the porch ceiling matches the flowers sprinkling the beds.

María keels over laughing when she sees a sign in front of her dad's home, declaring You Must Be This Height to Enter.

"Ha, ha, ha," Dodge says, tone as dry as the desert. "Your dad thinks he's so funny. You're how old? And Marcin still decorates like you're sixteen."

"You're just jealous that he always outdoes your handiwork."

He twitches his head, his brows furrowing as he considers her point. Since Julieta's death—María's mom—her father showered her with excessive attention and affection. As they

6

enter the house, Dodge folds the sign in half, taking it from six to three feet so that at five-foot-five he's allowed to enter. From the corner of his eye, he catches Marcin peeking through the window.

Did a party store vomit in María's childhood home? Maybe. It seems her dad had spent hours cleaning, shopping, and decorating. Piñatas, balloon bouquets, and banners litter the small space.

"Dad? What is all this?"

"It's not every day your favorite child turns twenty-six," he says with a chuckle.

"Dad, I'm your only child."

"See, my favorite, no competition." He gives María an enormous hug and kisses her on her forehead. "María Valkyrie Landowski-Jiménez, you look more and more like your mamá every day." His voice wavers on the last few words, like he'd shed tears any second.

He has a lot to be proud of. María is her mother's daughter, a natural-born leader, tough as nails, cunning like a fox, and brilliant. He didn't love the tattoos on her arms, but at least they showcased both her mom's Mexican heritage and her dad's Polish ancestry.

"So, what's brewing for breakfast?" Dodge smiles from ear to ear.

Marcin smirks at Dodge and gives him a firm handshake. "Perogies, eggs, grits, and fruit."

Dodge licks his lips. There's nothing quite like the blend of Marcin's cuisine.

María grabs Dodge's hand and heads into the kitchen, where Nicolaus and Akari are already chilling and drinking some organic wine at the wet bar. Akari's parents live next door to Marcin, so she and Nicolaus had coffee and a garden walk before venturing across the yard for the party.

They greet each other like they haven't seen one another in ages, exchanging secret handshakes and tight hugs. Their families have been through tough times together, and they would risk their lives to save each other. Family is blood.

"Where're your parents, Akari?" María asks.

"They're in the garden and thought we should have some time to ourselves. They mentioned Marcin has a special gift for you."

"Alright." Marcin throws his hands up in excitement. "The smartest human in the world is here." He beams at his daughter.

"Which one of us is that?" Akari asks, a beautiful twinkle in her cat-like eyes. "After all, we're technically tied in the brain's category."

María gives her a fist bump. "Third and fourth weren't that far behind," she says. Smiles spread across their faces. They won't let the guys forget they crushed the SATs and had higher academic grades.

"Yes, we know girls are smarter than boys," Nicolaus says, pulling Akari in for a kiss that has Marcin clearing his throat to remind the young couple that they aren't alone.

"Dude, we got paintball reserved for later today at the Warring Combat Zone. It's thirty on thirty. Army versus marines," Dodge says, while drumming his feet on the floor.

María's lips stretch into a wicked grin. "We are so going to take down those suckers. The Four Shadows of Light are unstoppable, especially against marines."

"Where's Herculano and Catalina?" Dodge asks while he piles food on his plate from the buffet breakfast.

Marcin takes off his chef apron and replies, "They can't join us with the hectic breakfast rush."

When Dodge made the move from Michigan to Texas ten years ago, he found a welcoming home with Herculano and Catalina Vargas. They became his guardians, allowing him to enroll in the same high school as Nicolaus, Akari, and María. The Vargas's managed the Texas location of Julieta & Marcin's Café, while his parents manage the Michigan location.

After they finish breakfast, Marcin and Akari put twenty-six candles on the homemade pomegranate and mango-filled, two-tiered vanilla cake. The level-of-detail Akari puts into everything, even the placement of candles, reflects her work ethic as the lead scientist at her parents' company, DaeChie Pharmaceuticals.

Nicolaus can't resist staring at Akari, and he doesn't even feel guilty about it. Earlier in the morning, while still in their pajamas, they had a deep discussion about how to solve Alzheimer's. Now she's in a sleeveless dress from her Hawaiian hometown, glorious tan skin, and Japanese-Hawaiian features. Few people—including modeling agencies—could turn away. Even after sixteen years of knowing her, he can't help himself.

"Nicolaus, you're doing the dreamy thing again," María says with a giggle.

"I'm sorry. She drives me wild. I was just thinking about a conversation we had this morning. She gave me some great ideas about my mechanical concept on a robotic prosthetic, mimicking every pattern of a biological arm."

"Kinda like that robot kills humankind movie," Dodge says, gazing at his spicy friend with benefits. "You know, where María would be the badass to take them all out?"

Marcin gives Dodge a hard look. "Like *Terminator*? Does everything with you revolve around movies?"

"Totally. Cause your daughter is like"—he motions his hands like he's holding a machine gun—"an angel of death while being a testosterone tempest," Dodge says, causing a flush to rise in María's cheeks.

Before Marcin can rebut, Akari lights the candles. "Nicolaus, no helping María this year."

Marcin sings an operatic version of "Happy Birthday," and everyone joins in while Akari walks to the table holding the vivid white cake with sunflower icing.

The Mexican sunflower was María's mom's favorite. María remembers the yard and flowerbeds lined with honey-scented flowers as a child. Julieta read María military strategy books on a rocking chair Marcin placed in the middle of the garden. Before María blows out the candles, she peeks at her dad, and a tear rolls down his face. She winks, and then, with a single puff, all the candles go out as if a sudden gale rushed through the kitchen.

After Nicolaus and Akari clear out the candles, Marcin presents María with her gift from Dodge. She rips open the wrapping to unveil a collector's edition army action figure that stands a foot tall and is still in its original packaging.

"That was like crazy to bid on. Some other dude was outspending me for it, but you know I don't quit until I win." Dodge shoots a dirty glimpse at Nicolaus, who can't help but laugh because he drove up the price. María leans over and kisses Dodge while her dad moves back to the kitchen to get the ice cream ready, avoiding the scene.

She opens Akari's gift, and just like every birthday, it's a new photo book of all their adventures from the previous year decorated with stickers and crafting supplies. Without delay, María dives in. The first photo is of the two of them posing beside the River Walk fountain in San Antonio. Their arms and a single leg were in the air for the cheesy social media photo op.

Akari places the first slice of birthday cake in front of María, kisses her on the top of her head, "I love you, sister. Besties and family for life."

María stands up, and they hug. "I love you too." As María wipes a second tear away from her cheek, she notices the comical grin on Nicolaus's face. "What the hell did you get me?"

He grabs a poster-sized gift and two smaller boxes and sets them in front of María. "I couldn't decide which one, so I got you all three."

María's eyes light up—shining like a kid on Christmas morning—as she opens the wrapping, revealing a collection of autographed football jerseys, rookie cards, and a game-day championship ball. María, no matter what team or sport, roots for a player who went through the military and joined professional sports. With her love for the Dallas teams, the choice was a simple decision. María hugs her cousin, while her dad finishes slopping the ice cream into birthday bowls.

After serving everyone, Marcin clears his throat. "Your mom asked me to wait until you were twenty-six years old to give this to you." He pulls a small jewelry box from his pants pocket and hands it to her.

She opens the box, unveiling a platinum, gold, and bronze diamond studded locket on a sparkling chain. In the center of the pyramid-shaped locket, an embossed symbol catches her eyes. "It's outright beautiful. What does the—"

Before María finishes, Marcin glances at the four of them. "Throughout your entire lives, you've known of your extraordinary physical, mental, and spiritual gifts beyond the norm. We didn't hide the fact that a Divine entity has blessed each of you. However, it's imperative to understand that the powers you possess serve a greater purpose than even what you achieved in the military. I don't know all the specifics, and I can only guess what the future will hold, but I know that this is the beginning of a remarkable journey y'all will do together. Be prepared, be steady, be faithful, be true to each other."

María and her father embrace when Dodge interrupts them. "Are you two done with the sappy crap? I want to get my ice cream and cake on."

Marcin huffs, and they unlock from the hug to eat the homemade cake and ice cream. Marcin's hearty belly and well-kept graying beard, and warm smile match his love for sweets almost as much as cooking at his restaurant.

"Remember when María went crazy ballistic after I sabotaged her go-kart?" Dodge says, swirling his ice cream.

Nicolaus grins with a slight glance at the necklace as he finishes his last bit of cake. "I actually won a race without my inventions."

"The only time you can beat me, cousin, is when Dodge pulls a prank."

He chuckles to himself, reflecting on how those outside his close circle often underestimate his intelligence. His father named him after Nicolaus Copernicus, the well-known Polish astronomer. With his captivating green eyes and strong, muscular build, he stands out as the tallest member of the group. His striking appearance comes from his South Korean mother and Polish father.

As the locket swings forward from María's chest, Nicolaus catches sight of the emblem, and like a sudden burst of salty ocean spray hitting his face. "María, I need a closer look at that symbol on your locket." She senses a tension on his scrunching face, lifts the locket out to him, and leans closer to provide him a better view. Nicolaus's eyes widen and the hair on his neck stands up. "I haven't seen this since I was a kid—"

"You've seen this before?" María glares at him.

"Well, I—um, my mom showed my sister and myself a drawing—"

Marcin interjects, "Wow—look at the time. You should get going."

"We'll discuss on the way to paintball." Akari rubs the back of Nicolaus's shoulder blade. "Don't be mister serious while we enjoy your cousin's birthday." He nods his head, and then a tiny clumping of icing smacks him in the face.

"Yeah, don't be the party pooper, even though you're not telling us something," María says, licking the evidence of her attack off her finger.

Nicolaus shifts his gaze from the necklace to the partygoers and musters a smile. "Sorry, y'all. I just need a moment to think."

Akari wipes the frosting from his cheek and then pops it into her mouth to break the tension. "Compliments to the chef."

Akari and Nicolaus leave the party first, strolling to their five-passenger battle cruiser parked in Akari's parent's driveway and spots Keanu and Chie gardening in the front yard.

"We're off to play some paintball," Akari says as she hugs her mom. Akari's radiant smile mirrors that of her moms, along with her athletic physique.

"You've got that inquisitive, confused look on your face," Keanu says. His eyes are warm, deep brown, with crinkles at the corners, gray eyebrows pulled in a tight line, and a smile wrapped in a full gray goatee. "What's bothering you?"

"Nothing . . ." Nicolaus's voice trails off before deciding to say what's on his mind. "Marcin gave María a locket, and something about it feels familiar."

"Regarding?"

Nicolaus pauses, sorting through memories he'd rather not revisit. "Something my parents showed me before. . ."

Keanu strokes his forearm. "There's no denying you four are something special, but even so, we've been so careful—"

"Stop discussing outside!" Chie says as she waves a hand between the men. Her long hair slants across her back, and her golden hue skin flushes red.

"Yes, my dear." He gives a chuckle, but something about it sounds forced to Nicolaus's ear. "If you want to avoid any conflicts," he cautions, "it's wise to agree with the ladies, as they are always right."

Akari directs her gaze toward Nicolaus. "I'll drive so you can think." With a nod, they hop into their tricked-out, off-roading 4x4 truck, decked out in army green and loaded with all the accessories needed for a bug-out vehicle or battle-grade encounter. Akari named the off-roading monster the Slayer, paying homage to her favorite anime show.

Meanwhile, Dodge strides out with his arms loaded with the gifts and begins putting them in his mammoth pickup truck. María hugs and kisses her dad near the porch doorway.

"I'll see you in a couple of days. Godspeed," Marcin says as she steps off the porch, his long, salt and pepper hair flowing in the wind. He smirks in Dodge's direction. "Why isn't María driving? I didn't think you were old enough."

Dodge huffs and squints his eyes at Marcin. "What'd they say back in your day—oh yeah—I'll get some telephone books." Dodge grabs the empty metal cooler Marcin left out on the porch for them to take on their paintball adventure.

Akari backs the rumbling giant out of her parents' driveway and pulls up next to Dodge's hulking truck. Nicolaus rolls down his window, "Let's go lay spray the marines!"

"Yo, why not the muscle car? That 1970s speed demon brings the heat," Dodge squawks.

"The art of war—intimidation," Nicolaus says, managing a cheeky grin, even though his mind is still contemplating the symbol and the locket. "Besides, Akari won't let me drive it. She's obsessed with keeping it in mint condition, and I'll ruin it with my constant coffee habit."

"Plus, he has such a lead foot," she chimes in, recalling his two speeding tickets in the past eight months.

María climbs up the beast of a vehicle, leers at Dodge, and points backward toward the road for him to get moving. Dodge shakes his head as he pauses for her to buckle up, and then, with a turn of a key, the truck starts with a loud rumble.

Before Akari drives off, she gazes at Nicolaus and asks for a kiss. Naturally, he agrees, and right as he does, the vehicle, inch by inch, creeps forward with the audible sound of the engine. They stop kissing, and he laughs at her. "Now who's forgetful?"

Akari blushes back at Nicolaus. "Your habits are rubbing off on me. Now focus and think—the locket stirred up something in your mind."

"I know I'm like an open book with my emotions, as you say. I wear them on my sleeves."

Nicolaus fidgets with a small glitter container in his pocket he kept with him for good luck from his sister. He ponders how they got so accustomed to their Divine sixth sense during their time in the army and in academics. He's frustrated by their lack of understanding of the origins, limitations, and full potential of their abilities. Their parents only told them so much, even as they pestered them with questions. *Why?* He knows the locket has a special meaning, but what? Nicolaus grips the bottle a little stronger with a sense of frustration slithers over his body. All they heard was "when the time is right" or "not the time"—*who's deciding the timing?*

Secret of Shamrock

3

Present

"Did you pack everything?"

Dodge laughs. "No, I forgot your mini war arsenal. Of course. I'm not an idiot."

"That's debatable, my little lover boy." María tightens her grip on her necklace, feeling a sudden pull toward the window. Lost in contemplation, she wonders why her father gave her the locket at this moment. What is the significance of this timing?

Dodge isn't oblivious to her wandering thoughts and wants to redirect María's attention away from memories of her mother and her premature death to happier things. He clicks the military-grade satellite communications device to connect with Akari and Nicolaus, who are driving ahead of them. "Are the drones, camouflage, and paintball goodies in your battle wagon, Nicolaus?"

When his focus doesn't shift from the landscape rushing past his window, Akari grabs the comms set. "We're ready for some logistical cremations. Nicolaus is in his own little world right now."

Chuckling, Dodge remarks, "María's doing the same trance thing. Must be a Landowski family thing, you know, all serious and dramatic."

"Let her think, Dodge, and we'll chat when we stop at Winnie's."

"Yes, ma'am," Dodge says with a cackle.

Nicolaus can't sink into the banter. His mind is stuck in a loop, recounting the Shamrock Lake trip. He recalls the cozy, vintage log cabin in the Cascade Range east of Seattle. It felt like a home away from home during their school vacation between Christmas and the New Year. The crackling fireplace, steaming cups of hot cocoa, and fierce competition in board games set the stage for their relaxed mornings. When dusk arrived, the sweet smell and warm taste of homemade soups, like rosół, a Polish chicken soup, or tteok mandu guk, a Korean rice cake soup with dumplings, filled the family's appetite.

Before their departure on New Year's Day, the family soaked in the landscape's beauty, with frozen waterfalls gracing the rocky mountain slopes. During their Cascade adventures in the winter, Nicolaus created nicknames for each family member. The leader, Dae, his mother, was Captain Whitehawk as her eyes darted back and forth, aware of their surroundings. The captain's first mate, Magnar, his father, was Snow Bear because he strapped a large backpack with the tent on his back, fishing rods, a shovel, and utility items while clomping through the snow-covered terrain, leaving giant footprints. His sister, Mi-Cha's, codename was Storm Fox, as she moved with sly grace through the adventures. When a forest creature revealed itself, she behaved like a thunderstorm, loud and booming, bolting toward the poor animal. Nicolaus named himself Ice Rock as he climbed faster than everyone, and his confidence never wavered.

Nicolaus noticed his mom, steady and aware, emitting an aura of tension and anxiousness like a pulsating beacon. Mi-Cha had asked why they didn't bring the skis or skates, and their mom mentioned this was a vital quest.

"You must focus as we near the three lakes and push through the evergreens." Dae motioned to the farthest body of frozen water. "That's Shamrock Lake." She peeked back at Magnar, walking ten feet behind her as they neared the east portion of the water, and then pointed to a mini cliff near the lake's southwest side.

"The chamber is over there." Dae leaned forward.

Before the family walked to the crevice, Magnar and Dae dropped their gear next to a solid, iced-over lake. The only item Magnar took with him was a worn wood and metal snow shovel.

"Take off your backpacks and place them next to ours," he instructed them. The family walked toward the towering cliffs, and Nicolaus observed his dad's double gun holsters with sidearms enclosed. An unsettling sensation churned in his stomach. *Why would he bring his sidearms?* He thought his dad had brought the rifle for hunting or scaring bears or wolves away. But his mom was carrying too. She had a white holster strapped to her thigh over her snow camouflage.

As they followed their mom onto the snowy mountainside, they passed boulders strewn about, with some hugging the bottom of the cliff wall. Dae moved to a grouping of boulders, some the size of a tire and others the size of a basketball. With her heart pounding, Dae's eager eyes locked onto her husband. "It's here." The family removed the snow surrounding the boulders, and then their parents worked in unison to roll the heavy boulders away, revealing a hidden iron hatch square door that was covered in ice. His dad picked up the snow shovel and, with a couple of loud clangs that pierced the silence, revealed a symbol. She waved for the kids to come closer.

"Mom, what does the circle's symbol mean? You told us before it was just drawings that you made at the ranch." Nicolaus asks, pointing to the image on the door.

Dae kneeled down, her eyes filled with a mix of tenderness and urgency. She stared her kids in the eye. "Remember the spot. Don't tell anyone, it's our secret. The true worth of what's inside will become apparent when the time is right." She extended her hands, and both kids grabbed onto them. "Underneath lies a glimpse of your Divine future." She let go and pulled out two lockets from her coat pocket. Their mom instructed Mi-Cha and Nicolaus to put the necklaces on. "I want each of you to touch the Divinities emblem. Mi you go first."

Mi-Cha rushed toward the grate, her eyes widened with excitement, and her hand made a loud thud against the Divinities symbol. A brilliant light shone from her skin, gleaming all around her and casting long shadows on the ground.

"Mom, what is happening?" Nicolaus squeaked. "Why is she glowing?"

Mi-Cha smacked her hands back and forth on the grate. "Mom told us we're special, and I'm now a human sparkle."

Unable to suppress a smile, Nicolaus was about to speak when his father interrupted. "Alright Mi, now it's Nicolaus's turn."

After Mi-Cha moved away from the grate, Nicolaus moved closer to the metal door. He paused for a moment. "Can we go inside the door like a treasure adventure?"

Dae smiled. "Son, it takes more than two lockets to open the door. Just like on an adventure, you need all the pieces for the map. Each of the lockets has a code to a specific person, so we will give you the lockets when you are older and you will come back to this spot."

"But who has the other lockets? And how many are there? And where does the glow come from?"

Magnar chuckles. "Nicolaus Vasili, just touch the door." He winks at his son, knowing the answers will arrive when the Divinities decide the precise moment. "Always so many questions, my little inventor. Trust us."

Nicolaus nodded his head in agreement, brushed his fingers over the door, and radiated with the same glowing energy.

Mi-Cha laughed and pointed at him. "Nicolaus, now you're shining like my coat."

"Alright kids, go with your mom." Magnar smirked as he exhaled; his breath materialized into tiny clouds in the cold air.

Dae grasped their hands and guided them to take a step back, allowing Magnar to maneuver the boulders back into position. Dae led Mi-Cha and Nicolaus toward their belongings and explained the significance of Shamrock Lake, symbolizing the Holy Trinity. "The Trials of Divinity will start when you're older. The *tri* means three."

"Kinda like you, Akari's, and María's mom together. Like triplets."

"Similar but different, Mi-Cha. The three represent tests to complete when the time comes. Right now, what I need you both to do is to stay focused on your academics, spirituality, and martial arts training." She glanced at Nicolaus. "The chamber within is your future."

They heard their dad grunting as he used the shovel to cover their tracks, flinging snow like a snowblower to ensure no soul detected a group of people had disturbed the rocky surroundings. While they put their backpacks back on, Nicolaus admired the view, contemplating about the chamber and the Divinities symbol, oblivious to his sister's machinations. A snowball smacked him in the face. Mi-Cha clutched her stomach and rolled in the snow with a bellowed laugh.

Dae motioned for them to follow, and for a mile, the family was silent. Only the crunch of the snow beneath their feet provided any accompaniment to their steps. Nicolaus noticed his mom still wore an anxious appearance, but was in better spirits as she smiled and kissed his dad on the cheek.

As they neared the three-mile mark on their return journey, they took a break, sipping warm green tea from their thermal cups and eating non-GMO fig bars while perched on a fallen tree. Nicolaus asked, "Can I tell my cousin María about the spot?"

"María, Akari, and Veton will see this spot for themselves without you two saying a word. When you all experience the Divine visions from Aamirah, it will unveil the locations. It's imperative for us to keep the secret for now." Dae smiled, taking in the serene landscape that stretched before her. She envisioned her children, with their unique abilities, shaping the world's future.

"The shimmering glow you just witnessed is the mere beginning of your transformation. As time passes, you will experience visions that will guide you toward the future, tapping into the ancient power of Divinity through the power of sight. The consequences of not choosing the Divine pathway are dire—darkness would consume every trace of light."

Those words etched into his mind like a burning brand, urging him to stay on the moral trail.

ᐁᐁᐁᐁ

"Hey!" Akari yells, shaking him out of his thoughts as she pulls to the side of the road. She points to his fading, shining arm. "You're glowing like a bio-fluorescent fish."

"What—um—I have no clue. I was just thinking about Shamrock Lake with my family—the locket." Even after all this time, he still hasn't brought up the iron door and the lockets to his closest allies. He realizes he would have to tell them soon, especially after witnessing his hand glow.

Akari views the nervous twitching of his fingers. She says, "Relax and ease your mind."

"When will we know it's the right time? It's frustrating to have some clues, but not all the pieces. I feel as if our parents blindfolded us and sent us soaring into a thick fog. Why don't they tell us more? Why give María the locket and not the rest of us?"

"Keep your patience in line and don't lose your temper." She extends her right hand toward Nicolaus, offering him the comfort of her warm touch. "I know how you are when you can't solve the problem in a flash. Take a couple of deep breaths." Nicolaus inhales and exhales while closing his eyes. As he attempts to calm his nerves, Akari contemplates María's mom's death. She ponders out loud, "That has to be the same glowing, ethereal aura coming out of you, Nicolaus."

Lost in contemplation, his confusion grows to understand his mother's insistence on keeping that trip a secret. Even after all these years, guilt gnaws at him for not telling Akari, María, and Dodge. Nicolaus exhales, regaining his composure, and finds himself unable to glance away from Akari, who beams with a smile, reminding him of a rainbow after a rainstorm.

"I don't know how I'd survive without you."

Akari nudges him. "You best remember that, or else!"

Beginning of Takedown

{4}

Present

The rolling grass stretches before María, a picturesque scene interrupted only by the occasional glimpse of cows ambling by in the distance. As she clutches her locket, the weight of her mother's last moments burdens her heart, each detail etched into her memory.

Julieta and María had dropped off her dad, Marcin, outside San Antonio to help her uncle rebuild the burned down barn on his ranch. With María riding shot gun, Julieta drove their beefed-up, camouflage green and brown, super-sized pickup truck to the south part of Texas to end a cartel dispute with their family.

Julieta's muscles tightened as she spoke to her only child, her voice filled with a mix of concern and love. "This is why I've pushed you so hard. I needed to know that when I'm gone, that'll you'll be able to protect yourself. Whatever comes at us today, especially if the Federation jumps into the mix, you must stay alive at all costs."

"I'll do whatever it takes—but I don't understand," María said, her voice trembling. Her fingers tightened around the grip of the handgun in her waist holster. *Why would the United Federation of Enforcement turn against her mom?* She helped start the Federation. "You won't die today."

"I'm hoping you're right, but promise me, María, if this goes wrong, you will let me go. Your dad will need you."

"I repeat: you're not dying today!"

Julieta sighed as her jet-black hair shined with a hint of mahogany. "Let's just pray the money Nicolaus's parents gave us will repay my brother's debt. These bastards only care about money."

She turned up the volume on the radio, reducing the tension with the rhythmic beats of traditional Mexican music. They listened for the remaining thirty minutes of the drive, winding down roads and through flatlands, before they arrived at the cartel headquarters—a one-story brown brick ranch house with broken shutters.

Julieta pressed the radio knob to turn off the music. "Remember, we have three plans. I will give you the signal if plan one won't work. Stick to the plan that I tell you."

María's eyes darted to the cluster of armed men smoking cigarettes and chewing on toothpicks past the entrance. Julieta parked near the top of the dirt driveway, where María's focus turned to an older Hispanic man. With rifle in hand, he leaned on the railing of the shabby wood porch that was patched with rot and pocked with overgrown weeds.

Julieta's senses tingled, and her intuition screamed a warning of impending danger. She had weighed the pros and cons and knew they had to finish the deal and resolve the dispute with the cartel.

She narrowed her rich chestnut-colored eyes. "Stay in the truck. Get your guns ready, just in case. Look for my hand signal."

Fourteen-year-old María nodded to her mom, then pulled out two sidearms to prepare for a lethal encounter.

Julieta stepped out of the vehicle, her hand gripping the suitcase, and closed the door behind her. She peered through the driver's side window and tapped the side of her head with her index finger, signaling to María to rely on her wits in case of any unexpected trouble. Julieta faced the broken-down house as a one-armed gangster, Javier, appeared from the doorway with his entourage of five tattooed criminals beside him, each armed with military-grade assault weapons they had received as gifts from the United States government.

Under her breath, Julieta muttered, "Fuck, fuck, fuck, clear your head, Julieta. Just clear your head and focus." With a deep breath, she let go of the lingering pain that Javier had caused her in her youth. She marched closer to the porch to complete the payoff as quick as possible, praying things stayed the course.

"I've brought two million dollars so you'll leave my family the fuck alone," Julieta shouted over the thumping of her heart. "Go ahead, count it." She threw the suitcase on the ground and backed up a few steps.

"Juan, count the money," the gang leader said, without breaking eye contact with Julieta.

The tattooed cartel member sauntered over to the case, flipping it open and sifting through the stacks of one-hundred-dollar bills.

"Why does a pretty girl like you have so much money to hand over? Makes me think you got more—Julieta." Things were about to become complicated. *How had Javier identified her so fast?*

She unbuttoned her camouflage vest, which matched her monster truck's camo, revealing a harness with four grenades. She didn't take her eyes off Javier. Julieta moved her right arm behind her back and signaled to María with two fingers, switching from plan one to plan two. Javier laughed, put a cigarette in his mouth, and lit it up.

Things were about to go sideways when the overlord, she guessed, recognized her as the girl who blew off his arm and killed his father and brother.

"You know, Julieta, I owe you. I owe you much pain."

"This is between you and me. You murdered my parents—so an eye for an eye. Stand down now, take the two million, and leave my family alone, or I'll blow this little shithole of yours to the moon."

Javier's nasty face wrinkled. "It's not me you must worry about. It's them." He pointed to the right, revealing fast-moving trucks about three hundred yards away. "I get paid the money no matter what—they paid me more not to engage and let them wipe you off the face of the planet. My job was to delay."

Julieta recognized the vehicles as part of the United Federation of Enforcement.

"Time to die, little heroines. You better get moving. They told me they're going to make you suffer." Javier grinned at Julieta's horrified face and took another puff of his cigarette.

She bolted toward Juan, kicked him in the face, grabbed the suitcase and the walkie-talkie he dropped to the ground, and ran for the driver's side. María vaulted out of the truck, her two sidearms drawn and aimed at their enemies. She fired a few shots, causing the men to scramble for cover.

"Don't fire back at the bitches," Javier yelled at his cartel members, while he ducked to avoid the gunfire. "The Federation will take care of them if we want our money."

María hopped back into their truck and felt the rush of wind as Julieta floored the vehicle, causing dust and gravel to swirl around them. María continued to fire at the cartel compound through the passenger side window as they escaped, the sound of gunshots echoing as she emptied her remaining ammunition. They'd made it a kilo away from the ranch when a fiery explosion flashed in the rearview mirror. Julieta smirked, seeing the lake of fire and sulfur, knowing that at least the Federation erased all traces of Javier, and her family can feel safe from the cartel.

The Federation vehicles turned their attention to Julieta's battle tank. The solid black SUVs with octane-tinted windows fired automatic rounds that pinged off the reinforced doors and windows.

"They couldn't even be original," Julieta griped, shooting a tremulous smile at her daughter. "Typical movie shit."

The three hulking vehicles raced down the country road, gaining on Julieta's truck. "We can't outrun them, Mamá," María said, mustering a courage that belied her young age. "We have to take a stand."

She reflected on the strategies her mom taught her since she was old enough to train in hand-to-hand combat and the endless hours of tactical practice at the ranch shooting range to prepare her. Julieta confided to her daughter that if she had the proper training when she was younger, she could have killed the cartel. Thus, María's grandparents would still be alive.

Over the open channel from the walkie-talkie Julieta stole from the cartel's ranch, a booming voice blasted through the speaker. "Disable that ogre of a truck. I will kill Julieta myself."

"Got it, sir. We've unloaded tons of ammunition, and we can't penetrate that truck yet. We'll have to pin them in."

"Don't fuck up! I have to take care of them myself."

María jerked her head to scrutinize her mom. "Who is that? Why us?"

"I've told you, there are outside forces that want our secrets for themselves. A long time ago, we negotiated a truce with both GREC and the UFE. The Federation has shown their true colors by betraying the agreement. There's a growing cancer in the Federation, splinter cells. In the past weeks, they have become very aggressive with Nicolaus's mom. Last night, they said one of us will die if we don't give them what they want."

"That's why Dae gave you the money last night. This wasn't just about my uncle. It was about DaeChie Pharmaceuticals?"

"Yes. We wanted to give truce money to the cartel working with the United Federation of Enforcement. Now let me focus." Julieta fought the splinter cells for the past year to prevent the Divine powers from falling into their grasp. Unable to gain a foothold on their secrets, the UFE turned their attention to DaeChie and extort the families.

They sped through stoplights and stop signs as they entered a small country town with Julieta weaving as the enemies tried to box them in. Julieta turned a corner, tires squealing as the attackers forced them off the road for a moment. Her eyes switched between the rearview mirror and the front windshield. The gunshots clanked off the metal truck, causing minimal damage to the custom bulletproof windows and military-grade exterior she and Magnar installed to protect her most precious treasures: her daughter and husband.

Julieta gripped the steering wheel, roaring over the gravel and gunshots. "That voice was Hamilton Parsons, the newly appointed UFE special operations unit lead. He won't stop until I'm dead. So, once we are out of this town, we'll make our stand. You can unleash Little Mamá on those suckers. We need to get past that church, and I'll spin a one-eighty, and you can play whack-a-truck."

María's muscles quivered as she clung to her sidearm for comfort, while Julieta gritted her teeth and felt the sweat trickle down her forehead. A black SUV blindsided their truck, plowing into their driver's side, and caused them to spin into the yard of a rundown country church. As their super truck thumped to a halt, a sense of unease settled in the pit of their stomachs. Six SUVs closed in, forming a tight ring around them.

Julieta grabbed the walkie-talkie. "Take me and leave my daughter unharmed." María's eyes widened in sheer horror.

"Mamá, you can't give up."

"We have no choice. They got to me, and so they can spin the truth to meet their grand plan. They are the Federation. I'm out of time."

A hail of bullets punctuated her words. They blazed through the weakened metal straight into Julieta, almost hitting María.

"Stop firing, you fucking morons! You're going to kill the girl," bellowed Parsons into the walkie-talkie.

With her last bit of energy, María's mom floored the gas pedal and spun the vehicle straight at the caravan of trucks. They smashed through the motorcade and rotated to the passenger side, facing the enemies at a standstill. María clicked the knob for the heavy machine gun, which popped out of the roof like a champagne cork. Little Mamá sprouted out of the cab. María grabbed both handles, spun toward the grouping of vehicles, and unleashed the wrath of God upon all the foes. Two trucks exploded after forty-five seconds of constant automatic firing.

Without even glancing at her mom, heart pounding like a race car, María slid down and snatched her reloaded guns. She dashed to the closest vehicle, unloading shots across the sides of the SUV, opened the door, and lambasted the inside. She repeated the process for the other idling trucks, ensuring no survivors.

Fueled by rage, she stowed her sidearms in her waist holsters before pulling out a grenade and hurling it at the SUVs farthest from her. Without hesitation, she uncorked another grenade and launched it at the remaining two vehicles. She sprinted back to their truck with an explosion behind her, completing a clean sweep of the attackers.

Julieta rested against the truck's rear tire, coughing, with blood dripping out of her mouth. She motioned for María to sit down.

Julieta leaned against her daughter, her head resting on María's shoulder, her breath scant. "I love you, Sunflower. Keep shining." Her mom gasped for air, then whispered, "Know that Nicolaus, Akari, and Veton are your most important allies, friends, and family. Tell your dad I love him and will miss his cooking. Remember, you're a child of the Divine."

Before Julieta muttered another word, a loud gunshot pierced the air with a high-pitched whistle. The bullet tore through Julieta's heart, causing a surge of crimson blood to spill from her chest. María let out a loud scream before collapsing across her mom's too-still body, tears pouring down her cheeks.

A seventh black truck pulled up beside them. Three men with black combat uniforms exited the vehicle with assault rifles aimed at María. A stocky, bald, European American man with a well-defined jawline, clean black suit, and polished shoes stepped out of the rear passenger side door and took in the sight of Julieta's motionless body. His eyes lingered on her before shifting his attention to María. "Your mom paid the price for not being honest about her knowledge." He pulled out his gun from his coat pocket. "We don't take kindly to that!" He points the gun at her.

María's eyes burned with the intensity of a thousand troops ready to charge into battle. She locked eyes with him, gripping her mom.

"Your mom double-crossed me." He spread his arms wide. "I'm Hamilton Parsons. Nobody fucks with me! That's right, no one!" With a grunt that sounded like a dog bark, he lowered his right arm and unleashed a flurry of gunshots through the driver's side door a mere foot from them. "We'll be watching your every move." Parsons edged forward with his handgun pointed at María's head. "If you don't finish her work, you and your friends will face the same fate. I will slaughter you all like pigs if you don't comply." María didn't blink, even with a gun pointed at her forehead. "We'll let you have her body so you can bury her. Think of it as mercy." Parsons climbed back into the vehicle, with the troops close behind. The death brigade drove past the fire and devastation in the little town.

María's body shook with each sob, refusing to let go of her mom. A scream burned her vocal cords and shattered the windows of the truck and nearby corner store. A blinding white light radiated from her, as if her anguish had unleashed her very soul. As she extended her left hand, it emitted a dazzling white light, casting a fleeting silhouette before disappearing.

Ignoring the blood splatter and glass splinters, María crawled to her phone, which had fallen out of the truck during the melee.

Her hands trembled as she dialed her dad.

"Is it finished? Are y'all heading back?"

She swallowed once, twice, ignoring the copper tang on her tongue. "Daddy . . ."

"María, what happened? Where are you?"

"She's gone," she whispered over the scream and the sob taking up all the space in her throat. Her lungs burned because there was no room left for her air, only pain.

A sense of numbness washed over María as she grappled with the devastating truth that her mom, her beloved G.I. Julieta, was no longer alive. "They killed her."

There was another long pause, and María heard her dad's anguish through the phone with the hitch in his breathing. "Are you hurt?" he asked, voice small and tight. "I'll be right there. Text me your location."

The police and ambulance sirens drew closer, and she scooted back to her mom's now cooling body. "When you get here, I'll tell you what happened. I tried, Dad," she said, her voice fracturing like the glass littering the ground. "But I couldn't save her."

"Sweetheart, I'll be there as soon as possible. Text me if they take you anywhere. I love you."

María dropped the phone and scooped her mom's head into her lap. She smoothed down the black hair that was so similar to hers, mind replaying her mom's last words, the windows exploding, and her body glowing.

She blinked, and the trucks were closer than she expected. María blinked again, and they were parking beside her. She blinked and the first responders were surrounding her, wheeling stretchers toward her.

ʘʘʘʘ

"María!" Dodge yells, clutching her shoulders with vigor. "Dude, wake up. You're lighting up like the sun. María, *wake up now!*"

With a sudden jolt, she turns her head toward him, her eyes wide as the glowing white halo disappears.

"How long have I been out?"

"Like, the entire trip. I just pulled to the side of the road before we got to Winnie's, and you're practically a human lightbulb. Akari told me that Nicolaus did the same solar flare stuff, too."

Her ears ring from Parsons's gunshot, the memory still vibrating through her mind. She clenches her fist, smacks it against her forehead, and mumbles, "Do you always have to be so extra?"

"Yep, there's no other way."

María can't believe she glowed like the night her mom died. It hasn't happened since. And Dodge just mentioned Nicolaus did, too. She grabs the locket, sensing the warmth of the metal in her palm as the shimmer dulls out of view.

Dodge revs the engine and merges back onto the road. "Let's go load up on some goodies. And then you and Nicolaus can discuss whatever you felt." He pulls into the parking lot next to the Slayer.

The sound of Akari tapping on the driver's side window startles them both. He rolls down the window, feeling a rush of fresh air on his face.

Akari clasps her hands together. "Let's go get changed and grab some food. María, I suggest you and Nicolaus have a chat."

"Aye-aye, captain," Dodge retorts with a salute.

María let out a deep sigh. "Dodge not now. My head burns, and Akari's right, I have to talk with Nicolaus."

Legends of Paintball

5

Present

After they change into their combat fatigues and grab their refreshments, Nicolaus and María inspect the paintball equipment in the back of her truck. The sweet smell of fresh cut grass fills their nostrils. "Hey, cousin. Dodge told me you were glowing like a Christmas tree."

"Not everyone has the luxury of Akari to calm them down. I'm just pissed right now." She closes her eyes and all she can see is Parsons's face. She grips hard on a paintball gun. "Plus, Dodge gets on my nerves with his sarcasm."

"Yeah, I know how you feel. Especially with Dodge." After a momentary pause, he smirks, and laughter erupts as he nudges her arm with his elbow. "Hey, I glowed too. I—umm—I don't know what this is."

"I think you do, and you're not telling us."

Nicolaus hesitates, scratching the back of his head, conflicted by his mom's words. *Keep it a secret until the right time.*

Before Nicolaus speaks, Dodge appears from around the corner. "Sorry to ruin the family love fest, but Akari wants to get moving. If we don't listen, she'll be all over us—like flies on shit."

"I heard that, Dodge," Akari responds, walking over to give Nicolaus an organic granola bar.

Nicolaus smirks at Dodge. "You know better than to mock her. She'll only make your life more difficult."

"It's not any worse than María telling me to shut up all the time, which I ignore because she likes me keeping things lively."

María slams the rear hatch on the truck. "Let's cut the chitchat and roll. We have a twenty-minute drive to talk and complete the plans."

Moments later, Nicolaus clasps the communications handset to talk with María and Dodge driving ahead of them. "Are you all listening to metal or cyberpunk, and are we rolling up badass style?"

"Cyberpunk, of course. Don't forget the shades and the pissed-off straight face when we get out. Distraction is our first tactical advantage," María responds.

"Cousin, I think you are salivating over this."

"You know it, and same with the lovely assassin sitting next to you."

Nicolaus glances at Akari as she turns up her rumble playlist of K-Pop and hard style dubstep while bobbing her head back and forth, psyching herself up, ready for the action.

They pull into the gravel-strewn lot of the Warring Combat Zone, parking their vehicles side by side at a forty-five-degree angle with the front ends almost touching. The bass from their music rattles the rocks beneath their cars. Akari gets out first, turning heads with her stride, and then María follows, commanding even more attention. The girls flip their hair backwards for accentuation. Nicolaus and Dodge exit, moving towards the rear of the battlecruiser. They grab their guns and accessories while Dodge unloads his beloved childhood toy, a small black metal wagon, to transport the equipment. The paintballers taunt him as "the small man with his petite trolley," and it gets his adrenaline pumping even harder.

The Four Shadows of Light approach the pavilion entrance and staging area. "Hey, Lawrence, how's it going?" Nicolaus shakes hands with the former army cadet they met in bootcamp. "Are you ready to dominate the marines?"

"Yes, sir," Lawrence snarls. "Ready to silence the enemy and plant the army flag in the ground."

The four members of the Divine team equip themselves with two small sidearms fastened to their lower legs, along with a utility harness that they wrap around their chest to hold grenades or more handguns with extra clips for any close encounters.

María leads the way to buy the ammo and grenades. Dodge fills the tanks, and Akari gets to work laying out the weapons organized for each game. Nicolaus launches two drones with cameras, one landing on the building's roof to guarantee nobody messes with their possessions. The other he navigates to the first game of capture the flag, memorizing the landmarks as the facility shifts the playing field around each week.

They shake hands with all the veteran marines and their squad leader, Vincent, talking trash about how they beat the navy last week.

"Y'all are like rock, paper, scissors—marines beat navy, navy beats air force, air force beats marines, and yet you lose to the army," Dodge cackles.

"That's just because of you four crazies," Vincent replies, pointing at the Four Shadows of Light. "Today is going to be different, you'll see." He winks at Akari.

She strides to Nicolaus and gives him an immense kiss as his hand rubs down to her backside. Their hormones rage while a few of the paintballers whistle and yell, "Whoa, get a room."

She declares, "I have one man and Nicolaus has one woman, so dream on and prepare for an ass-kicking."

"See, the four of you are fucking nuts," Vincent replies to Akari.

María exclaims, "Twenty-six enhanced automatic elite guns, multiple scopes, five expandable shields, utility belts, grappling hooks and every option of camouflage netting."

Vincent adds, "And a partridge in a pear tree. We get it. Y'all go overboard even for a paintball match."

Nicolaus holds a remote control for one of his drones. "One can never be over prepared. We are the chosen ones." María flings a clump of paintballs at him.

"I said it once—I'll say it again: crazies."

Dodge cuts in, "How do you think I got my nickname? You got to be a little crazy, lucky, blessed, and have talent. On our first mission, bullets whizzed around my head and María asked how I dodged all the bullets. Thus, a Dodge was born."

María shakes her head. "Third person. Really, Dodge?"

"I'm the show, baby. That's what you said last night."

Nicolaus glances up while he finishes polishing a skull helmet to see the referees making their way onto the scene with zebra striped shirts and black cargo pants. "We're starting with Capture the Flag. Army, south. Marines, north. Once you're on the field, we'll give you fifteen minutes to plan. When the whistle blows, the game begins." The referee sweeps his hand, reminding everyone a thorough velocity check is mandatory before bringing any guns onto the field. The head referee glares at María and Nicolaus. "Leave your grenades, vehicles, sentry guns, and drones in the pavilion." Nicolaus shakes his head, considering the last event where he snuck in the drone. "We got six stations for checking your guns. Waste no more time. Start moving now," the referee demands.

Walking toward the starting point, the marines converse about how they were going to take down the badass foursome. María's hand clasps Dodge's, while Akari intertwines her fingers with Nicolaus's.

Akari whispers in Nicolaus's ear, "Remember— it's just a game. Loosen up and have fun."

"Did you talk to María too?"

"Yes, and she agreed to at least let them have some minor victories."

"What if we are losing?"

With a firm grip on his hand, "The purpose is to help us let go of our anxiety and tension. You don't have to prove manhood, so check your first-place pride."

They strut to the army's home base and Akari snaps her fingers to get everyone's attention. "The idea is to have sixteen members go up the right side, weaving between trees and pushing forward with some ballers on the ground, wearing camouflage. Six guys move up the middle, laying constant paint fire to draw attention away from the sides. Dodge will head left to the first thick tree and snipe the moving targets from above. María, Nicolaus, and I will rush left, pushing marines right to grab the flag."

With the team in position, the shrill sound of the whistle signals the start, and the Four Shadows of Light waste little time. In just sixteen minutes, María plants the opponent's flag in their base camp and howls.

"Army one. Marines, zip, zero, zilch, nada, nothing," Dodge jokes, walking back to the staging area, giving a high five to María. "I got the need for a flawless victory."

The next event setup is reminiscent of an urban city, with towering buildings that stretch three stories high. The goal is to eliminate every member of the opposing team. By winning the second competition, the team gains the advantage of using grenades in the final all-out battle.

"Just like Ukraine or Mexico," Nicolaus says, rubbing his hands together and winks at Akari, who loads her sidearms.

The whistle blows for the second competition. María takes out seven. Nicolaus, Akari, and Dodge have five as the army completes the victory lap by galloping around the marines.

Lawrence shakes his head at María. "At some point, can you allow us to take out more than one?"

"Nope. Show no mercy, have no favorites, and hold nothing back."

Akari pulls Nicolaus to the side. "I saw your body illuminate for a moment. Just like in the truck. What is going on? This isn't good. If this is the Divine power coming out, someone will see it."

"I don't know how or what it is. Something is triggering it." In all their operations around the world, Nicolaus never experienced a shine or a glow. This seems like a dormant periodical cicada waking up after sixteen years of being buried in the dirt.

Dodge pokes his head in the conversation with a mischievous grin. "María had a slight glow, too. Maybe it's the golden goose of a locket she's wearing that's doing some of this to you two."

Akari exhales. "You both are such pains. Dial back so we can figure this out."

In the last event, participants scatter throughout the forest, each with a unique starting point, before converging on a field that spans three acres. While each person fights their own battles, the four Berets move as a unified force. Realizing they are the final five left, they launch an attack on Lawrence, laughing as paintballs smack the unlucky former army cadet. "You fucking fools. Stop shooting!"

After Lawrence leaves the field, the four of them stare at each other. Akari holds her gun toward the ground and her other hand on her hip. "Last month, we were the only ones left. We went all out in a raging battle against each other. I got a nasty black welt on my stomach from the shot fired from three feet away from María. I don't feel like going through that again. How about you all?"

The three of them give a resounding no, except Dodge. The sight of defeat washes over his face.

"It's María's birthday," Akari says while she sets down her gun on the ground. "She gets to shoot each of us from fifteen feet away." María snipes Nicolaus first, then Akari, and for fun, whacks Dodge five times.

They return to the pavilion, where the rest of the players are hanging out and packing up. One marine jets up to Nicolaus with a smirk. "Why do you even take part? You know you're going to win every fucking time."

Nicolaus responds, "Target practice."

"It's a warm-up to get the blood and hormones flowing, too," María says, while flexing her muscles.

The marine shakes his head and then salutes Nicolaus. "I'm glad we are all on the same team. Stay hungry and alert. Let any of us know if you need anything, especially if the UFE turn against our armed forces."

"You got it, and ditto. Let us know if you get into trouble or want to hang out, united as one force." They give a salute, and the marine does an about-face before leaving. Nicolaus reflects on the immense power now held by the United Federation of Enforcement. Last week, a major announcement included the disbandment of NATO. The new international organization approved by a unanimous vote at the World Coalition Meeting signed into international law as The Reclamation of Falsity. His cousin María works for the top contractor of the UFE. She's only there to infiltrate and gather intel, like a spy, just like he and Dodge are doing at Pierce Roosevelt Financials & Investments.

Vincent approaches Nicolaus before departing. "You the man, and damn, you and Dodge are some lucky suckers. Don't you ever let them down." He points to Akari and María. "Like I did to my ex-wife."

"Thanks for the advice," Nicolaus replies, eyes fixed on Akari. "We won't. Plus, they'd kick our ass, anyway."

"By the way, how's your Godfather Casey doing? I haven't seen him around the ranch or at paintball since he moved my ass out of my former house."

"He's been crazy busy with his moving company and told me he'll be down in Texas in the next month."

"That dude is a baller, for sure, on the paintball field." Vincent nods and heads to the parking lot, throwing up the peace sign.

On the way home, they stop for some world-famous jerky at Winnie's. Nicolaus ponders the announcement and plays the press conference. He watches Veda's thank-you message on his phone. Her poised and confident regal posture that commands the entire audience's attention combines with her elegant Indian flowing black hair and rich golden-brown skin.

After her speech, Wei Zhao, CEO of the Global Reform Establishment, presents a counterargument to the Reclamation of Falsity. "We are the gatekeepers now and the future in advanced manufacturing, agriculture, aviation, capital markets, chemical industries, digital communications, education, and emerging technologies. We are also here to further help in food security, infrastructure and development, mining and metals, oil and gas, plastics, sustainability, and digital transformation for artificial intelligence. You see—the Coalition is here to lead. As a military faction—I implore that a new legislation enables Coalition oversight of the Federation. The last part we are proposing is the assimilation of the United Nations into the GREC, which enables a streamlined approach to humanity. . ."

Startled, he jumps when María's voice comes from over his shoulder. "We can't trust them."

"Agreed. I can't believe how fast they are progressing with their initiatives." He scratches his goatee. "María, tomorrow after work, let's discuss your vision. I just want to review again now that your dad gave you the locket."

María huffs as they arrive at their vehicles. "We've been over my vision a hundred times." Every time she revisits her vision, it pulls on her heart and reminds her of losing her mother.

"I know. I know. This whole thing is gnawing at the back of my mind, especially since we both glowed."

Dodge blurts through the rolled-down window, "The locket is a magical key to unlocking the unknown universe. IN A WORLD . . ."

"Shut up, Dodge!" María jolts her head as she gets into the driver's side, with Dodge already in the passenger seat.

Akari, sitting in the Slayer, replies over the intercom, "Children behave. María, write your recollection of the last day with your mom. Nicolaus and I will write everything he recollects about that night with his family. Tomorrow, over dinner, we'll review together."

"Great, sounds like a fucking plan." María scowls at Nicolaus as she clicks the button on the handheld intercom. "Also, see if you can get my cousin to open up on whatever he's hiding."

Akari arches her eyebrow. "If he's hiding something, he has a reason. But if it's important, now's the time."

Nicolaus pivots, his body now facing the complete opposite direction. "There's nothing I'm keeping from you, so can we

42

move on?" Nicolaus shakes his head, hating himself for keeping them in the dark.

Corporate
of
Bureaucracy

(6)

Present

It's six o'clock on a blue-sky Monday morning, and the alarms wail on Nicolaus and Akari's phones from their two-toned farmhouse-styled antique nightstands. They wake up, fling their cool sheets off the bed, sit up, and rub their eyes. With the room bathed in muted light, they lock eyes, feeling a strange tension. Nicolaus breathes in the gentle fragrance of island starfruit wafting through the air from the misting diffuser. Without a word, they reach over and turn off their phones, plunging the room into silence.

"I had a rough night's sleep," Nicolaus says, glancing at Akari. They had both tossed and turned, as if a possessed angel had woven its way into their slumber.

She fidgets with the comforter and moments later, mumbles, "Yeah, I feel this weird sensation in the pit of my stomach. I don't know. My mind is a whirlwind of jumbled thoughts." She exits the bed and makes her way to the bathroom.

Nicolaus's eyes track Akari as she departs the room. *Was it a dream or a Divine vision?* He rises with a yawn from the chic cottage-style white king-sized bed and goes to the upstairs second bathroom. As he styles his hair with gel, his gaze fixates on his reflection in the mirror. The dream felt lifelike, but he knew it couldn't be real. It was just like María's explanation after her mother's death—the vision that's been strangling her mind for the past eleven years. Amid getting dressed in dark gray slacks and a powder blue dress shirt, he debates if he should discuss it with Akari now, even though they're both in a hurry.

When he returns to the bedroom, he peeks into the main bathroom. Akari stares at the mirror in her alluring violet lace nightgown.

"Hey, what's going on?"

Akari snaps out of her trance and meets Nicolaus's gaze through the reflection. "I just feel different, angry, and confused—I'm trapped in this endless cycle of work and relentless research, and I can't seem to break free." She takes a deep breath, already making the mental decision to discuss the vision later, as she turns on her heels to face Nicolaus. "I'm just trying to figure out the elusive rest of the equation for the cure for breast cancer." Someone had ripped out half of the research journal that Nicolaus's mom, Dae, left behind.

Nicolaus puts his hands on Akari's waist and puts his forehead against hers. "I know you'll figure it out. I wish I could assist you." Her area of expertise is in biology and biophysics, while his lies in mechanics and robotics.

They embrace and Akari whispers, "I love you. We'll ask my mom again in a week or two for her blessing to get married."

"We've only been asking for eight years, and she keeps saying no."

"Patience and persistence, my confident boy. My mom's stubborn, but my dad's been getting through to her."

Nicolaus kisses her on the cheek. "Get ready for work, and we'll stop for coffee on the way."

She nods and before he exits the rooms Akari adds, "Can you please check on my cat, and make sure she's got food, and that the litter box is in good shape?"

Never having pets while growing up, he grumbles about Kaili the cat and how irritating she can be. While Akari completes her morning routine, Nicolaus steps outside to water the flowers and trees in the front yard. The sun shines bright, enveloping everything in a warm glow. As he refills the bird feeders, the soothing chirping eases his anxiety.

While the garage door is moving upward, Akari flicks the ignition, and the roar of the 1970s muscle car rattles the air. She backs out, and Nicolaus enters through the passenger side door.

During the drive, the exhaust drowns out the sports talk radio. They pull into the parking lot at Ammunition Coffee Café. Nicolaus runs into the coffee shop, picks up their two steaming coffees, waves and says hi to the former military baristas, and walks back to the car.

He opens the door. She takes the large dark roast from Nicolaus and smiles. "That's why I chose you. You're great at getting coffee." She laughs, and they both take some sips.

En route, they discuss paintball matches, while in the back of their minds, the nagging vision lingers. Akari pulls up to the Pierce Roosevelt Financials & Investments North Dallas headquarters. The campus comprises four seventeen-story buildings in perfect toy soldier formation, with skywalks connecting them in perpendicular perfection.

"Don't forget we've got training tonight," Nicolaus says as he climbs out. He leans back into the car to snag a kiss, then walks to building number four. Akari zooms off to DaeChie Pharmaceuticals, where she leads research for her and Nicolaus's late mom's company.

He goes through the shining metal front glass doors and eyes Dodge leaning against a marble wall.

"Yo, what's the word? You ready for another awesome day of bureaucrats in back-to-back meetings, arguing and defending their empires of nothingness and getting paid fat coin?"

Nicolaus cracks up, and they give each other a bro hug. "Thanks, needed that. It's been a different morning. Any lunch place in mind for later?"

"Let's roll down the street and grab some homemade fresh tacos. I feel like that Texas-meets-Mexico flavor," Dodge says as they scan their badges while traveling through the contemporary museum of an office.

Both stroll into their respective elevators, since Nicolaus works on floor fifteen and Dodge works on floor seven. They wave goodbye like young kids as the elevator doors shut.

Nicolaus's behavior annoys a director, Zander, who works on the same floor as him. "Real professional. Makes me want to promote you."

"So, can I hope that one day—fifteen years from now—I'll receive recognition for my talents? No, thank you. Plus, it wouldn't hurt for you to relax a bit. You seem, I don't know, a little rigid."

"Keep that up, Nicolaus, and you'll be pushing papers for the rest of your career." The elevator opens, and Zander sprints not to miss one of his seventeen back-to-back meetings.

Nicolaus ambles to the designated area for the business unit he leads in digital application architecture. Before he sits down at his desk, Michele, a cheerful new hire, bursts into the space.

"Are you ready for the sustainability presentation in two hours?"

"Absolutely, and it's an unequivocal game changer. Give me a moment to get settled, and then we'll rock the presentation."

As he reaches into his pocket to remove his keys, he feels the delicate petal of a flower brush against his fingers. He pulls out a single stemmed baby's breath, gazing at the small white ethereal flowers. It is now clear to him that the dream he had was a vision. Before he ponders further, his computer blares with a loud notification for his upcoming meeting.

At ten o'clock, his team presents two sustainability methodologies for the four buildings and skywalk roofs covered in algae for natural power, using an algorithm to maintain constant supplemental energy.

The senior vice president of investments stops Nicolaus midway through the second proposal comprising a variable solar panel without cadmium metal and other toxic metals to create energy using the potent Texas sun. "Nicolaus, thank you for the presentation. It was quite impressive. However, the cost-to-energy ratio makes little sense."

Nicolaus urges the board of directors to consider the positive impact of the company's public relations and marketing. "Also, if we go this route, we can learn more about making algae consumption more efficient and seeing how a nontoxic solar panel system will work."

"Nicolaus, we applaud your tenacity. We also know that Walter Roosevelt gave your team permission to work on these side projects. However, these concepts are for energy companies, not finance companies. We are an institution who provides loans and financing for energy companies. If they go against our energy supplier allies, it will only defeat our shareholder profitability and long-term investments. As a board, we overrule any determination from Mr. Roosevelt. We commend the effort of the entire team."

Nicolaus returns to his office, muttering under his breath how they got rejected twice in the past week. First, his team created a patentable solution for predictive analytics, and now implementing a sustainable energy solution is no longer possible.

ᘓᘓᘓᘓ

Walter Roosevelt, the CEO, taps a pen on his desk. "Mr. Zhao, there are no signs of the Divinity powers or Aamirah. I thought Nicolaus's inventions might work."

"It was worth trying. So far, nothing we've attempted has triggered Aamirah to return." Zhao pushes buttons through his virtual reality visor. "When you're in Manhattan tomorrow, we'll devise another plan."

Roosevelt clicks the end button. *Damn them all!* He exhales and then sets the pen down. *The Vargases, the Landowskis, the Ionas, all of them.* They hid the details of how to awaken Aamirah and her nemeses, Medium, and Sinrye. He sighs and pulls out a picture of Nicolaus's mom, Dae, from his top desk drawer. His biggest regret hangs over his conscience. If only he had made better choices. Dae would have been alive today, and they would have been sharing their lives together. His arrogance got the best of him all those years ago, and didn't see that Dae wanted companionship, not the money. She chose Magnar, Nicolaus's dad, because he gave her what Roosevelt couldn't or wouldn't— vulnerability, intimacy, support, trust and a best friend. His lust for money and power shattered the hope of any relationship beyond a fling and a business partnership.

ᘓᘓᘓᘓ

At twelve-thirty, Dodge and Nicolaus exit the building and stroll towards the outdoor café. After ordering, they sit down and Dodge asks, "Dude, you look thrown off. What are you thinking?"

Nicolaus glances at Dodge while covering the meal with the hottest sauce. "Had a bizarre vis—um—dream and didn't want to discuss it with Akari this morning. Would rather talk to her tonight. She also appears stressed, like we both felt somewhat off."

"Probably because María and I outscored you both yesterday."

Nicolaus chuckles. The best friends salute and tap their tacos together before chowing down.

As they walk back to the hollow glass halls of their workplace, Nicolaus grumbles. "Every day is a repetitive routine: scan, meet, sit, stare, listen, book, and leave."

"We both know why we have to work there," Dodge replies.

Nicolaus nods. It's all part of their investigation to figure out if Pierce Roosevelt is financially behind the UFE and what role Walter Roosevelt plays. María remains steadfast in her belief that the GREC is the mastermind behind it all, yet if her theory holds any truth, the Coalitions' ability to conceal their actions surpasses that of any other entity in existence. They first have to see if Roosevelt is funding the Federation. "I get it. It's just boring. I'd rather work on all the inventions in the media room."

Dodge stops and eyeballs Nicolaus. "Dude, like, you've had some things since sophomore year in high school. Either finish them or throw them away."

"Now you sound like Akari—you both are right. I just can't figure out the last steps to get them over the finish line. It's maddening." He feels like there's a veil over his mind, not allowing him to complete the last steps. "Hmm, maybe I'll toss them and start over?"

Dodge smacks Nicolaus on the back. "Start fresh. Easy-peasy."

"Umm—I haven't mentioned that I found this in my pocket when I got to work." Nicolaus pulls out the baby's breath flower.

Dodge directs his gaze towards Nicolaus, and his eyebrows furrow. "So, you saw a vision, like María did when her mom died?"

"I believe so, bro."

"Why didn't you tell me, like, when we arrived?"

"The flower appeared after I sat down in my office."

Dodge whispers to Nicolaus, "You have explaining to do for dinner tonight."

"After Akari and I have our training session later, then I'll tell her."

"Good, and you know she's going to kick your ass again."

"Thanks for the encouragement, short stuff."

The moment Nicolaus steps into his office, the image of the vision lingers, the fragrance of the baby's breath flower fills his mind, making it impossible for him to concentrate. The hours tick by, and he remains transfixed by the blank screen, his frustration mounting with each passing minute.

Clash
of
Lovers

(7)

Present

Akari rockets across campus, zipping past the financial buildings and arrives at Nicolaus's regular pickup spot. He swoops into the car, craving to bolt as fast as possible. As he fastens his seatbelt, Akari floors the vehicle, heading to the Asa Dojo a couple of miles away to continue their training, practice, and synchronized fighting techniques.

She glances at Nicolaus. "Are you still tense?"

"Work made it worse. Dodge did his best to cheer me up. But after lunch, all I did was blank stare at the computer. What about you?"

"I can't focus. I'm anxious and stressed." She and Nicolaus seldom felt this way at the same time. When one is feeling overwhelmed, the other is always there to help them unwind and let go of their tension.

They pull into the parking lot of the martial arts center. Akari turns with a fluttering feeling in her chest. "How about we do some Bōjutsu today to eliminate our edge?"

"I'm good with that. Smashing the bo and taking our aggression out with some intense fighting should help us both."

Over the years, Akari and Nicolaus have trained in Japanese martial arts such as Jujutsu, Karate, Aikido, and Judo, along with Korean Taekwondo. They incorporate their army tactical training to create mixed scenarios, including a fictional scenario where they work together to take down invisible targets.

Nicolaus reaches over to tuck her hair behind her ear. Their lips meet in a fiery embrace, accompanied by a gentle caress as his hand slides down her arm. María and Dodge can't help but tease the couple, as they seem to be lost in their own world. Their spiritual connection grows stronger with each passing day. As they step out of the car, they grab their backpacks and prepare for the clash.

Akari and Nicolaus stride hand in hand toward the martial arts center. As they approach, Akari glances at Nicolaus and says, "You haven't beaten me in a month, or maybe longer?"

Nicolaus lets out a sigh and replies, "You move quicker than anyone, and you're the only one who memorized my tells. I crave the challenge even though it's frustrating."

"Well, maybe you'll have the support of an invisible army to take me down today," Akari says with a sly grin.

Nicolaus opens the door to the building. "I won't need the invisible army, only my skills."

The Asa Dojo resembles a peaceful outdoor Japanese setting with tranquil gardens and authentic architectural details. A river with bridges is nestled amidst a backdrop of vibrant greenery and artificial turf. The winding pathways lead to traditional-style structures with thatched roofs, tatami mats, and sliding panels. Akari and Nicolaus head to their respective locker rooms to change into their keikogi uniforms and prepare for their one-on-one fight.

Akari finishes first. She exits the locker room and heads to the right side of the building where they often spar. She notices Asa, the dojo owner and their instructor, standing underneath the realistic artificial cherry tree which accents the mini arena. Since their elementary school days, she, Nicolaus, María, Dodge, Melodi—Dodge's sister—and Mi-Cha trained at his dojos once a week. Despite the passage of time, his physical appearance remains unaltered; he looks exactly as he did years ago. A long, trimmed beard, sides of his head shaved, silver-streaked hair pulled back in a bun, his bronze skin shows no signs of weathering. Donning a judogi robe with the color split down the middle, one side white and the other black, with a long green lapel and a green cloth belt. The Divinities symbol, embroidered on his right chest, shimmers in the light as he bows.

Akari enters the sparing arena clasps her hands together in praying position and bows back. She glances around, noticing the emptiness of the building. The only noise breaking the silence was the soothing sound of running water. "Asa, where is everyone?"

"I thought it would be better for you and Nicolaus to have some privacy today." They bow again, and he leaves the sparing circle, strolls over and climbs the steps to a sky bridge that reminds her of a bird's nest overlooking the dojo.

As Akari begins her stretching routine, Nicolaus arrives. "What took you so long?" she asks.

"María and Dodge called to remind me not to get frustrated if I lose. María saw a discerning glint in your eyes today when she visited you at work and worried you might lose control."

"She is right. I'm in a feisty mood right now."

Akari whirls her wooden staff, crossing the markers for the sparring space and out-of-bounds line. Nicolaus follows, jumping into the ring with his bo jetted forward. They feel a tug in their hearts, as if something is speeding up their heartbeats.

With a quick darting glance at each other, the tension from the vision reaches its boiling point. Nicolaus taps his bo on the ground, baiting Akari. She flashes a wintry smile in retaliation.

"Alright, queenie, show me what you got," Nicolaus declares in a cunning tone.

"You're going with a chess reference? You know, queens always beat knights. So, I'm going to lay the wood, wizarding style, on your ass."

They bow and circle each other, surveying for a tactical advantage. Nicolaus jolts headfirst, but Akari responds with an easy deflection. The two of them continue to strike at each other, with each move being predicted and countered by the other because of their countless hours of training and intimate connection. Akari's agility and lethality mesmerizes Nicolaus as she floats through the air, flipping and striking with more tenacity than most people with their feet on the ground. The clashing of their wooden staffs echoes throughout the building, striking harder with intense strokes of wrath. Akari's masterful footwork allows her to sidestep Nicolaus, hook his bo, and swat him to the ground.

"One nothing, Nicolaus," she says, with her eyes squinting and tightening.

He peeks up to see Asa wave his arm forward to continue. Akari and Nicolaus served together on over a hundred operations, taking out the world's filth, and all the world's problems seem wrapped up in this battle. They stand back to start again; their movements are graceful yet powerful, and their focus is unwavering. With all that fury, Akari launches at Nicolaus, striking his bo so hard the sound reverberates throughout the building. The impact cracks his staff in half, and the ground rumbles. From the depths of Akari's soul, a burst of light erupts, casting a spellbinding display. Repeated silhouettes float around her, and pulsating energy emanates from her. Akari appears stunned, and the anger dissipates as if someone woke her with a bucket of ice.

Nicolaus drops the two pieces and sweeps her legs out as she falls flat on her back. He glances with narrowed eyes at Asa, standing with arms crossed while Akari lets out a soft groan. He reaches out his two arms and pulls Akari to her feet. "We need to discuss what just happened. We should go."

She nods, unable to open her mouth from the shock. He grips her shaking hand for comfort.

Asa drifts toward them and bows. "Use your extraordinary gifts for humanity. I've been waiting to see Akari show the power of the Divinity."

Akari stutters, "H-h-how do you know, and what do you know?"

"Your parents and I have a long history together. I'm a magus or sometimes referred to as a sage. I built this dojo for them and the children of the Divine." He examines Nicolaus. "This training facility your dad helped me design."

It dawns on Akari like a kindled flame, that even in Hawaii, Asa would instruct their lessons. His teachings were not just for the martial arts but for training the Divinities.

Nicolaus runs his hands through his hair. "So, you've been watching over us, too?"

"Not watching—instructing. Your parents have reasons not to tell you everything, as you must experience this journey for yourselves. I understand that's not what you wanted to hear. I'll be here to support you on the arduous journey that lies ahead."

Nicolaus grits his teeth. "Another clue, with more rhymes and riddles, but no logical answer."

"I cannot guide you. Only the Divinities give you the visions. The time is coming soon. Akari showing hints of her powers, sets the true battle between light and dark in motion." His pupils flicker, changing colors from brown to green to white and returning to brown. "Go with these last words: You will face hard choices, and those choices have consequences. Choose wisely. Now go. Discuss only with María and Dodge."

Before they can reply, Asa turns around and walks away.

Akari and Nicolaus glance and nod to each other. They jog to the locker rooms, snatch their backpacks, and bolt out the front door without changing. They stride to the vehicle, holding hands in silence until they reach the speedster.

Akari's skin prickles with goosebumps. "You're driving. I can't right now." He starts up the roaring beast. "So, now we know I glow just like you and María." She taps her index finger against her lip, contemplating it's not a Landowski thing. *Could the connection be with their moms? Why are they hiding the details?*

Nicolaus grips the steering wheel, revs the engine, and throws the vehicle into drive to travel home. His mind runs a million miles a minute. *Asa is a magus sent from the Divinities? Does he have powers? They've been training with him for ages, but this is the first time he's mentioned it.* All Nicolaus hears from Asa is lecturing—*you must move faster, quicker, heighten your senses, push yourself, and never give up.*

While waiting for the traffic to clear, Akari blurts, "I had a vision last night!"

"Me too—"

Akari speaks in rapid fire, interrupting Nicolaus from telling her about the baby's breath. "Fragmented images are all I can recall, a hand reaching out, a library, chapel, flashes, writings, three lakes in winter, and a metal door at the ranch."

Shocked, Nicolaus stares out at the front windshield. "Slow down, breathe. You're doing the crazy, speed-talking thing when you have too many thoughts. Why didn't we talk about it this morning?"

"We both looked agitated, and I needed the day to piece it together." Akari waits another moment to collect her thoughts. "A glowing body and a voice saying the Divinity—"

Nicolaus interrupts Akari, finishing her sentence "—is in you, and your choice is coming." Nicolaus stops at a traffic light, and they stare at each other. They had the same vision. Their mouths hang wide open, unable to speak, as they gawk into each other's eyes.

They snap out of the shock when a driver behind them blows their horn and swings his hands in the air. Nicolaus hits the gas pedal, and the car roars, shaking the ground. He removes his eyes from the rearview mirror.

Akari rifles through her backpack and pulls out her notebook. She finds it more accessible to take notes on paper and write random thoughts. Per company policy, and her boss, Seok, she cannot dictate on her phone or use her phone for company work.

"I scribbled pictures of the scene from what I remember. In front of me, there is a cylindrical edged box made of glass the size of a refrigerator. Inside the glass, there is a body lying completely still. Lights strobe and spark from left to right, and top to bottom, like a printer at a rave. Then I'm standing next to three lakes in the snow surrounded by mountains and evergreens facing cliffs off in the distance."

Nicolaus focuses, his muscles tense as he navigates on autopilot.

"Then the scenery changes to the ranch. I'm standing peering down at the ground. There's nothing special about the ground, just like grass in the field. Then I entered an underground room. There's a metal wall ahead, with four shaped circle inlets, beckoning for a diamond shaped object to be inserted. Next, a gothic-style library that's filled with more books than I've ever seen. Then a chapel with a throne." Akari takes a long breath. "A glowing lady whispers her name is Aamirah—saying she's the Divine—and the faint hints of ancient writings in a book. Last," Akari peers at Nicolaus, "your voice calls to me as you repeat my name and shout, 'We must complete the circle.' Then images of burning buildings blast me when we woke to our alarms."

Nicolaus pulls into the shopping center parking lot near their neighborhood entrance, puts the car in park, and peers at Akari. "Can I see your drawings?" Akari hands over the notebook, and Nicolaus studies it for a few minutes while she gazes out her passenger side window.

Breaking the awkward silence, Nicolaus says, "We had the same vision. Seriously, what the fuck? So that's why Asa shut down the dojo for us. Aamirah must have spoken to him or sent him a vision. The Divine is in motion—" Nicolaus goes silent. His mouth gapes open as he contemplates.

From her purse, Akari retrieves a delicate baby's breath flower, and Nicolaus follows suit, pulling out his own flower. "Both of us experienced our first vision, just like María did. The baby's breath flower appeared in her hand when she woke up." Akari unbuckles her seatbelt and leans on Nicolaus's shoulder. "The Divinities or Aamirah placed us all together, intertwining our fates with our parents at the center." She gazes at Nicolaus, feeling like they are the only two people in the world.

He hesitates and takes a deep breath. "You know I've shared everything in my life with you except one secret that my mom told Mi-Cha and I never to discuss. It's the only thing I've never told you, Dodge, or María."

"Is this what you've been holding back?"

"Yes, María was right, and it's important. You all need to know because we saw it in our vision last night. The two places that were shown to us. My mom showed my sister and I the Divinities symbol on a grate by the Seattle cabin sixteen years ago."

Akari leans back so she can gaze Nicolaus in the eye and grips his hand as if squeezing a lemon.

"Underneath lies a glimpse of our Divine future. My mom put the same locket that Marcin gave to María today on Mi-Cha and myself. We touched an iron door, and that was the first time I experienced the flow of the Divinity." He chuckles, reflecting about his sister. "It's different from how you did today, not as powerful or bright. My mom mentioned the chamber." Nicolaus tightens his grip on her hand, unsure if she would be angry or empathetic or somewhere in between.

"You've known about the Divine presence and the locket since you were ten years old?" She pauses. Her voice rises in pitch. "Damn, you knew even before María battled the cartel and the factions of the UFE, and you never said a word."

"There's one more thing—my mom mentioned the lockets are coded for each of us. Believe me, I wanted to tell you all for so very long. It's been on my mind, and every time I went to say something, I could hear my mom's voice saying it's our secret. It hurt so much to lie to the three of you, but she—"

Akari moves her hand to his cheek. "Your mom had her reasons. I guarantee my mom is hiding information from us, like my locket."

"So, you're not pissed at me?"

"I am, but I'm not. I feel like our whole lives are an evolution of secrets. Now, I can't ensure María won't smack you."

"That is the truth." He exhales. "Wow! I feel so much better. Like so much better. Who knew a secret causes such stress?"

Akari caresses his face. "Let's go to our house and eat. Me hungry." She wonders why their parents wouldn't give them the lockets at the same time, and what is their purpose? Asa knew more details and even closed the dojo for them. She glowed like Nicolaus and María did. When's Dodge's turn? She giggles, imagining Dodge having an ethereal glow.

Blocks
of
Mackinac

8

Present

A giant black heavy-duty pickup truck rests next to Nicolaus's five-passenger, off-roading Slayer as the couple turns onto their street. The view of Dodge's truck displaying four massive flags—the army, Albania, Texas, and the United States—brings a smile to Nicolaus's face. Akari breathes a sigh of relief at the sight of their best friends waiting at the house.

Akari beams. "They are the best. And I bet Dodge has dinner ready."

Nicolaus pulls into the driveway next to the towering truck and their manicured 3,000-square-foot brick house, which they built a year ago. Akari taps her foot on the car mat. "María texted me. Then poof, she appeared at work. I shared some details with her until Seok interrupted and had us review financials in her office." Seok's decision to have them work in her office felt peculiar to her, as if she had ulterior motives to overhear their conversation.

Nicolaus turns off the car, and they stroll to the house entrance. María opens the door. "You didn't kill each other? Excellent! Well, then, dinner is served, your majesties," she says as she curtsies.

The sweet smell of homemade Hawaiian pizza, a specialty of Dodge, permeates through the house. "I figured pizza night with a splash of Akari on it." Dodge laughs, setting the table for the quartet.

"Nicolaus owes you for this." Akari hugs Dodge from behind.

"I get to choose the lunch restaurants for the next week."

Nicolaus replies, "Tex-Mex every day?"

"Of course. A daily dash of my future wife."

María exhales, grasping her wine glass. "How many times do I have to tell you, Dodge? I'm not marrying someone who doesn't want to grow up and drives me up the wall with childish antics."

"So—we just stay friends with benefits for all of eternity?"

"You like that, so don't complain." María circles to Nicolaus, pointing to a pile of papers. "We've got the competition for tonight: recreate Mackinac Island. We've got the building block kits set up. Dodge did his design thing and broke the competition down in timed steps."

"How can we turn down Mackinac Island? The last time we were there—" Akari stops Nicolaus by clanging a fork against a wineglass.

María shakes her head. "You two don't take too long changing. I know after your intense training battles there's another battle on the sheets."

Akari blushes. "We're going to shower together, and then we'll be downstairs to eat and discuss what happened today. And then the competition." She turns to Nicolaus. "In that exact order. We're just showering, so behave."

Dodge replies, "That's a good doggy, Nicolaus. Sit and roll over."

"We both are on a leash." Nicolaus smiles.

Fifteen minutes later, Akari and Nicolaus descend the stairs wearing matching camouflage green tank tops and black shorts. Dodge and María sit together on the couch, trying to agree on what to watch on the television.

"We were thinking girls versus boys for the competition," says María, taking the remote away from Dodge as Nicolaus heads for the table.

Akari responds with a voice firm, "No, I can't do that today, not after what happened in martial arts. I don't want to compete against Nicolaus. I almost caused him serious harm. We're still trying to make sense of everything."

María and Dodge glance at each other, raising their eyebrows. "Let's talk about this over dinner. Let me guess, Nicolaus the prideful lost his cool?" María says, setting down the remote and approaching Akari while Dodge gets up and pours wine for everyone.

"Believe it or not, he kept his cool this time. It was me that made a mark for sure." Akari shows María the baby's breath flowers.

María listens as Akari describes the visions, with her elbows resting on her knees and her palms supporting her chin. She stands up and wraps her arms around Akari. "So, it's not just my cousin and I who can glow. I thought it was a dad connection thing. Then, is it our moms? Or something else?"

"Well, I guess I'm the normal one." Dodge forces a smile while he taps his fingers against the wineglass and slouches in his chair. He considers, *So the three have abilities.* What about him? Why is he here? Is he a boat anchor? No, he can't be. Dodge moves around on his seat, sitting upright. He saved them many times in their army operations, and after all, he's the best sniper the military has ever seen. He'll be able to tap into the Divinities' power too. *Patience, Dodge.*

Nicolaus springs up, takes a deep breath. "María, there's one more thing. I told none of you, well besides just telling Akari on our way here. My parents took Mi-Cha and me to one of the chamber spots sixteen years ago. My mom clasped the lockets around our necks. We touched the Divinity symbol and experienced the surge of power. She made me promise not to say a word."

"So, you knew, and didn't tell any of us?" After their parents passed away, Nicolaus and she agreed to have total honesty and no secrets between them. María grinds her teeth and wonders how he could not let her know? "What the fuck, Nicolaus?"

"Look, she said not to." He rubs his fingers together to calm himself.

Akari raises her hands. "Our parents have reasons." She grabs María's hand. "My parents are holding back information, and Marcin is, too. He just gave you the locket with the Divinities symbol. At least we know some more details through visions."

María glares at Nicolaus. "What good is the locket? It's a shiny piece of metal with a circle symbol on it? Did your mom tell you anything about it? Is it magical? What does it do?"

"Well—each locket has a specific code assigned to us." He's been contemplating how many lockets there are. The four of them, Mi-Cha—does Melodi, Dodge's sister, have one? "Maybe your dad knows more about it?"

"More mysteries for us to solve. Anything else?"

"No. That's it."

"From this fucking point forward, any details we find out we all share. Deal?" María loosens her fists.

They sit down to eat while they delve deeper into the vision and meanings, but don't get any further than they were before. After they finish eating, Dodge makes his favorite beverage,

Turkish coffee. Nicolaus stares, while he sips on the coffee, at the EpicBloxx for the Mackinac Island competition and reflects about the battles he had with his sister growing up.

ᑊᑊᑊᑊ

When Nicolaus could crawl, his parents bought corrugated cardboard building blocks that filled the family room. His dad would build fortresses, cityscapes, forest layouts, and mini houses at night, which Nicolaus would then demolish while drooling and chewing on the cardboard the next morning. At six years old, Nicolaus graduated to the next level of building blocks, called EpicBloxx. The company focused on building historic landmarks and recreating famous cities. He had over seventy sets organized into themed categories in his room.

One evening after school, Nicolaus's mom, Dae, noticed him playing with his military action figure sets. "Organization leads to clarity, and building these sets inspires your innovation. Complete one task, and then you can move to the next." Dae smiled with her warm honey-toned brown toned skin and full lips. "I see your father in you, jumping between different activities and never completing the previous mission. Stay focused on completing a task. Do not procrastinate."

Nicolaus peered up at her with emerald-green eyes. "Yes, Mom. I just get bored so fast."

Dae grinned as her dimples appeared and she caressed his cheek. Her shoulder length hair bobbed forward. "That's why I'm pushing so hard. Your focus and concentration need improvement to inspire the world."

Nicolaus considered the calming nature of his mom the day Mi-Cha started building, as Dae scrutinized both. "This will teach you to harness organizational skills and, most important, patience. Patience will be your best friend to deal with kids who don't have your extraordinary talents." Shifting between English to Korean, their mom said, "Patience is vital."

Mi-Cha was less patient than Nicolaus, who had developed endurance by building, deconstructing, and rebuilding sets. Mi-Cha preferred to create her own inventions without having to follow instructions.

Their mom suggested that Nicolaus and Mi-Cha compete in a timed competition with the same set ten times to see who built it faster. As they repeated the steps in the instructions, they memorized the procedures. She was faster than Nicolaus once she memorized the instructions, which she only had to view once.

Once they completed the memorization competition, their parents elevated the stakes.

"Creative problem-solving skills are the next adventure," Dae said. "You both will recreate full global city layouts or countries by building famous landscapes, wonders, or landmarks not part of the sets."

Both Mi-Cha and Nicolaus spent hours studying printouts of the GPS views of each city and country and replicating the arrangements of structures and landmarks with the EpicBloxx.

Their mom critiqued and suggested ways to improve their craftsmanship. At first, both kids defended their work, as they spent so much time creating their masterpieces. Magnar, their dad, a slim, toned, and tall body with a clean-shaven face, featured a prominent nose and intense green eyes, pointed out why they needed to let go of the frustration.

"Listening skills and mindfulness will keep balance. Also, being mindful ensures you won't be brats and collaborate with others without bullying, even though you might be the smartest in the room."

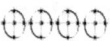

Dodge waves his hand in front of Nicolaus's face. "Earth to Nicolaus. Space monkeys calling you."

Akari notices his distant gaze and places a comforting hand on his leg. "Wake up, sweetheart."

María can't take it anymore and yells, "Snap out of your fucking daze, cousin!"

Nicolaus jolts backwards, almost falling out of his chair. "I'm sorry—I was just thinking of my sister and the competitions." As he shakes his head, his military instincts kick in and he stands up, his posture rigid and ready to march. "I'm ready to throw down in building Mackinac Island."

Gallivanting to the living room, they see two identical stations with ten thousand pieces in different containers and instructions on the floor. María clicks the timer on her watch, and the two couples slice and dice the instructions to construct the foundation for the island. Just ten minutes into the competition, Dodge and María pause their construction to marvel at Nicolaus and Akari's remarkable speed and synchronicity. A subtle, intertwined glow radiates from them, reminiscent of connected strands of Christmas lights.

"Hey! Stop. Stop! Look at your progress." María waves her hands in the air. "That's insane. I've never seen you move that quick, or that crazy united." Akari and Nicolaus pause with a couple of blocks clanking on the ground. They gaze at what they have constructed while the Divine glow fades out of sight.

"I've always felt so connected to Nicolaus, but now I feel we are like one, like truly one." Akari wonders, is that what true telepathy is?

"I agree. I feel like one conscious. How is it even possible that I feel we have one mind? Do y'all think it's because Akari's ability showed or the vision?"

María's eyes dart between Nicolaus and Akari. "Talk with your mom, Akari, you have to."

Akari shakes her head and crosses her arms. "No, not until we piece together more. I know there's a reason she is holding back. Am I upset she hasn't told us more? Yes. But my mom always has the best intentions. Plus, what do I say right now? 'Mom, here's a crazy vision. I glowed, and I broke a bo staff.'"

Nicolaus pulls at his ear. "María, we'll hold off on discussing your vision again. I don't know if I can handle it tonight. Not after the events today."

"You think?"

"Sweet, hands in the middle, go team." Dodge puts his hand out and María shakes her head.

"We brought our clothes with us and already got the spare bedroom all set, so we're having a sleepover tonight." Akari hugs María, and they sit on the couch and talk while Dodge and Nicolaus clean up the dishes in the kitchen.

After the cleanup, they give each other a jumping man bump for a well-done job.

"Let's go, soldier," Akari says, fingers intertwining with Nicolaus's. They rush up the stairs to conclude the day with a romantic touch.

"Seriously, that's like all they do," Dodge says, flicking on the remote to watch a new streaming movie release.

"Let them go, and we'll entertain ourselves with a great action flick, and then we'll go get some rest."

Once the movie ends, she and Dodge go upstairs, lie down in bed, and drift off to sleep.

ᘓᘓᘓᘓ

María witnesses the reoccurring vision, a haunting image that has plagued her since her mother's death. For her, it feels like a broken record or looping the same music track for hours.

She stands near the altar of the church gawking at the stained-glass windows when a voice rings across the air. Her mom, Julieta, appears in front of her as an illuminated Divine figure, creating a beautiful play of colors on the walls.

"My precious sunflower. Know that you're my most important legacy I left behind in the world. I did my best job raising you to be a strong, independent, intelligent, and compassionate young woman who's not afraid of anyone. You will feel something burning inside you, a feeling you can't explain. You will have visions in your dreams, which will evolve. This is only your first vision. There will be a time you will unleash your full abilities and talent upon this world." When Julieta points at the statues of saints, María realizes they are unlike any figures she has ever witnessed.

The church dissolves into the chaos of a war. The smell of smoke and burning debris fills her lungs. She can hear screams and explosions in the distance. María can't speak as her mouth feels sewn shut. Julieta's blue, flaming eyes focus on María, her words flowing like a steady stream, carrying both wisdom and conviction. "Take down the oppressors by calculative force. You can only fight against the villains if you can strike fire with fire. Follow in my footsteps into the Army Special Forces with Nicolaus, Akari, and Veton. Remember, the balance between darkness and light, and you will shine. The actions that led to my death are not the workings of a single government but a new global threat, a united one government, a single entity controlling the masses in the darkness. It's best if you play a clever political game to get inside. Remember when we used to pretend to be spies when you were a kid? This time, you're working as a spy for your team and humanity, rather than for a government institution or corporation."

A bombshell ignites around them, circling with a ring of fire that changes from orange to blue. "My last request is for you to find the courage to fight the powers of corruption and solve the puzzle of the Divinities. The Divine will reveal themselves on the challenging journey, and you must follow their righteous pathway. Each of you has a special gift; together, you *will* change the world."

The flames form a sphere around their two illuminated bodies. "I love you with all my heart and already miss those blue sparkling eyes peering at me. Whenever you need courage, support, or a casual conversation, I will always be by your side. I'm there listening."

María reaches out to touch her mom's hand, causing the blue flames to burst into a labyrinth of light.

Coalition
of
Parsons

(9)

Present

Hamilton Parsons, who now goes by the name of Alexander Taylor, dressed in a black pin-striped suit, paces in front of six large windows, every so often scrutinizing the Dallas morning skyline. A chime sounds, and a bubbly voice announces, "Mr. Taylor, it's time for you to join the coalition meeting."

He stops pacing and clicks the intercom button, responding in a heavy New Jersey accent, "Thanks, Elena—oh, clear the rest of the day for us. I'll need the full treatment after this call. I'll meet you at my digs in two hours."

"Yes sir," replies his administration assistant.

Parsons clears his throat and selects the meeting invitation on his phone. "How can I be of service to the board at such an ungodly hour?" he asks, his tone dripping with condescension as he raises an eyebrow. He sits in his chair, spins to face the glass windows.

Wei Zhao, the CEO of the GREC, rubs his gray brow. "They have one locket now. We need to ensure all four have the

Divinities' powers." Zhao pauses. *Their dormant powers are surfacing.* He's waited twenty years to get his hands on the Divine abilities. The decision to have Hamilton kill Julieta had a dual effect—it bolstered the UFE global foothold while accidentally breaking the connection to Aamirah. "It's crucial to hold off on attacking them. Our goal is to use the powers, not kill them. Don't be impulsive."

"Have I ever disappointed you? Please let me know when I have. I'll wait." Parsons stands up and taps his foot on the marble floor. After he killed María's mother, Veda solidified his position by giving him a new identity and changing his appearance through plastic surgery. In fact, he found his new facial appearance more appealing. His directives emphasized the foundational progress in the UFE's efforts for worldwide surveillance. He takes great pleasure in the mercenary work, the acts of torture, and the power he gained from them. "That's what I thought . . . nothing. Now, let me tell you something, Zhao— Veda, confirmed this morning that the Coalition doesn't drive the tactical side. The Federation does."

Wei Zhao replies, lifting his chin, "The military may back Veda, but politically, neither of you has the authority. The Coalition possesses absolute supremacy and influence. Our tactical operatives drive the governments. Pay close attention. According to the deciphered details, the four must unlock the visions and unleash the Divine. We must allow them to gain their strengths to see how we can harness their potential."

Parsons kicks the chair. "I know they are lab rats for our experimentation. How do you know so much about their powers, lockets, or Divinities? How are you gaining insights, and why haven't you told me?" Irritated, he listens to the board's conversation while glancing at the peasants walking on the sidewalks. "We have sent troops, used our latest technology to scan the ranch property. Veda and I have a plan. We need to take action now. Stop all the deliberating."

"I asked Veda to pull back all the troops right before this call," Zhao says, voice remaining calm. "We don't need a massive negative public focus on GREC, especially with our takeover of the United Nations. I've assured the United States government that we will continue to operate unnoticed to the American citizens. That means the UFE cannot form a massive military presence."

Parsons's fists tighten as his fingernails dig into his palms. "They still don't know about their abilities, and you are always looking at the political angle."

"You need to recognize that your role is only in operations, not strategy. Veda and I work together on the overarching vision. I saved you from a lifetime in prison, did I not? You murdered Julieta in front of María and killed the Landowski's against my authority."

Parsons sits down in the chair, rolling his eyes before he speaks. "I won't repeat that mistake. Veda told me if I do that again, she will end me herself. So you both have my word I won't kill them yet. But I am getting close to shitting on some of the board members." He rubs his left hand over his shaved head.

"Veda told me her initial plan of stealing the first locket," Zhao replies. "I instructed her to wait until all four have theirs. Once they do, then you can move forward. Their lockets will guide us to the next step."

Parsons loses his patience with Zhao and the seventeen members on the line, grunts, and smacks his desk. "You still haven't told me where you're getting the information from after all these years?"

"That's for me and the board to know, not the UFE or you. You might be Veda's number one, but you're still a foot soldier. I pulled you out of the abyss."

"I have to run. Let me know if there are any more limitations or decisions discussed." He pauses as his beautiful assistant walks in wearing a pink body con dress and motions that she's leaving. She turns around and shuts the door with the lofting smell of vanilla perfume.

Distracted by her backside, he realizes he hasn't finished his statement. "I need to focus on getting some answers on another case." Parsons slams his laptop shut, frustration etched into every line on his face. The anger bubbles inside him like a volcano on the verge of eruption. Taking a couple of deep breaths to calm down doesn't erase the freshness of Zhao's taunting words. Memories flood his mind as he contemplates the origins of it all.

۞۞۞۞

Jackson and Hamilton Parsons entered the marines against their wealthy New Jersey parents' request. The twin brothers, born seven minutes apart, wanted to prove they were more than spoiled elitist children who attended boarding schools. They both desired to outdo their parents' fortune, but they both had a dark side. During their elementary school days, they would capture rabbits or squirrels and subject them to agonizing torment until the animals met a miserable demise. In middle school, they would tamper with the brake lines of random cars parked outside restaurants, expecting the chaotic aftermath. Although they achieved top honors upon graduating high school, a lack of fulfillment in academia plagued their psyche. The duo knew that strategic lessons from the marines would help them navigate the corporate landscape and allow them the freedom to kill without repercussions.

Five years later, Jackson and Hamilton Parsons shipped out on their sixth and final tour in Afghanistan. They survived and thrived in the war zones and wanted one last taste of enemy death.

"Jackson, be careful. Keep your head on a swivel when the bridge goes down."

"Brother, we got this. Let's roll it, and then we can go home. Only six months left, then we're done."

"Oorah!" Hamilton replied with a corded neck.

The Taliban waited and lashed the first couple of battalions from the United States. They were part of the third wave that crossed the bridge. As marines, they didn't quit and moved farther into the first city, and then it happened. Multiple children and women strapped with bombs exploded around their unit, and in a single moment, Hamilton viewed his brother, Jackson, blown into a million pieces. Erupting in rage as his brother died, Hamilton unleashed. He slaughtered fifty civilians and about twenty Taliban fighters. When his ammunition ran out, he used his knife to butcher anyone in reach until a fellow corpsman jumped on Parsons's back and pinned him to the ground. Multiple other troops helped detain Hamilton while the rest of the force moved forward. "I will kill every one of you; release me. I'll win this war alone," Parsons yelled, seething for retribution.

A few weeks later, Hamilton had already received a dishonorable discharge and was awaiting the court-martial. The morning before he entered the courtroom dressed in an orange jumpsuit, his well-connected parents had a deal worked out with some of their wealthy and influential friends in the government and private sectors.

Hamilton sat by himself in a holding room and waited for the felony court to begin. Wei Zhao thrust the door open, shining a light in the darkly lit room, telling the officers to leave and not ask questions.

"We have a deal worked out," Zhao said to Hamilton, slamming his fist in his palm, "and I will change the outcome of your punishment as other-than-honorable discharge only if you agree to work for me for the rest of your life on this planet."

"Fuck you, fuck the world. The only way I would agree to some bullshit is if I can unleash hell on Earth."

Zhao sneered. "Deal. I wanted you to be the lead on operations with light restraints, tons of money, and power. The special operations unit has the pull in certain bureaus and in the United States Armed Forces. You will work for the Global Reform Establishment Coalition as the boots on the ground."

"I want revenge, power, and I won't be afraid to take it. I just watched my brother blown to shit. I still feel his blood on my face."

"The Coalition gives the instructions, and you execute them, and receive enormous money and power. If you follow my directives as ordered, then we will fulfill my ambitions to create a global military force without limitations, giving us global control."

Parsons knew if he didn't take the deal, he would have no freedom, no revenge, no power, and someday, down the road, he would control the Coalition Zhao mentioned. Parsons stood up, "Deal. When do I start?"

"Now. I'll have them release you, no panel, and we'll take care of the political details." Zhao handed him a stack of papers in a wrapped folder. "Your first ten missions start now. You will work in collaboration with my two leads, Julieta and her protégé, Veda. I want you to review the tactical and strategies report for all of them and execute the operations in four weeks. If you cannot deliver or you go offline, your life will end. Are we clear?"

"You won't be disappointed," Hamilton responded, "and I'll reward you ten times over for the opportunity."

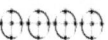

Hamilton Parson hurls his wireless mouse across the office. He knows Zhao gave him the opportunity, but he's tired of being controlled like a puppet. With every word he utters, his neck veins pulsate, and his eyes held a mesmerizing glint of orange, and body radiated a fiery silhouette. He wants to be the puppet master, not some academic bureaucrat. Before leaving, he texts Veda: *The Coalition is so useless. Power to the Federation.*

She replies: *Hamilton. Don't blow your top.*

۞۞۞۞

Wei Zhao pushes the button in the center of the wood-grained conference table to disconnect the call and turn off the blank dial tone. His well-defined and athletic build, accentuated by a dark burgundy, cashmere tailored suit, contributes to his authoritative presence. A former spy for the People's Liberation Army, he addresses the Coalition members. "I can't argue with his results, but that man gets on my nerves. For twelve years, he has accomplished what was necessary with minimal failures. We'll handle the Veda problem later." Zhao exhales while deliberating how Veda is the brightest mind in India, the most talented tactical operative in that region. That is all thanks to the UFE secret head of research department scientist and her pharmaceutical experiments.

A lady sitting three chairs down from where he was standing says, "Sir, if I may?"

Mr. Zhao nods for her to speak.

"We have infiltrated the schools, divided the populace based on race, religion, and sexual orientation, weakened all the world military, enabling the sheep to tear each other apart while we rule in the shadows." She has a heavy Russian accent. "We have the world where we want it. Why is Divinity so important?"

He walks to the front of the conference room, gazing at the black monitor. His body jerks around as he takes notice of the reactions from the other members sitting around the table. "Each of us has wealth and riches, and we will soon have the power to remove all potential threats. That is why. It leaves no room for revolts, uprisings, or hope. History has taught us that when we squeeze too hard, we lose, and the endless cycle begins again. This time, we leave the population with no alternative. We ensure that our ruling class, our children, and our way of life face no threats, and we have pawns to govern and manipulate." Mr. Zhao places his hands on the top of the chair in front of him, leaning over to review the audience.

He fixes his eyes on the newest member of the board, an uncomfortable looking Arabic American gentleman seated near the back of the gray walled room, who stares at the pure whiteboard, which gives the impression it was a recent purchase. Mr. Zhao jolts him out of his train of deliberations. "Saleh, have something to say? Say it."

"How can we trust nations not to in fight when they cannot even agree on a governing style, religion, money, who's in charge—"

Mr. Zhao interrupts, "Once we deter any possibility of an uprising, each division sitting at this table can choose how they govern with no global police, as we all will agree on an equal portion, splitting up who reigns what countries."

A man on the right side raises his hand. Wei Zhao moves his chin up, signaling the man to speak.

In a heavy British accent, he says, "Why have you allowed the Federation to gain so much power? They can control us now—and they are."

Before Mr. Zhao rebuts, the main door for the conference room opens, and a taller, clean-shaven, European American man walks through. As the door shuts behind him, he says, "Hope I'm not interrupting. Just got here from Washington. Those bureaucrats in Congress couldn't even tie their shoes without us." The entire room turns toward Walter Roosevelt, the CEO of Pierce Roosevelt Financials & Investments. He pulls out the chair at the end of the table, sits down, crosses his legs, and asks, "What did I miss?"

"The members seem confused by the UFE role, the Divinities, and the overarching plan." Mr. Zhao smells the obnoxious cologne. "Would you explain where I failed to?" Mr. Zhao placates with his arms spread out.

Mr. Roosevelt, who obliges, takes control of the room. "When we get what we want, then we kill Parsons and Veda. We control the world. Remember that—it's our products, our marketing, our silencing of threats, our influence, our laws, us behind the scenes creating riots, chaos, falsified news, AI-generated search manipulation, and history alteration, keeping the population angry. Then we will silence the populace once we become Divine. Isn't that right, Seok?"

The CFO for DaeChie Pharmaceuticals stands up. Her short silver hair complements her piercing dark eyes—windows into a brilliant mind, and youthful caramel skin. "That is correct, Roosevelt. We've been planning and experimenting for a long time. We are close to a solution." She ponders to herself about the new revelation in her research, a breakthrough that occurred six months ago. The board, Roosevelt, Zhao, and Veda, in her eyes, are the beasts of the field, and she is the sword. *In due time, the world will learn who the dragons are and who are the carcasses.* "The solution is a secret weapon, so to speak."

"All the top finance companies are manipulating the markets and world governments." Roosevelt cracks his knuckles. "We have the population's most personal data, retinal scans, DNA samples, and fingerprints—the last thing we need to do is shut the door on any hope of an uprising. That's why we have chased the golden egg for twenty years." He pauses, scanning the room as everyone's eyes fixate on him. "If anyone or any country gets in our way, we will delete them from the planet. We must push those four naïve twits to reveal the energy source, and then it's all over. That's why Parsons and Veda are playing the game. Believe me. I know Hamilton is power-hungry, driven mad by his need for retribution for his brother's death." In the back of Roosevelt's mind, he believes that if Parsons holds the lockets, he'll wipe the Middle East off the map and become the world's czar through his narcissistic and psychotic mindset. The guy is crazy, messed up in his head on the edge of insanity—all thanks to Zhao. But only Seok knows how to kill him, because he was the first experiment to replicate the power of the Divinity. "Our plan is to get rid of him after those four children unlock their abilities with the lockets."

Seok leans forward and studies Roosevelt. "I've been keeping a watchful eye on the Four children of the Divinity ever since they took their first breath. We won't rush and still have a lot to figure out now that we have a Scepter to help us."

"Seok, you might think you have a plan, but this is a race, and my little star pupil, Nicolaus, is the centerpiece, just like his mom. You, of all people, know that I decide how we proceed."

A man sitting near the back of the room groans.

Roosevelt shoots him a dagger-like stare. "Say what you're thinking, don't hold back."

The man with an Australian accent speaks up. "Torture them, get the details, and then be done with these games. Twenty years of this, we're no closer than before. You're just holding out on us to maintain your power. Who's saying you don't just eliminate this entire room and become,"—the man gestures air quotes—"Czar?"

Roosevelt pulls out his phone from his pocket and uses his thumbprint to unlock the device, which already has an application opened. "Well, you don't, because I hold your life." He waves his index finger in the air and then presses down on the phone screen. The Australian man gags. Foam pours out of his mouth, and his face slams into the table. The coalition board, horrified, gapes at Mr. Roosevelt, and as he stands up to walk out of the room. "There's a button for each of you. Don't question me, Seok, or Zhao." Without a second thought, he opens the door and exits, leaving the audience in a state of shock. As he parades out of the building, a mischievous smirk dances across his face. His investments always return a positive gain. *The implant device Nicolaus and Akari created to wipe out the European Union's lead assassin works wonders.* He sneers. *When those four work as a team, no one can stop them, not even Veda or Zhao.*

Office
of
Influence

(10)

Present

That afternoon, during their stroll back from lunch, Nicolaus says to Dodge for the tenth time, "Thanks again for coming yesterday, making dinner, and listening. The day was intense." Going back to high school, Dodge and Nicolaus relied on each other for support and bro talk. In football, they pushed the boundaries with their relentless effort, working in sync as the team's quarterback and running back.

"Dude, enough. That's why we are here. What do you have planned after lunch?"

"It's my favorite part of the week: mentoring and uplifting sessions. What about you?"

"I've got logos to design that they'll decide to farm out to a vendor, anyway. They'd save crazy cash with how fast I crank out dope designs."

Nicolaus nods in agreement.

Dodge shakes it off, and his fingertips tingle with nervous energy. "I don't want to sound like Akari, but have you found more links between Pierce Roosevelt, GREC, and the UFE?"

Nicolaus sighs and tugs on his dress shirt sleeve. "I wish. Cybersecurity won't let me into the main databases. I've asked for clearance, but my boss told me Walter Roosevelt himself declined my request."

"That's not fishy or anything. That guy is such a d-bag."

"He is, and if our assumptions are correct, he hired us to observe what we're doing. So, both sides are measuring each other. If Akari logs into my computer, she can hack the system."

"The clock is ticking, bro. I want to get out of this hellhole. Plus, like Asa said,"—using his fingers, Dodge mimics air quotes—"the time is coming soon."

"What did he mean by that? It's so frustrating that he knows more than us." They've asked Marcin, Chie, and Keanu, but they just ignore them, telling them they need to wait.

"I guess we'll find out soon. But it's cool that Akari's now a sparkler like you and María."

"I dare you to call her a sparkler to her face."

"Done, and she'll smack you for it."

After the two friends enter the building, and head up the elevators to their office spaces, Nicolaus turns his chair to face the door. He notices one of his aspiring candidates, Raj, passing his office with a heavy breath and a scowl on his face. Raj carries his laptop bag with one strap, which appears odd, and his sweat drips down his forehead. Nicolaus recognizes the situation and sends a text message to Dodge, alerting security to evacuate the building as something may happen on his floor. He shuts his laptop and reaches into his backpack for his expandable bo staff, which he carries everywhere, same as Akari, who brings her nunchucks.

He walks out of his office toward Raj's manager's location down the other side of the commercial skyscraper, increasing his pace as he moves.

"Shut up and get on the ground," Raj yells.

His coworkers scream, "He has a gun!"

Nicolaus walks toward the scene where Zander, Raj's manager, is on his knees with Raj waving the gun around.

"Stop or I'll shoot everyone." Raj's hands shake. "Set down the weapon, Nicolaus!"

"I'm setting down my bo." Nicolaus sets the staff down and straightens. "Raj, this isn't you," Nicolaus says, noticing Raj's finger pressed alongside the barrel. He doubts Raj has ever held a gun. "Why don't we talk? You're a very talented developer, a family man with a loving wife, daughter, and son. Put down the gun. We can still salvage this situation. Think about your family. You'll be throwing your life away."

Raj scrutinizes Zander. "I work eighty hours a week. He takes credit for everything, and I get laid off. I have nothing. We came with nothing. I have a house now. My family is happy here. My visa will expire, I'll get deported, and we'll have nothing."

Nicolaus edges closer. "It's not him. Politics stink, but it is the corporation's machine, not him or anybody here. Raj, point the gun at me, not Zander." Raj's eyes widen in surprise and raises the firearm at Nicolaus.

"That's it—focus on me, Raj, and me only." Nicolaus's eyes shimmer with an intense, bright light green glow. "This is not you. Do you want your kids to live knowing their dad was a murderer? I can help you." Nicolaus is now a yard from Raj, ignoring the gun pointed at his forehead. "Zander, back up, and go slow." Nicolaus keeps his mental concentration aimed at Raj while raising his voice. "Everyone, move towards the doors. No one make a noise."

Sweat cascades off Raj's face onto his blue dress shirt. "Nicolaus, I don't know what to do—" Raj finds himself unable to peek away from the piercing gaze in Nicolaus's eyes. He feels suspended in time, as if everything around him has come to a halt.

Nicolaus's emerald eyes fix on Raj's face. "You did nothing wrong." His eye color shifts from emerald-green to brilliant orange. A grim male voice in a low tone permeates Nicolaus's mind. *Let him do it. Let him kill everyone.* Nicolaus hears the soft tone of Aamirah fighting back. *Ease your mind. Don't let evil enter.* Nicolaus grunts and shakes his head and his eyes transition back to shining emerald-green.

Raj stands like a statue. His face becomes pale, and his pupils transform to solid white. Nicolaus yells, "Let it go! This is not you."

Raj's hands tremble with his finger slipping on the trigger. Nicolaus grabs hold of Raj's wrist and applies pressure to force him to loosen his grip on the gun. With a sudden twist, he disarms Raj, snatching the weapon out of his hands. Nicolaus's fingers curl around the cold metal of the gun and release the clip, which clanks on the floor as Raj drops to his knees. Nicolaus kicks the clip away, kneeling before Raj, and sets the gun down. "You made a wise choice, Raj. Just keep looking at me."

As the police barge in, they charge toward Nicolaus and Raj, screaming at them to lie on the ground and put their hands behind their backs. The officers handcuff them while Nicolaus's eyes fade to their normal shade of emerald-green.

Emerging from the trance, Raj blinks several times, his complexion returning to normal, as if he had just quenched his thirst, before locking eyes with Nicolaus. Raj whispers, "What happened? I blanked out. I—Nicolaus, I didn't want to—" His voice cracks. "Nicolaus. I never meant to hurt anyone. I wanted what's best for my family, and the stress I'm under . . ."

Nicolaus responds in a soothing tone, "We'll get through this together."

The police escort them to the main floor. When they reach the building lobby, Dodge and a few other officers greet them. Dodge points to Nicolaus, "That's not the dude. My boy just saved lives."

Nicolaus peers over his shoulder at the police officer. "Look, I neutralized the threat with no civilian casualties. Do you want my statement now? I'll give it."

"I did it," Raj says. "Nicolaus stopped me. He's innocent. I'm the one you want."

Nicolaus blurts. "Look, I disarmed Raj and avoided civilian losses."

The officers exchange glances and release the handcuffs. "Guessing you're former military?"

"Yes, sir." Nicolaus stands up, eyes Dodge while rubbing his wrist. "Served in the Green Berets."

"Let's get your statement going, and that was very brave of you. You're a hero."

"It's not about being a hero. The aim is to improve the world. Today we saved lives, and that's all that matters. He's a good guy put in a horrible situation." As the officers lead Raj out of the building, Nicolaus steals a quick glance at him, and Raj responds with a nod, acknowledging his fate of going to jail.

While Nicolaus gives his statement, Dodge calls Akari and María to meet them at the financial headquarters. They wait, standing behind the police line, as Nicolaus walks up to Akari and kisses her on the forehead, and hugs María.

The Four Shadows of Light leave the financial campus and arrive at Nicolaus and Akari's house. Dodge fires up food for the crew. Akari sits down on the couch, petting Kaili. "Let's recap the past two days. To start off, Nicolaus and I had visions for the first time."

"Identical visions, to be exact," Nicolaus adds, still contemplating the voices in his head while at gunpoint.

María taps her marker against the paper. "Yes, identical. Can you let Akari tell the details while I write on the easel, Nicolaus?"

"We have identified two locations: the Texas ranch and the Washington mountains," Akari says, while María writes on the board. "We also know that Aamirah is the Divinity contacting us, but we don't know who or what she is to us or our parents yet."

Dodge enters the room with a plate of organic mozzarella sticks and places it on the coffee table. "Just appetizers, and I'll get dinner kicking while y'all do the yapping thing."

María glares at Dodge. "Go make food, chef boy." He chuckles, waltzing back to the kitchen.

Nicolaus reflects how Raj seemed frozen when he stared in his eyes. This wasn't like in Russia when he got lucky with a mafia drug lord's son with guns pointed at him. He negotiated his way out of it and, of course, it helped that Dodge had the red dot pointed at the son too.

"When I disarmed Raj—" Nicolaus clears his throat. "I felt this strange sensation in my eyes, and Raj complied, entranced."

Akari glances at Nicolaus. "Was there anything else with it or just the sensation in the eyes?"

"It was like—Aamirah or the Divine power mind-controlled Raj—There was another voice, a deep-toned male who tried pushing me to allow Raj to shoot everyone. Aamirah helped me make the right choice and disarm him."

Akari takes a deep breath. "So you had to make a choice, and you chose the right pathway."

Nicolaus nods while rubbing his hands together.

She glances at the painting of Hiku and Kawelu climbing out of Poe, the land of departed spirits. She then observes Nicolaus's grandfather's heirloom painting of Lucifer falling from the heavens. Hiku and Lucifer both chose the wrong path. They have to make the right choices. Unlike the paintings or stories, Nicolaus made the right choice today. *But what about tomorrow? Who was the voice who spoke to Nicolaus?* Akari gets up and takes the marker away from María. "Recall the vision out loud to see if there is any correlation with our recent discoveries."

María paces in front of the entertainment center while retelling the details. Akari jots down notes on the gradual development of their powers and ponders the interpretations of Divinity statues as representations of saints. Akari writes *a new world order or a global threat* on the board—the potential link to UFE or GREC. Nicolaus shuts his eyes, leans in, and absorbs the details, envisioning the scene unfolding before him. As María completes the last part of the vision, she lets out a long exhale.

Akari reaches out to touch María's hand. "Sit down and collect your thoughts."

María shakes her head, not wanting to let herself relax. Her face twists with anger from missing her mother. She grabs a marker from the living room table and paces to the board. She writes one word on the board: *choices.*

"I'm done sulking. The thing is, we've made choices so far. We've chosen to not trust the UFE investigation about my mamá and Nicolaus's family. We've chosen to train, stay united. Whatever comes at us, we have each other's backs. We're listening to our instincts."

Nicolaus pulls out the glitter bottle from his pocket and twirls it in between his fingers. *The flawed investigation from the UFE claimed they would eliminate Hamilton Parsons and shut down the rogue faction—case closed. They wouldn't kill an agent who took out someone with the skills of his aunt. The UFE started as a back brace for global protection. Julieta knew the GREC wanted complete control, so she made the choice to help set up the UFE as a deterrent with its own priorities to balance out the global elitist takeover. But now it looks like the Federation is gunning for the complete control—like Julieta did too good of a job setting their platform. Was her mission driven by the Divinities? If Hamilton Parsons is still alive, where is he?*

Nicolaus puts the glitter bottle back in his pocket and peers at his cousin. "The GREC, UFE, and Pierce Roosevelt, they are the trifecta we are looking into. If Parsons is still alive, and this is a coverup, we will get retribution."

"Alrighty. Let's channel your rage into devouring kimchi stew. Come dig in." Dodge, wearing an apron and patting a silicon serving spoon, hoping to ease their minds with his fantastical meal.

María bangs her fist on the easel. "I want Parson's head on a stick, Vlad Dracula style."

Dodge points the utensil at María. "Now we're talking! You're busting out my Eastern European and Albanian roots. Skanderbeg and Vlad. My heroes."

Akari motions her hands downward. "María, let's go eat— like Dodge said—and enjoy some good home-cooked South Korean food."

María's conspiracy theory about the Global Reform Establishment Coalition goes back to how they work as a team. She's the strongest in enduring pain, and the grunt of the crew, but the foot soldiers take their orders from the strategy of their commanders. In their team, Akari is the lead on strategy. UFE, being the lead, doesn't add up in her mind. It makes more sense if Wei Zhao was the one pulling the strings.

Conspiracy
of
Loss

(11)

Present

Tuesday morning arrives, and Nicolaus reaches for his phone to check his emails. One particular message from Walter Roosevelt catches his eye. Roosevelt granted him some time off and wants to discuss yesterday's situation, along with a promotion. Nicolaus grins at the idea that he might, after playing the waiting game, gain access to the financial data he needs to complete the triangle between Pierce Roosevelt Financials & Investments, Global Reform Establishment Coalition, and the United Federation of Enforcement.

After reading the email, Nicolaus checks his unread text messages and finds one from María. She tells him that her father wants to throw a mini celebration tonight at his house in honor of his heroic actions from yesterday. She also mentions that her dad requested Nicolaus to examine the locket and make it "magically work," followed by a winking emoji. He shakes his head—*how can he make it work*? What did his mom mean by coded? He snickers, recalling Dodge—*IN A WORLD…*

Akari rolls over in bed and places her hand on Nicolaus's chest. "What's so funny?"

"My uncle is throwing us a party tonight as a hero celebration. He wants me to look at the locket. And Mr. Roosevelt emailed, giving me a promotion and some free time, and now maybe we can move forward with getting access to the financial data or an opportunity for you to do the hacking thing."

Just as they chat, Akari's cat jumps on the bed and rubs her whiskers against her.

"Your cat drives me crazy."

"Oh, leave my cat alone. She's adorable, and you need to be an animal person at some point."

"She looks like a fat tiger striped rat."

"Jealous of a cat, I see. Well, I'll take my cutie and fix us some breakfast, and you can have cereal unless you apologize to her."

"Really? Fine. I apologize. You're a cute, spoiled cat who makes Akari happy, so I like you too."

Akari gets up, and Kaili trails behind her into the kitchen. As he gazes at the ceiling, memories of the night his sister died flood back like a hurricane rushing ashore.

꧁꧂꧁꧂

Dae Landowski loved taking her family on work trips, in particular to Seattle, where they went hiking, enjoyed fresh seafood, and visited museums. Her tragic death occurred after a cancer research fundraiser event in Bellevue, Washington, hosted by DaeChie Pharmaceuticals.

Chie, Julieta, and Dae founded the company to save lives and eliminate life-altering conditions like spinal cord paralysis. Before her death, Julieta served as a silent partner who had worked behind the scenes, handling the threats in the shadows.

With the help of a Divine vision, Dae and Chie pressed on with their research, aiming to uncover more potential cures.

After the black-tie fundraiser ended, the Landowski family was the last to leave the lavish banquet hall, close to eleven o'clock at night. Nicolaus and Mi-Cha still had plenty of energy for playing tag. However, their parents were eager to get into the limousine and return to their penthouse hotel room after a long day.

Magnar, Nicolaus's dad, noticed that a different driver opened the door for them to step inside the limousine. He paused, reaching for his sidearm, and then a man dressed in a black suit with a burgundy tie approached him. He poked a gun in Magnar's lower back and advised them to climb in without causing a scene.

Another Federation operative sat in the vehicle, holding the family at gunpoint, directed them to sit in the back row of the car and confiscated both parents' firearms. Nicolaus noticed they were all wearing the same outfits María had described the night her mother died. Two of them wore black combat fatigues with United Federation of Enforcement patches, while the other wore a black suit, tie, and dress shoes.

The man in the middle was of French descent. "We told you to hand over all the information you have, and yet you keep the secrets to yourself. Let's see. We registered a massive energy spike from your ranch, and then your company created a diabetes cure. Then, another energy spike and a spinal synthesis infusion cure enabled the paralyzed to walk again. Then a third energy spike, and now you say you're close to finding the breast cancer cure? Which, by the way, you've been working on since Julieta's accident."

Magnar spoke through his teeth with forced restraint. "Don't you say her name. You all fucking killed her. We've given you everything. Let our family be."

The muscular arms and broad shoulders are about to break out of the suit. The man leans back against the seat. "We'll see what my boss says. He's interested in seeing you both now."

Dae held Nicolaus and Mi-Cha's hands during the menacing commute, while Magnar glared at the three men, wondering if there was any way to escape the situation.

Thirty minutes later, the vehicle pulled into a dark area in the Cascade mountains. The GREC representative waved his gun for them to exit the vehicle.

As Nicolaus's dad got out, he glanced at the kids. "Do nothing, try nothing. Let this happen for both of your sake." Nicolaus noticed his dad's eyes flickered from green to white to orange. An orange glow lifted out of his body, like a spirit rising out of his dad. Then his eyes shifted to green.

Mi-Cha shouted, "No, please. No. Why is this happening?"

The entire family exited the limousine on the gravel beside a deep cliff edged with snow-laden evergreens. The air smelled like fresh pines, and a sharp shiver struck the spine of Nicolaus's back. A large black SUV maneuvered next to them, and another fifteen combat-geared men circled the family.

Dae peered down at Mi-Cha, kissed her, and said, "I love you for all eternity. Stay strong." Dae stood up with a nervous twitch in her fingers. "Take care of Mi-Cha."

Nicolaus felt a suffocating sensation, as if he had sunk into quicksand, rendering him immobile, and all he could manage was a nod. It was then that he realized the importance of his parents' preparation in martial arts, military training, education, and life lessons. As they came to terms with their mortality, the harsh reality set in that he and Mi-Cha would soon be alone.

A tall, muscular, clean-shaven man dressed in a suit with an open-collared dress shirt got out of the last vehicle with an evil swagger and a broad smirk. "We don't need you sniffing around our business anymore."

"Parsons," Dae said, hands clasped together with her plea. "I'm begging you. Please don't do this."

"It's not my call. Leadership ordered me to eliminate any unnecessary pieces." Hamilton Parsons squinted at the officer with his gun aimed at Magnar. "Shoot him."

The UFE officer pulled the trigger. As Magnar's body hit the gravel, Mi-Cha screamed at the top of her lungs, and before she could run to her mom's side, Parsons shot Dae in the heart as the officer grabbed hold of her. Parsons surveyed Dae's body with an evil grimace and arched eyebrows. He cackled and shouted, "We only need one of the kids. As they say, two's company."

"Sir, that wasn't our orders—"

"Do as I say!"

Mi-Cha wiped away her tears while she observed the handgun placements on the officers, and how their hands trembled with fear in front of Parsons. Nicolaus felt the tip of the troops' barrel in his back while the officer swallowed heavy and eyed the demented distraction in Parsons' gaze as he stared at their parents' lifeless bodies on the ground. Their martial arts training from Asa and their battles against each other prepared them for this moment. She nodded at him with a sharp focus, like a finely honed blade, as they had no alternative but to gather their strength and kill all the UFE troops.

Nicolaus's nostrils flared. He struck the officer standing beside him, seized the automatic rifle, and shot the man in one motion. Mi-Cha spun around with an increased sensation of strength and ripped the gun from the Federation trooper in back of her. Nicolaus let out a primal roar. He eliminated nine men in rapid succession, improvising a human shield by using the officer's body beside him.

Mi-Cha shouted as she maintained a steady aim on the targets, firing her gun while evading the projectiles that zipped by in her direction. "That's for my mom—that's for my aunt—

that's for my dad." She killed four officers before falling victim to an isolated bullet shot by Parsons, who fled back into his fortified vehicle and jetted away from the scene as only a coward would do.

Nicolaus fired multiple rounds at the vehicle and emptied the remaining ammunition into the last two troops. He surveyed the area for his sister, and spotted her crawling toward their parents, shivering, with a pool of blood spreading beneath her shuddering body.

He bolted to her with his veins straining against his skin. Taking a deep breath, he turned her over. His hands trembled as he lifted her fragile body in a protective embrace. Mi-Cha spoke her last words, "At least we had one last battle together," she whispered, her voice strained as she coughed. "Promise me you'll change the world."

Tears surged down his face. Nicolaus kissed his sister on her forehead, and she stopped breathing. He screamed so loud it echoed through the valley below, and his body fell to the ground, still holding his little sister after a tranquilizer dart pegged him in the neck.

Three hours later, he woke up in the limousine's trunk when a police officer opened the door and discovered him duct taped and hands tied. A flashlight blinded Nicolaus's eyes, and his ears thumped from the sounds of the sirens.

Bewildered and angry, Nicolaus thrashed about. His heart raced as the officer took the duct tape off.

The officer peered at Nicolaus. "It looks like a carjacking gone as wrong as it can go. The culprit is lying over there, and your dad must have shot him."

Nicolaus turned to scrutinize the crime scene and noticed an unfamiliar area. The color drained from his face. He relayed to the police officer what had happened, and realized the scene was different. Nicolaus assumed the guns were scrubbed clean, along with the limousine and the crime scene staged by the Federation and the man named Parsons.

How could he move forward without his parents and sister?

ὉὉὉὉ

Kaili hops onto the bed as Akari shouts, "Breakfast is served! Get up and come eat with me."

Nicolaus peeks at the purring cat. His anger dissipates into a smile. "She sent you in, huh? Well, I suppose I'll have to get used to you." As he walks into the kitchen, he's greeted by the mouth-watering aroma of eggs, Portuguese sausage, and savory rice. "Wow, you're going all out today." He plops down in a white farmhouse chair.

"I figured it'd be nice to have a nutritious breakfast together this morning, especially after the past couple of days," Akari replies. "I called into work and let them know I'm taking the day off."

Nicolaus nods and asks, "What time are we heading to Marcin's for the celebration barbeque?"

"María said to be there around five o'clock. She's also tried a couple of things to get the locket to do something, but to no avail. That's why Marcin wants you to look at it and figure it out."

"Got it," says Nicolaus, still pondering what the locket does. *Coded—what the heck does that mean?* He's speculated about it for years. When he touched the locket and the gate, he illuminated an ethereal glow. But when Marcin gave the locket to María, nothing happened. "Did she say who else is going to be there?"

"Our usual family combination," Akari answers. "Oh, and Dodge invited your direct reports from your work. And some of my coworkers from DaeChie are coming over too."

As Nicolaus puts barbecue sauce on his plate, he says, "While you let me rest, I recalled my parents' and sister's deaths. I'm with María. I just want the actual answers, and then we take them out."

"Revenge is not the only answer," Akari cautions. "We need to get firm proof and the full depth of your work's involvement with the Federation." Their investigation hypothesis is that UFE's good intentions evaporated at the very beginning, and Julieta acted as a dam to hold back the onslaught of corruption. Nicolaus's godfather, Casey, used Thomas Jefferson's quote for them to see how far the rabbit hole goes. *The end of democracy and the defeat of the American Revolution will occur when government falls into the hands of lending institutions and moneyed corporations.* "Once we have the proof, then we know all the players in this game."

"Let's game-plan how you can hack into the system to get what we need since we don't know the financial implications," suggests Nicolaus.

Akari pours pineapple juice for herself and Nicolaus. "Let's focus on beating María and Dodge in euchre later."

"Dodge can't stand that we beat him and María in horseshoes," Nicolaus chuckles. "He adds in the euchre flavor to at least win at something. Makes his ego feel better." He reflects on his and Dodge's competitions like rock climbing, paragliding, and even a forty-yard dash. Everyone hates to lose, but he and Dodge take it to another level, keeping a tally of their wins and losses. They never forget the importance of challenging one another. When one person is exhausted and ready to give up, the other person helps push them—no soldier left behind. Dodge is so talented at design and him with IT architecture they joked they could set up their own software development company and squash the large consulting companies.

"After we're done eating, let's get some housework done. Then I want to practice some violin with you as an audience, and then maybe a little extra playtime for both of us," she says as she strokes Nicolaus's hand.

"Housework, beautiful music, and romance. It's going to be a great time today."

♪♪♪♪

Later that evening, Dodge shouts, "Boom! Born and raised in Michigan, baby! I'm an euchre expert here. It's nine to three, after my two loners. Y'all better pack."

"Akari and I beat you both in horseshoes with seven ringers in a row." Nicolaus clenches his playing cards.

Sensing Nicolaus's agitation about losing, María deals. "Dodge, let's finish them before he explodes."

"Calm down there, my tiger. It's just a game. And I pass, by the way." Akari strums her left fingers against the table.

"I have hearts, the left, right, and the ace." Dodge slams his down his cards. "Like, game over."

Nicolaus scrapes his hand over his face as he notices Michele, his new direct report, and her fiancé, approaching. "Your uncle is hilarious. He's telling us stories about you all growing up together."

"My dad is a bit of an animated storyteller," María admits.

"It was so nice meeting all of you. We're taking off. Thanks again, Nicolaus, for stopping Raj . . . for yesterday."

Nicolaus and Akari wrap their arms around her and extend a handshake to her fiancé.

"Thanks for coming. Are you both the last ones left?"

"Yes, we couldn't get enough of the food. It's why we always visit Julieta & Marcin's Café. María, your dad is an amazing chef." Michele giggles. "Plus, watching you all compete against each other is beyond fun."

As the young couple leaves around nine o'clock, Akari says with a playful grin, "Let's go make smore goodness around the fire."

Locket
of
Light

12

Present

The Four Shadows of light sit down on the Adirondack chairs, each grab organic dark chocolates, graham crackers, and marshmallows.

"I remember the day we signed up for the army," Nicolaus says to the group.

A smile lights up Dodge's face. "It's funny. We walk straight into the recruitment center, and the recruiter explains things. Then María tells him mid-speech not to waste his breath and show us where to sign."

"He was so shocked that all four of us had already made up our minds and were ready to roll," Nicolaus adds.

Akari directs her gaze toward María. "The recruiter was more surprised that all four of us came in full camouflage gear with SAT and ASVAB high school scores all off the charts. He suggested we consider enrolling in one of those elite schools. Oh, and you totally intimidated him, María."

"Speaking of intimidation, we haven't talked about our operations in a long time," Dodge says, drumming his hands on his thighs. "How about we pick our favorite or funniest moment from our missions together?"

"Why? Do you need a break from the corporate world?" Akari says, while placing her marshmallow over the fire.

"Just some sort of action, instead of this same crap every day. We had like so many crazy adventures and then, boom, it feels like we smacked a wall in the boringness."

María says with a raised eyebrow, "All right, then you start it off."

"Cool, I enjoy being first for once," Dodge replies, beaming while María giggles. "We have so many missions, all successful, but my favorite moment was in the Middle East when twenty dudes ran straight at us with swords swinging in the air while we were all holding automatic weapons. María looks at us like 'Really?' then turns and, action movie style, cuts all of them down within seconds."

Akari confesses, "I have absolutely no idea what they were thinking."

"It's such a shame," María comments. "Veda wouldn't allow us to keep any of those swords as souvenirs."

Akari twists her head toward Nicolaus. "Your drone mishap in Africa is still my favorite." Everyone laughs.

"I'm never going to live that down, am I?"

"Nope. Your half-baked invention almost ruined the operation."

"The key word here is 'almost.' If my memory serves me right, the odds were skewed, with a ratio of seventy to four. Akari and María, doing the stealth-like reconnaissance, freed the ambassador with Dodge in overwatch with his sniping abilities. Once you all got back to the safe zone, their alarms wailed, all to plan. We heard sentry dogs barking and their makeshift trucks with turrets and machine guns roaring toward us. That's why my plan worked. We saved the day."

María chirps in and rolls her eyes. "So, let me get this straight. You added an explosive device to the drone without considering its weight, and then you blamed it on the wind when it fell right next to the guard."

"Sometimes I overthink or under think things when excited about an invention," Nicolaus responds, a wry smile forming on his lips. "My confidence in my abilities never falls short. But hey, the guy picked it up and ran into the barricaded stronghold, and then we lit them up. The entire compound erupted in flames. He did the job for us." Nicolaus punches his fist in the air.

"You never admit that you're maybe wrong or you messed up." María cocks an eyebrow at her cousin.

"Nope, it always works out."

"Well. We already know your favorite."

"Mission forty-two." Their commander said Nicolaus couldn't use explosives to neutralize the Iranian third in command. Nicolaus leans forward. "So Dodge and I were looking through our sniping scopes and not firing one shot."

"I hated that mission," Dodge blurts. "I didn't get to take out one bad dude. The girls had all the fun."

"Hey, we got to chill for once. And you can't tell me you didn't enjoy watching the action. Anyway, Akari and her swagger took out ten dirties with a knife, and María took out thirteen with her sidearm. Absolutely brilliant. Then he wanted you to retrieve the satellite documentation. That's when we noticed the UFE supplied the militants with government support."

Dodge glances at María, knowing she's about to bring up something serious, and asks, "What's your favorite moment or operation?"

"Project Seraph. Where we added on to our missions. We freed thousands of girls and women from human trafficking in Central and South America and Asia." María shifts in her chair, her movements gentle and deliberate. "Sure, our commands sometimes said *don't* free them and we did what is right. Man, all these global governments in partnership with the drugs and shipping women for profit are so messed up. It fucking pisses me off. The global elitists are never called out for their messed-up minds." María's eyes burn while gawking into the fire pit. "After taking down all those fuckers, we found ourselves in deep trouble because our directives didn't include freeing the girls."

Akari places her hand down on the armrest. "We did what is right. I only wish we had the resources to free all women around the globe held hostage by corruption."

María snaps out of her deliberation and changes the subject to the office aftermath. "So, what happens to Raj now?"

"He's in custody. He'll go to court, and they'll sentence him for a long time. I'm going to testify on his behalf. He's a good guy, put in a horrible position. However, he made an awful choice." Nicolaus frowns into the flames. "I've talked with Chie to sponsor his wife at DaeChie Pharmaceuticals, since she's a great coder. Chie said she'll have to hire her in India and cannot sponsor her in the United States after what Raj did." Nicolaus pauses. "Not to change the subject, but I'm still a little rattled by the voice that wanted me to let him shoot up the place."

Dodge glances at Nicolaus. "Have you tried closing your eyes and asking Aamirah?"

"Hilarious Dodge. She doesn't work that way, it seems." Last night, Nicolaus kept asking for an answer before he fell asleep, but he received no response.

María rubs one hand down her pant leg, closes her eyes, and takes a deep breath. "I found out today they granted me access to the Federation archives in the basement of Fort Cavazos." While she's talking, the fire crackles, crickets chirp, and neighbors chatter at a birthday party nearby provide a background symphony of sounds. "When I reviewed the archive's internal database, searching over the names and descriptions, I came across the classified area that somehow I have full access to."

Akari, Nicolaus, and Dodge sit on the edge of their chairs, hanging on every word. María leans forward, her elbows on her knees, hands crossed, as she simulates a praying position. "Divinities, Level 10—Contact Alexander Taylor for Access."

They all sat back in their chairs in silence.

"Get into that boxed archive," Dodge says, cutting the silence with an unusual serious face.

"What can I do to help?" Akari asks.

"I'll get the confirmation of what the UFE knows about the Divinities. You and Nicolaus have to get the financials to confirm Roosevelt's involvement." María fiddles with her necklace.

"Akari is the computer super expert," Nicolaus says and nods in agreement. "So when I meet with Walter Roosevelt, she can search and find out. We've got global security all set with Wayne on overwatch." Nicolaus grins and lifts his bottle of non-GMO beer. Wayne cracks him up. They've known him and his two sons, Henry and Mack Irons, since they were little kids. The three of them are former Air Force pilots and the air transportation for Kazanowski Moving Forces, Casey's company.

Akari taps the metal marshmallow roasting stick against her chair. "It's Hacking 101, no biggie. Just make sure I can use your computer on the network, and you keep him and your coworkers away from me in your office."

"No problem. I'm a hero now." Nicolaus smirks. He peers at María. "Would I be able to look at the locket?"

"Yeah, sure. Dad asked me to let you look it over, and it slipped my mind."

"He's asked me like ten times today. I felt like he was my sister. 'Are we there yet? Are we there yet?'" Nicolaus pauses.

Akari puts her hand on his. "Every day, she is here with us. There's no way we survived all that combat without help from above."

María stands next to Nicolaus, removes the necklace from her neck, and drops it into his open palm. His fingers twitch as he recalls when his mom fastened the same locket around his neck. He inspects the intricate design of the piece. As a young child, he didn't have the chance or inclination to study the locket.

"It's a beautiful necklace. And obviously, it does something for us." He knows that firsthand, *but how does this thing work?* "Let's go to the kitchen where there's more light," he suggests.

Dodge chimes in, "If it goes all sparky and stuff, we don't need the neighbors looking at María going all Zeus-like." Dodge's playful nature brings a smirk to Akari and María's faces as they shake their heads in amusement.

They move toward the back patio door, taking off their shoes, and settling around the kitchen island on the vintage leather bar stools.

Nicolaus examines the necklace. "Hold on. Now I see why your dad wanted me to look at it. Dang, I wish my mom would have let me check this out." He discovers there are two openings. The main locket fold has pictures of the Divinity symbol, and he guesses it's Aamirah. There's a small slit on the beveled edge. "Get me a paper clip, María."

She hands him a paper clip, and he uses it to poke into a little circle hidden in a sculpted crevasse on the side. The second door on the locket pops open, and María, Akari, and Dodge step back, startled. Inside, there's a blank white paper on the right and some writing on the left: *Only a Divinity can Awaken with a Touch.*

Nicolaus smiles. "Man, I'm so glad my dad taught me well. He stressed details, details, details when working on the cars or mechanical inventions." He hands the necklace and locket back to María. "Notice it says 'with a touch.'"

Akari contemplates, it doesn't refer to a simple tap of the finger or a technology algorithm. It signifies a blood connection. She interjects before Nicolaus finishes his statement. "Our blood is the key. María, you need to touch the paper with your blood. That's how it's coded."

"Sweet. Blood opens the locket. That's so dope," Dodge says, eyes wide with excitement.

María gives Dodge a sharp glare as Nicolaus passes her his pocketknife. As she pricks her finger, a tiny drop of blood appears. She presses her index finger on the parchment paper. A white flash blazes through the kitchen, causing the lights to flicker and the sweet smell of baby's breath permeates the air.

"Are you alright, María?" Akari views María's unsteady head and tight grip on the countertop.

"I'm—did you hear the woman say, 'Welcome our child?'" she pauses. "Welcome to the Divinity."

Nicolaus, Akari, and Dodge stare at each other, confused, and then Akari says, "No, we heard nothing, but a burst of light surged out of you."

"That was just like your light surge at the dojo." Nicolaus says as he glances at Akari. "But it felt ten times stronger."

"I feel like fainting. I need to lie down." María touches her forehead, attempting to keep her eyes from closing.

Nicolaus catches María just in time, preventing her from tumbling off the chair.

"Bring her to her old room and place her on the bed," Akari says. He nods and lifts her up in his arms.

Dodge grabs a chair from the kitchen and places it next to her bed. "I got this. Go home and get some rest. Marcin is sleeping right now, too. I'll have María text you both in the morning."

"Are you sure?" Akari shakes her head in apprehension. "I'd rather stay by her side. She's like my sister."

"Dude, she's, like, sleeping. You know I love her more than anything. I'll stay by her side all night."

Nicolaus leans over, kisses his cousin on her forehead, and then gapes straight into Dodge's eyes. "If there is anything, anything at all, text us, and we'll be right there."

"I can handle this and it'll be good for me, too. Show some maturity, and María may want to be more than friends with benefits at some point," Dodge says with a grin.

Akari and Nicolaus hug Dodge, leaving him alone with María.

Over the next six hours, Dodge watches María's reactions to the Divine visions with growing anxiety. She jerks back and forth, muttering in an unfamiliar language and sweating. Dodge gets up from his chair, rushes to the kitchen, and grabs a towel. He runs cold water on it, wrings it out, and hurries back to María's side. He places the towel on her forehead and holds her left hand, which calms her down. The unrecognizable language fades into the background as mere murmurs.

ꭾꭾꭾꭾ

Aamirah bellows to María, overlooking sand and rock formations. "Divine Child, you must stop history from repeating itself." María surveys her surroundings. She's in the Chihuahuan Desert in Mexico. A Mexican gray wolf runs toward her. Her instincts kick in and she reaches for her gun, but it's not there. "My child, you must meet this head on. The evil destroyed the Divinities from within." The wolf launches at María. "You must embrace your role. Let it engulf you. Let it become part of you."

María closes her eyes, feeling a bolt of lightning that jars her eyes open. The desert landscape is gone. Only white sand and cacti are visible. María walks toward the plant.

The soft voice continues. "Do what is righteous. Fill your soul with love. We selected your parents because their hearts were pure. Rid the world of evil and hate, even when the choice is painful."

María stands next to the cacti. Her arm moves without hesitation, and she pricks her finger on the sharp spines. Blood drips on the white ground, and a searing pain she's never felt before vibrates through her body. She screams multiple times. The crimson beads falling on the clean surface reverse their course, flowing back into the minuscule hole in her finger, which closes up, leaving no trace of her pricked finger.

"Seek the vital spark of the chamber. Open your senses to the visions I share."

A familiar voice calls to María. A searing pain forces her to drop to her knees, screeching. The sound of her mother's voice reverberates in her ears.

"The necklace acts as a protective barrier, preventing any mortal harm from coming your way while you wear it." Like a thunderstorm passing, the pain subsides. María's chin quivers as she holds her stomach. "You must seek the remaining seven to unite the chamber, dispersed in five parts."

María yells, "Mamá, where are you?"

"I am here with you."

A breeze rolls over her cheek, and she closes her eyes. The fragrance of sunflowers intoxicates her senses.

"My daughter, a Divine child of Nativity. You are the enforcer; the soul clears the pathway of the four. Veton is the protector, Akari guides. Your cousin Nicolaus is the creator." The sweet smell of flowers changes to burning wood, suffocating her lungs. "Hamilton Parsons is still alive, and he's biologically

morphed. Be cautious and don't act out of uncontrollable hatred."
Her lungs burn and smoke clutters María's sight. "I love you
always and forever, my daughter."

Julieta's voice transforms into Aamirah's tone, but with a
roar of anger. "He will surrender completely to the blood of the
Divine. He must surrender. His heart and soul belong to her, and
the pair shall unite the world. The three are children of Divinity,
and the one is the protector. The four will fuse to eradicate the
evil. Take heed of the remaining four. The Accursed haunt their
presence."

María coughs, feeling the hole open up in her finger with
blood streaming as she falls flat on her stomach. The searing pain
flows from her legs through her spine to her brain, feeling a
thousand electrical arcs. She screams, hearing the voice in her ear
as the arcs stop. She cannot lift her arms. "He must not betray her
or the Divine."

Rain sprinkles around her, calming her fire-ridden skin.

At around four o'clock in the morning, María's eyes open,
and she turns her head to find Dodge sitting next to her bed. Tears
roll down her cheeks.

He leaps to his feet, his heart pounding with relief. "You're
up. I was so fucking worried." He pushes the chair aside.

"Shut the fucking door," she whispers, and Dodge obeys,
closing it behind him. He returns to the bed, slipping under the
covers beside her. He wraps his arm around her waist, touching
their foreheads as she leans into him.

"My mamá spoke to me." María grips his arms, her eyes
fixed on his. "Parsons is alive. There are eight lockets." She
pauses, gathering her strength, and recalls the vision. Dodge
listens, his heart racing with the weight of her words as her nails
dig into his arms. Once María finishes, she kisses Dodge.

After a minute, he moves his lips away from hers. "So, like,
the Divinities get you all . . ."

Before he finishes his statement, she replies, "Stop your fucking yammering and kiss me."

They press their lips against each other, hearts racing. She rips open his buttoned shirt as he pushes down her jeans, both tearing at the barriers between their bodies, desperate for release. Their moans fill the air, sweat beads form on their skin, and they grip onto one another, anchoring themselves against a passionate tumult that culminates with an electrical jolt. They collapse, holding each other, staring into each other's eyes as their heartbeats slow in the aftermath.

"Dodge, we must do everything we can to keep Nicolaus on the path."

"We will. He's a big boy who can handle himself. I don't think he wants to battle you and Akari or be part of a band called the Accursed." Dodge kisses her forehead. Before they drift off to sleep, María smells the freshness of a flower. As she glances at the nightstand, a single sprig of baby's breath undergoes a remarkable transformation, growing from a tiny bud to a blooming flower.

Light
of
Darkness

(13)

Present

At sunrise, Marcin bursts through the door, his cheerful good morning echoes through the room. He surveys the surroundings while María and Dodge attempt to open their eyes.

"Really?!" Marcin asks in shock. "Don't you two have your own houses to do that?"

Dodge pulls the sheets up to his neck, while María's voice reveals a touch of amusement. "Dad, let's talk over breakfast, and then you will understand."

Marcin's disappointment is apparent as he shrugs his shoulders.

"Dad, I had a vision in my sleep last night. It's the locket. It worked."

Marcin's face shifts from a frown to a flicker of excitement as he awaits to hear about the vision. "Your mom told me some details that occurred. I'll go, umm—go make breakfast. Will omelets, coffee, and biscuits work, María?"

"Yes, Dad," she answers. "We need to freshen up, and we're excited to fill you in on everything." He leaves to fix breakfast and avoid the awkwardness.

Dodge gawks at María. "Wow, that's the first time your dad didn't filet me with his eyes."

She kisses him. "He loves you, but he still thinks of me as his little girl, and he's jealous that we are always together. I'm sure you'll be like that if we have girls, too."

"I'll probably be worse. Chastity belt, anyone?"

María slaps him on his chest. "Let's get ready, but first, did we miss any messages?"

Ten missed calls and texts, all from Akari and Nicolaus. Dodge smirks. "They're stupid worried. I'll call Mr. Brainiac. Also, you admitted that we might have a chance for kids."

"I'll call Akari and have them come for breakfast. Go tell my dad they're coming over and then go take a shower. And we have plenty of time in the future to see if kids are what we both want." She eyes Dodge's body as he crosses the room. "By the way, I like your ass, but you can't go naked to tell my dad to make more food."

"I think your dad would throw me out." He struggles into a pair of athletic shorts. "Hey, so check this out. You had a vision when your mom died. Akari and Nicolaus just had a twin version, and now you have a locket vision. Should we call this, like, an Evolution of Vision or something? Cause that's what the Aamirah is doing. Giving us ingredients, so to speak, to make the meal?"

"That's good, Dodge. You're actually thinking—with the foodie analogy."

Dodge snickers and leaves the room.

Nicolaus and Akari arrive at Marcin's house a half an hour later and exit their shiny silver muscle car. They walk toward the front door while Nicolaus sips his Ammunition Coffee. Akari peeks at him and says, "Your impatience for caffeine is amusing."

"After last night and this morning of passionate lovemaking," Nicolaus replies, winking at Akari, "I need the caffeine to invigorate me." She beams back.

Akari rings the doorbell, and Dodge opens the door. "Hola, you two are always smiling. Another great night for you both?"

"Thanks for letting us know María is alright." Akari blushes and walks past Dodge.

Nicolaus gives Dodge a bro hug. "You know how we are. It's like a romance novel 24/7." They walk to the kitchen after Dodge shuts the door.

"I'm so happy you're okay," Akari says as she hugs María. "What happened? Dodge texted us that, in his words, some poop emoji went down, and we have to come over."

"Can you just not use emojis for once?" María rolls her eyes in exasperation.

"No way, they're so fun, and they tell a story without typing an entire sentence. Genius they are." María shakes her head while they sit down.

Marcin places a Kona coffee at each person's table. "Akari, your parents' coffee is fantastic. The blend is perfect." He glares at Nicolaus. "My nephew ought to stop doing the six-bucks coffee and make the homebrewed style."

"The place is local and owned by veterans. And Akari and I are working with them to source the Iona Farms coffee and set up a coffee chain. Plus, sometimes you need a quicky." He winks at Akari.

She shakes her head, her hair swaying, and then brings the warm cup of coffee to her lips for a sip. "Alright, enough chit-chat. María, tell us what happened."

María places the baby's breath on the table and describes her vision to the group. Nicolaus stares at the floor, spinning the glitter bottle in his hands. He darts his eyes to María's and then back to the ground. He can't focus on anything else besides Parsons being alive.

Akari listens, breathing in deep while taking in the vision. She concentrates on the word biologically—*did they experiment on him? Create their own super soldiers? How many are there? Which pharma did this? Could she emulate whatever their scientist did—create an antidote?*

After the recollection, while rolling a piece of fruit in her hand, María says, "I'm just glad these are new visions. For eleven years, I've only rehashed the same single vision from the night my mom died. Honestly, there's only so many times I can see a hand touching my shoulder and saying we are the blood of Divinities." Her gaze lingers on the fruit, her concentration slips away as she theorizes about finding Parsons for closure. She shakes her head. "And by the way, Dodge actually came up with a name. It's an Evolution of Vision from Aamirah that will lead us forward."

Akari peers at Dodge. "Look at you. For once, you're ahead of all of us."

"Hey, every once in a while, I'm dope like that." He points at the locket around María's neck. "So, there is another seven of those buggers."

Nicolaus purses his lips, not hearing anything but his own thoughts. *Are the Accursed a legion of wickedness?* He stops twirling the bottle and grips it in his left hand. *Parsons is alive. Coded lockets for the chamber. What is the chamber? How do they find all the lockets? There's four for them, and he knows the fifth was Mi-Cha's. Where can they find Parsons? What if they hack into a government retinal scan database? They could track him down.*

"The only thing I haven't mentioned I saved for last—," María says before Dodge can answer. "It's for you both." She makes strong eye contact with the Akari and Nicolaus. Akari grabs his hand, pulls him back to reality as a scowl fades from his face. "He will surrender completely to the blood of the Divine. He must surrender. His heart and soul belong to her, and the pair shall unite the world. The three are children of Divinity, and the one, the protector, will fuse to eradicate evil."

Akari's forehead wrinkles with worry, and Nicolaus is speechless, both understanding the meaning. They gawk at each other.

"You have my heart and soul," Nicolaus says while peering into her eyes. "I know I need and want you, and we cannot do this without each other, always together, always forever."

Akari knocks Nicolaus off his chair, kissing him, and with Marcin breaking up what could be the couple's fourth time in ten hours. "Hey, not in the kitchen. Man, to be young and in love again. First, I walk into my daughter's room with you two," pointing at María and Dodge, "and now you two are in a love fest."

"I'm sorry, Marcin," Akari says while they pull away from each other's grips. "This whole thing . . . it makes so much sense that our souls are together."

"That's how Julieta and I were, too." Marcin says as he stands beside the table, taking off his apron. "Passionate romance."

"I don't want to hear it, Dad." María chimes in.

"Let's eat before the food gets cold," he chuckles. "Then you can all gather in the living room to discuss your plans." Akari and Nicolaus finish breakfast first. "Leave your plates, both of you, and relax while Robert Oppenheimer and Edward Teller finish up."

Dodge looks up with a biscuit hanging out of his mouth and says half audible, "Really, the atomic bomb reference."

"Well, you are like organized destructive chaos with all the best intentions. So would you rather me call you Ada Lovelace and Charles Babbage?" Marcin asks with a smile.

Dodge gives two enthusiastic thumbs up as María sketches the visions into her notebook.

Once Dodge finishes breakfast, he and María get up together, walking into the living room with Nicolaus and Akari sitting on the couch, snuggling together, touching the side of their heads while holding hands. When one of them has a bad day or feels bothered by something, the other is always there to offer emotional support and comfort. Akari strokes his hair and Nicolaus runs his hand down her arm. Akari sees the anger in his eyes for Parsons, but there's something else in his thoughts. The Accursed nags at him—*could GREC and UFE use their spirit?*

"I guess we get the two chairs on opposite ends of the room," Dodge says to María.

Nicolaus blinks multiple times, shakes his head and suggests to Dodge, "Pull the two chairs closer, and we can discuss the plan around grandma's old coffee table."

María and Dodge grab the two reclining chairs and sit. She picks up the notebook she left on the table and continues writing and sketching the visions.

"María," Akari asks, drawing her friend's focus. "Can you repeat the line about the chamber?"

María closes her eyes and concentrates, a small wrinkle appearing between her eyebrows. "You must unite the chamber, which is separated into five parts—"

"Let's talk about the necklaces first," Nicolaus interrupts.

"You gotta pick a path and stay with it, cousin," María retorts, rolling her eyes.

"Sorry," he utters, holding his hands up in placation. "Do your thing, and I promise I'll be quiet until—"

She doesn't give him a chance to finish. "When you wear the locket, it shields you from any mortal harm. You must seek the remaining seven."

Dodge's knee is bouncing so hard that it shakes the coffee table. "So . . . we are on an Easter egg hunt to find the lockets and a quest to assemble some magical chamber. Does anyone have any idea what it's supposed to do? Is it like one hundred percent pure adrenalin? Like we can beam to another galaxy?" He taps his palm on his chest.

María huffs. "Let's focus on one thing at a time. We must get our lockets first."

"Okay." Dodge's leg resumes its bouncing. He can't seem to focus without moving some part of his body. "So, the first locket was with your dad. The second for you, Akari, is probably with your parents. The third, for me, is probably with—hmm."

"Maybe with Catalina and Herculano," Akari suggests. Akari peers at Nicolaus before Dodge can reply. "Nicolaus, where do you think yours is at?"

"The most logical place is the ranch." He reflects about his dad and mom always mentioned hiding spots there. "They tried disguising their intentions in Korean and Polish for Mi-Cha and me not to eavesdrop. We only recognized certain words—like hiding it at the ranch. We just need some sort of clues as a starting point."

Dodge laughs. "Yo, so your parents used two actual languages and my parents used pig Latin to disguise their plans as me and my sister totally could understand them in Albanian."

The doorbell rings, propelling them to all jump up. They hear a thud as someone drops a package on the doorstep.

"There's no way," Dodge exclaims as they stare at each other.

Marcin walks through the living room humming and glances at them. "I can see all of you are jumping beans today. I'll get the door." Marcin opens the door, squinting with the sunlight beaming into his eyes. He bends down to pick up the package from the porch and looks around, surprised not to see a delivery truck. He closes the door, unseals the box sent from Nicolaus's godfather, and pulls out a piece of paper. "It's from Casey. I told him I was giving the locket to María, and he wanted Dodge to have his locket. He didn't want to text the location, just in case the UFE hacked into our phones." He pauses and peeks at the Four Shadows of Light, reading the note aloud. "'It's buried underneath the cross in Catalina's backyard garden next to the house and the two fountains.'"

"See, I know what I'm talking about." Akari's dimples gleam, glancing at Nicolaus.

"Yes. You are always right, my goddess."

"Dad," María asks, perplexed. "You wouldn't keep two necklaces a couple of doors apart. Where was mine?"

"Casey dropped it off the day I gave it to you. Your mom told me over and over that you would be ready on your twenty-sixth birthday."

"Why didn't Casey say hello to us and at least let me see him?" Nicolaus asks.

María glimpses down at the locket, and something occurs to her. "Why didn't Mom wear this the night she died?" She clutches the locket tighter. "And if it saves us from mortal harm, then why not give them to us sooner?"

"They said y'all would be ready on your twenty-sixth birthday to harness the gift."

Among the four, María was the youngest, turning twenty-six last in the season of renewal. Akari was born in summer, Nicolaus in fall, Dodge in winter.

Marcin sits on the chair's sidearm. "Not sooner and not later. They claimed that if we were to give up the gift sooner, we would lose this world. They said—"

María interrupts and asks, "The Divinities?"

"Yes. The Divinities gave the lockets as spiritual artifacts, so to speak, and only those whose blood can harness it." Marcin clears his throat. "Akari, your parents and I agreed not to disclose the details we know to the four of you as instructed by Aamirah through Dae's first and only vision. I can say for sure you must figure out the major players trying to take these gifts. And you will discover the sanctuary soon enough. Last, assemble the chamber."

Staring at Nicolaus, he says, "You must be ready to lead from only your heart. They will tell you more. So, your focus now must be on finding the companies and people responsible for killing our families to seek the rest. That's what I know."

"So, my mom experienced a vision, and no one said a word? And what's the sanctuary?"

Ignoring Nicolaus's questions, Marcin turns to María. "If that could have saved your mom, believe me, she would've had it on her, and if she thought you wouldn't have survived, she would have put it on you." Marcin chokes up. "She was the first. They chose her to have you."

Marcin stares at Akari and Nicolaus. "That is the same for both of you." Now Marcin glares at Dodge. "They chose you, like a root on a tree, to maintain balance, so to speak." He eyes the four of them. "Focus on your goal this week, and the rest will happen in a short time."

María hugs her dad and turns to Dodge, Akari, and Nicolaus. "Let's get planning and deal with the logistical systematic nightmare."

Before leaving the room, Marcin gazes at his daughter. "The phrase that stuck in your mom's visions drove her to keep going after the Coalition and the Federation, as she couldn't figure it out—you must seek the darkness and turn it into light."

Two
of
Lockets

Marcin's living room converts to the command post for the day as the Four Shadows of Light continue their strategic planning.

Akari turns to María. "Start your observations tomorrow and then strike on Friday."

"The schematics for the UFE building are not public," Nicolaus advises. "I need you to note the advanced security measures near the vault, such as retinal scans or keypads." He envisions the UFE Fort Cavazos building laid out in a familiar arrangement, much like the other secure Federation buildings where they stored their mission documents. It's always better to double-check and avoid putting his cousin in a vulnerable position. Measure twice, cut once or as his dad used to say—think what could go wrong so you can find the solution.

"María, take pictures, so we don't have to hear Nicolaus say what model number or which variation is it?" Akari smacks him on his leg. On their military missions, he programmed his inventions based on the facility's reconnaissance details. That way, they'd get in and get out as quick as possible. If they didn't have the details, pictures, or blueprints, they would provide cover fire while he programmed on site, encountering some interesting diversion techniques and a few close calls.

"Akari, you just don't want to hear Nicolaus bitch about the lack of preparation." María laughs.

Nicolaus sighs. "The devices owned by the UFE have some pretty complex tech—and yes, I get a little frustrated when they don't work the first time." He visualizes his mother standing in front of him, delivering a stern lecture. Then he hears Asa, their martial arts instructor, whom they have discovered is a magus. *Patience, Nicolaus, you can't force it to work if your mind is not clear.*

Amused, María interrupts Nicolaus, causing him to snap out of his trance as he feels Asa swatting his wrist. "When do you meet with the CEO?"

"Ah—umm—according to the latest email, Akari and I meet with him on Friday around noon. Akari will do her thing while I keep Walter Roosevelt distracted." Nicolaus peers at Dodge. "You'll need to drive her to work, so if something goes wrong, you both jet out together."

"You mean she'll drive there, and then I'll find something to do. Then she'll push me out of the driver's seat when we're bugging out," Dodge says with a smirk.

María replies, "I've trained you well, my apprentice."

Akari clears her throat and turns the screen of the phone to Nicolaus. "I have all the applications on my phone ready to go. I'll find the corporation's financial trail and download all the pertinent information from your laptop and the network. We must ensure he doesn't see me on your computer. As a precaution, since everyone in the office comes to you for advice cause you're so loveable, I'll have my laptop as a disguise to make it look like I'm working."

Nicolaus nods and then peers at María. "I know you told us your full vision—but was there anything you might have missed? Did Aamirah show a glimpse of how to propel our abilities through our bodies? Any chance that she can use her telepathy to help us out?"

"I told y'all everything that happened in my vision." María exhales. "It's infuriating that we have this Divine power, but we can't unleash its full strength." She grips the locket. Curiosity fills her mind—*how do they unleash the power?*

Akari stares at María playing with the locket. "We survived all those operations worldwide. The lockets, whatever potential they hold, are essential for unleashing the raw powers." She wants to examine the locket under a microscope as soon as she has the opportunity. She and Nicolaus could dissect and analyze the elements, metals, and biomaterials used in its construction. A strange sense of unease washes over her. With Seok's recent behavior, she's hesitant to bring it to DaeChie Pharmaceuticals.

María nods in agreement. "I guess it's all about patience. I hate that word so much."

"Like your dad said, we just focus on this week." Akari exhales.

Dodge chimes in. "Dude, it'll be like our weeklong destroyer missions in Asia, but with no guns, which stinks."

Nicolaus chuckles to himself, reflecting the army slogan they shouted before every mission: *For Freedom, For Life, For Love, Death to the Vile.*

During the group's discussion of the plan, Marcin heads over to Catalina and Herculano's house, located a couple of doors down. He grabs a shovel and some other tools from his house and unlocks the eight-foot cedar fence gate to enter their backyard. As he walks past the brick patio that he and Herculano installed, he spots Catalina's garden, which she calls the garden of Christ. The garden is a paradise of South American-styled plantings, and there are several two-foot-tall angels with cement accents and multiple crosses throughout the ten-foot subsection of the garden. As he gets closer, he recognizes two four-foot-high angel fountains with birds flocking around them. Marcin steps next to a mini three-foot replica version of Christ the Redeemer from Brazil, takes a breath, and murmurs, "Here we go. The moment of truth."

He pushes the statue aside and notices fresh dirt covering the white gravel rocks. While removing the stones, he feels the rough edges of the torn blackout weed tarp, realizing that someone had already made their way through. He claws through the dirt and finds a square plastic box that is a foot and a half in size. After dragging out the box from the ground, he sets in between the guava plants. Opening it, he unveils a sturdy metal vault box. On the front, a six-number key combination awaits, already aligned with Julieta's birthday. Marcin mutters under his breath as he opens the box and pulls out the bubble wrap, revealing a smaller jewelry box. He opens the two-inch box, but there is no locket inside. He pauses, seeing only a piece of paper the size of a fortune cookie note.

Frowning, he reads the note. *I'm back from the dead. Ironic isn't it? —Hamilton Parsons.* He slams down the jewelry box and runs back to his house, bursting through the door. "Parsons has the locket."

"What! How?" Nicolaus jumps up from the couch.

"I have no clue."

"The UFE and Parsons must have intercepted or been watching Casey. Call him right now."

"Fuck. Can I put Parsons's head on a stick now!" María pounds the chair's armrest.

Akari stands up, straightening her legs. "We'll get it back. This presents an issue and throws off our plans. He can't do anything about it, since his blood won't be from the Divinities. Let's focus on tomorrow and we'll plan around this speed bump."

"It's more than a speed bump. He continues to haunt us, and I just want him dead."

"Consider what your dad said. You must seek the darkness and turn it into light."

"I know what my dad said, Akari. Unlike you, I have faced Parsons. You don't know how much I hate him, and how could you? Both of your parents are still alive, just like Dodge and his perfect family. My mom is dead, and Nicolaus's parents and sister are dead because of that bastard. I want retribution now!"

It takes all of Nicolaus's strength to restrain María as he wraps his arms around her. "Do not use your vengeance against us. That's exactly what Parsons wants. He wants to fuck with us. Akari and Dodge are your best friends. I feel your pain every day. You're talking about my family, too. I want revenge just as bad as you, but we must stick together like we always have. We are a family—we have gone through this together. And we will continue to protect each other. Think about the big picture. He isn't the only one who haunts us."

María grunts and relaxes her muscles while Nicolaus releases her arms. "Why are the Divinities delaying this?" She yells as she steps away from her cousin. "They give us pieces like breadcrumbs—I want the full fucking loaf!" *It's just not fair. Why did my mom have to die?*

Akari sobs in the chair.

María walks over to Akari and touches her hand. "I'm sorry. I just have all this rage. When we were Green Berets, I could take all this frustration out. But it's boiling inside of me."

"You're right, I don't understand your and Nicolaus's pain. But I've been around you since we were kids and loved your mom and miss Mi-Cha every day too—and Nicolaus's parents. I'm doing my best to keep us together." Akari went with Marcin to pick up María from the police station after her mom died. She was the shoulder for María to cry on. Akari was her go-to sparring partner whenever she needed to unleash her anger and engage in martial arts practice.

"I know you are. Sometimes your calmness, Nicolaus's rationalization, and Dodge's stupid, self-gratifying crap gets under my skin. You've kept us together. I love you so much. My cousin and I would have gone over the cliff without you."

Akari can't help but consider her parents. *What if they died? How does Nicolaus keep himself composed every day? How does María fight her internal demons of revenge?*

"And here I just thought it was me and my comedic sense that drove María to lose it. Now I know the three of us drive her batty." Dodge chimes in.

Nicolaus punches Dodge in the arm. "Really, at this moment."

"Hey, it's my locket missing, and I know that we'll totally get it back." He eyes María. "I know I'm lucky to have my parents and sister. That's why I have all the faith in us. It's a mission possible every time. We never failed in our operations, and for sure won't fall flat on our face now."

Standing up from the chair, Akari wipes a tear from her cheek. "I'll call you later. Go get some rest for tomorrow." She embraces María.

"We'll devise a plan and see what we can come up with." Nicolaus fidgets with his small goatee. "I'll also talk with Casey. Like Akari said, rest up for tomorrow. You have a super important day."

On the drive home, Nicolaus taps his fingers against the steering wheel. "Text Casey that I'll call him in ten minutes."

She nods. Within seconds of her text, a reply comes back.

"I'm so pissed right now," Nicolaus mutters. "How did Parsons know the locket was there?" He clenches his jaw.

Akari reaches over and places her hand on his thigh. "Once you talk to Casey, we might know, or y'all will come up with a solution."

Nicolaus deliberates. *Did Veda or UFE take the locket sooner? Could someone have bugged Casey's house?* The questions pound his head. "I'm sorry about my cousin blowing up at you."

"It's okay. I'm glad María got the frustration out. You know we need to let off some emotion now and then. You could use some of that too. Both you and María have pent up your frustrations. I've been telling you both for years meditation will help."

They pull into their driveway as Nicolaus smirks, visualizing his cousin meditating and throwing her arms in the air. *Fuck it, this is so boring.*

"Let's get inside, and you can call Casey. I'll make some dinner for the both of us." He nods, and they head into the house.

"Parsons has the locket," Nicolaus barks through his phone.

Casey replies, "What? Parsons is alive? I thought—shit. How are you and María holding up with knowing that he's alive?"

Nicolaus clinches his fist. "It doesn't matter right now. What matters is he has the locket."

Casey stands up and walks around his kitchen. "Relax, Nicolaus. He might have found out a while ago, since he's been hiding this hold time. Just relax."

"No. I will not relax. I've got María losing her cool, a stolen locket, a bunch of jumbled clues from our parents, Aamirah, and the Accursed messing with our minds with incoherent random visions."

"The Accursed?"

"I'll tell you later about that."

"Let's look at the positive," replies Casey while scratching his beard.

"It's a good thing that the Federation has the locket?"

"The note didn't say UFE. Parsons left the note. Right? Look, when you worked for me and my trucking company, you saw firsthand the UFE operations. This whole Divinities thing with Parsons and Veda is off the books for them, so keep in mind why and what you learned at the moving company. It will make sense."

"That makes little sense right now."

"Nicolaus, stop trying to rationalize every little detail. Divide and conquer is the mantra with the lockets. Greed and control are our friends. If Parsons took it for himself, then does Veda or the UFE know? They will fight against themselves if that's the case."

"That's a pretty big hunch."

"Strategy, not hunch."

"But they have a locket."

"They do, so what? They can't unlock it without you. So, we'll get it back. We are staring at Big Brother straight in the eye. Sometimes we'll have to make a deal with the devil, and then burn them down. Do me a favor and just trust me. I have to go."

Casey hangs up the phone, and Nicolaus glances at Akari. "He wants me to relax and to remember us working for him and our transporting the military and Federation materials across the United States."

"Nicolaus, we will figure this out. I'm upset that Parsons has the locket, but he can't do anything about it. Let's eat, and then you can go into your invention room and think about the trucking company."

Forces
of
Moving

15

Past

A couple of weeks after returning from their last mission, Casey showed up on Herculano and Catalina Vargas's doorstep.

Nicolaus opened the door. "Dude, not even a call." He eyed the cobalt blue semi-truck with a super cab parked on the street in front of the suburban neighborhood. "You just show up, big rig parked in the front."

"Of course—give me a hug, godson."

Casey wrapped his arms around Nicolaus. "Damn, you're ripped." He peeked inside the house. "Where are the brains of the operation?"

"She's out with María, shopping for dresses. They've been craving a dress-shopping adventure for the past couple of years."

Casey laughed. "I guess they're a little over camouflage and pants."

"Come on in, let's catch up."

"I can't. I just completed a long haul for the marines." Casey rubbed his calloused hands together. Nicolaus admired him. He's blue collar, in shape, business savvy, and most important, a family first man. "Chloe and the kids want me back home for family time on the lake. I came to offer the four of you jobs moving top-tier money makers and high-ranking officials nationwide."

"Hold on, like chauffeurs driving limousines? Or do you mean moving their belongings?" Casey's business includes nationwide moves with his big rigs and air transport for faster deliveries. His favorite way of making a profit is to create personalized trip adventures for the individuals he's moving— such as travel packages with hotels and destinations for someone moving from New York to Texas. Nicolaus knows not to call it a travel agency, because it contradicts Casey's marketing messaging, plus he'll get punched.

Casey shakes his head. "It's white glove service. You meet the people you're moving. Move their stuff into the big rigs."

Akari and Dodge, during their last year in the service, created an app for Casey so his customers could track the shipments. Dodge boasted about being a unique all-in-one shopping experience for moving, unlike anything ever seen before. Akari rolled her eyes about the design, because the code was so streamlined that its loading times beat the top fifteen retailers' applications.

"Nicolaus, it's big money, you get to stretch your legs—get that degree going—and learn all the bug out routes and get an inside scoop on the UFE—you know, for when that moment hits the fan," Casey carefully stated to Nicolaus.

"We're in, but don't have the licenses to drive them."

"It isn't a big deal. Each of you will sign up for my truck driving academy, and I will provide the wheels and a plethora of jobs. Pass the test, and let the quests begin. Also, since these are money shakers, you'll find the perfect jobs to continue the mission. Let's say—" Casey leaned closer to Nicolaus and whispered, "María can continue to investigate government stuff under the radar, or if you want to figure out the financial business stuff."

Casey moved backward, and Nicolaus leaned back on the door frame. "When do we start?"

"When you're ready." Casey cracked his knuckles. "Talk it over with the crew and text me. I'll get you all signed up in the classes and fly your butts to Michigan."

Nicolaus and Casey gave each other a mighty handshake and bumped their shoulders. Casey turned around and walked to the semi-truck, waving two peace signs, then collapsed his index fingers, only showing two birdies in the air.

Nicolaus snickered. It's a move Magnar and Casey always made.

An hour later, María and Akari walked into Catalina and Herculano's house.

Nicolaus addressed the group. "All right, I know we have only been home for three weeks. This should be good timing since Akari and I are looking to build a house which will take, like, ten months. And you two," Nicolaus pointed at Dodge and María, "you have to decide to build a house or townhouse. So, the timing should be good."

"To-to-today, Junior," Dodge interrupted Nicolaus.

"We got an offer from Casey to start the next phase in our Divine mission."

Nicolaus told the crew about Casey's plan.

Dodge's smile broadened. "Road trip, adventure, sightseeing, making bank, studying—I'm in."

María laughed. "Of course you are. It's a big truck." She turned to face Nicolaus. "I'm game. I finally get to drive a big rig as a civilian and see how far I can push it."

Akari emptied their shopping bags. "Of course I'm in. We can now solve the riddles in our past, present, and future, and,"—

she raised her eyebrow at Nicolaus—"we can have romance in forty-eight states."

With a gentle lean, their lips met in a compassionate kiss. Nicolaus stroked her cheek with his hand.

"Dude, you got time for that. When do we start?" Dodge asked.

They stopped caressing, and Akari said, "Let's leave tomorrow after we all have breakfast with my parents and María's dad. There's no sense in waiting. We'll get the party started."

María pulled out her phone and texted Casey, and he texted back. *See you all tomorrow night at the airport. I'll spring for first class.* "Dodge, let's go see my dad and let him know." María gawked at Akari and Nicolaus, kissing again. "Will you stop and go tell your parents, Akari?"

Nicolaus and Akari separated. "Yes, commander," he chuckled.

"We'll go by the restaurant and let Catalina and Herculano know, too," María replied.

"Wonderful, and then after we stop at my parents' house, Nicolaus, let's stop by DaeChie so I can continue my research work on the road. It will be our mobile research lab." Akari stroked his hair.

For the next four weeks, Nicolaus, Akari, María, and Dodge trained in truck boot camp, finished in half the time of an average newbie driver. María finished with the highest marks in the school's history, and Akari finished with the second-best marks ever.

"You boys got smoked by the girls." Casey laughed while he stroked his long brown beard, which complemented his sun-kissed white skin, and poked fun at Nicolaus and Dodge.

"That just means I get more time studying since I'm like a third of the speed slower than these three." Dodge peered at Casey with a smirk.

As the five of them sat in his office, Casey said, "Shut the door. I'll explain the plan for next year."

"Each successful run, you get a point. At certain levels, you move up in the rig's quality. Like a small little bitty cab to start—to a mega cab—a living room on wheels, and a full trailer wrap of your choosing with the Kazanowski Moving Forces name and tagline Operation STEAL is on all four sides."

Nicolaus interjected, "You really want us to use Strategically Take and Extradite to Alternate Locations on the side of the trucks? Don't people get freaked out about seeing the acronym STEAL?"

Casey responded, "No, the tagline helps because people realize we are a serious moving company willing to protect their assets at all costs." Casey exhaled and took a deep breath. "You will learn all the primary routes in the country and mark the quickest side routes just in case you all need to leverage those in the future." Casey stared straight at all of them. "This is the most important list of all: no wrecks, no tickets, no fines from being over the weight limit, keep your sidearms handy, watch your back, help fellow truckers if they need help, treat the customers like the President of the United States, and for the love of God, Dodge, stay off the damn radio with your antics." They all cackled and glanced at Dodge while he waved his arms in an outward motion.

Casey cleared his throat, eyes still dancing. "I'll work out the jobs. María, I'll make sure you get all the UFE and their contractors so you can sweet-talk them. You two will also get all the armed forces shipments. Dodge, do your thing and get them to trust you with your humor, and you're in like Flynn with figuring out the military government involvement. María, this will help follow through on spying on what your vision was the night your mom died." María's skin flushed and nodded.

Casey then turned to face Nicolaus and Akari. "You two will get the c-suite, like CEO's and CFO's for big technology and financial companies. Nail this to get in and find out who's funding the whole UFE operation. Also, you both will get all the GREC shipments to see what their involvement is. The goal is to understand all of their facility routes, the contents, and get a feel for the locations. That will come in handy later on."

"One question." Dodge stood up with his hands spread apart. "Why are you in league with GREC and the UFE?"

"First off, I'm not. Second, the whole reason is because of . . . well, for your quest. This was the plan Julieta had in place. Spy, uncover, understand their operations. Third, someone's going to snatch the golden toilets cash. Might as well be us, right?" Casey stood up. "Let me show you all your trucks."

The Four Shadows of Light followed Casey to the truck yard full of every high-end and low-end truck. In the front were two older trucks, painted brown and orange. "These are the starter twins. You do a good job, you elevate up."

"They are the ugliest and oldest trucks on your lot, straight up from the nineties." Nicolaus scrutinized the two trucks.

"They are oldies, but goodies."

María added, "Alright, this is like an initiation to the trucker fraternity. We'll be out of those rigs in a month."

"Seven weeks is the record. My guess for you all is three weeks, so get cracking, and the list of all our approved repair shops is in the truck." Casey good-naturedly smacked Nicolaus on his back.

"Let's ride 'em and roll out," Dodge replied, walking toward the rigs.

Over the next year, the two couples memorized the UFE and GREC transport routes, creating custom maps with escape paths.

Each group brought workout equipment, trained in martial arts at truck stops, and kept their edge with their guns at shooting ranges. They all completed their associate degrees within a year and continued moving toward the bachelor's degree during the downtime in the passenger seat. Akari delved into her breast cancer research, that Dae started before she died.

Akari and Nicolaus selected their lot in a subdivision in Prosper and built a farmhouse style, open floor plan with a rustic character. It was a two story, four bedroom with over three thousand square feet for future family expansion. Every time the house conversation came up, María and Dodge fought the entire time. They couldn't agree on anything and settled on two separate new-build townhouses as next-door neighbors. If they committed to live together, they agreed to rent out the townhouses for passive income.

Both trucks arrived in Michigan one year after they started and handed the keys back to Casey. "Goin' miss the massive profits next year without you all. You did an unreal job, but I expected nothing less than perfection from all of you. I'll support the land transportation and the Irons' brothers with the air transportation." Casey smiled ear to ear. "What did you all learn in the past year?"

Dodge replied, "Akari and Nicolaus never stop with their romance."

Casey scowled at Dodge and then surveyed Nicolaus. "What did you learn?"

"Let's see here. Planning, strategy, and networking."

María jumped in. "Adjusting to civilian life. And my most hated word, patience."

"Trust. Trusting that you have our best interest in mind. Also, even if we game-plan scenarios, they might not go as planned. We've learned better ways to adjust on the fly," said Akari.

"The UFE is spreading its wings across the United States without Americans realizing it," María said, crossing her arms. As she shifted in her chair, she couldn't help but dwell on Veda and the complete lack of trust she felt towards her.

Nicolaus added, "The art of deception. You had us mingle with elitists to gain insights and wiggle our way into where we needed to be. Just like how we did on our missions. We couldn't have achieved what we did without deception."

Casey replied, "Excellent. You all get A plus." He furrowed his eyebrow with a slow and deliberate tone. "When the UFE comes knocking on your door to halt your divine purpose, the four of you have the knowledge to blast across the United States."

ᘐᘐᘐᘐ

Nicolaus makes his way downstairs. As he reaches the lower level, he finds Akari curled up on the couch, absorbed in her reading. The soft, melodic tunes of traditional Hawaiian music create a soothing ambiance. "Trust in us and roll with the punches. We'll figure how to make a deal."

"Very good, my little brainiac. If, let's say, the UFE goes head-to-head with the GREC or Parsons faces off against the UFE, then they're split."

"Nicolaus, it's the same approach we had in the Green Berets. That's why you nicknamed me the Graceful Assassin, María the Lethal Reckoning, Dodge the Sniping Jokester, and you the Intrinsic Inventor. We strategized to our strengths."

He reflects about mission thirty-five, the Columbian cartel—where they made the enemy feel like they were winning and then they crushed them. Nicolaus places his chin in his palm and reflects on how they gave the cartel rockets and guns in a terrorist deal brokered by María, who was undercover. Without warning, they unleashed a wave of violence, slaughtering every member of the cartel.

Akari eyes Nicolaus, staring off. "We've got this. We just need to be ready when we need to act."

Base
of
Plans

16

Present

The next day, María and Dodge set out from their home at six in the morning, embarking on a two-hour journey to Fort Cavazos. As Dodge sits in the passenger seat, he ponders over the information that the UFE, GREC, or the army might have regarding the Divinities and their connection. He's dressed in his cowboy boots, his western-style shirt, and a pair of blue jeans. María finds him charming when he dresses in true Texas fashion.

While browsing the military base website, Dodge turns to María and asks, "Just to confirm, today we focus on the plan, and tomorrow is D-day, right?"

María replies, "We've gone over this countless times. My boss only granted me access to the basic United Federation of Enforcement archives. So today, I'll familiarize myself with the lay of the land. When we return tonight, we'll meet with Akari and Nicolaus to strategize." As an analytics expert, María's refuge is the realm of math. No matter how overwhelmed she may be, and even if a tough workout doesn't help her unwind, she finds comfort in sitting at a computer or analyzing numbers on paper. It's her form of meditation.

"So, like a P-day? Prep for a mock interview, a game plan run through, putting your order in a cart and waiting a day."

María sighs. "Yes, yes, and yes."

"Got it. And why did you get access now, and why not earlier?"

María submitted for access six months ago. Her boss walked up to her two days ago and handed over the case files. The timing of Akari's surge of Divine power and María's access being granted is not accidental. *Was it Veda? Parsons? Or Both?*

"The documents I'm going through were unsealed twenty years ago. After being exposed to biological weapons, each troop developed cancer and died within two years. The other bioscientists, investigators, and analytic researchers haven't found the right compound that was used against the troops."

"My guess is UFE has some crazy secret formula that the US military doesn't have access to and flooded the war zones with their dirty shit."

"It totally seems that way. I'll have Akari help analyze too. It's a biological compound, and the numbers don't add up."

"Can we say deep state?" Dodge adds.

"We have been involved with the deep state all our lives, especially my mamá."

"Not to mention we've been the poster children for black ops." Dodge fidgets with the seatbelt. "After yesterday's blowup, I thought you'd be like, totally anxious."

"It's game time for us. When we suited up for battle, we blocked all the other crap out of our minds. The endgame is taking them down." For two years, María has worked inside the Federation, gaining insights into their operations. In her blunt analysis, the UFE possesses the autonomy to go wherever and whenever they desire. The initial intent is an improved iteration of NATO, but they are advancing into a platform for dystopian control.

Once they arrive at the military base, they step out of the vehicle, share a kiss, and Dodge says, "Success is yours. Do your badass thing and don't forget to smile. The glasses are pretty tight on you too. It's like a fashionista thing."

María giggles and walks towards the gate, and a gentle breeze blows through her hair. The military base is a sight that brings about a feeling of nostalgia, as if it were a home she had long forgotten. When she was younger, her mom would take her across the country to the different armed forces bases along with the UFE centers. For María, stepping onto a base is the equivalent of warm sand between a shell collector's toes at the beach—comforting.

Dodge jumps in the extreme battle wagon and drives off to spend the next five hours enjoying literary life at a bookstore and enjoying some coffee. He grabs at least fifteen books and skims everything from mechanical engineering to information technology architecture design, searching for ideas that can help Nicolaus and Akari discover the next revolutionary innovation or inspiration for his product designs.

María passes through the security checkpoints and enters the military base. She inspects her surroundings and acts like an average person to avoid any suspicion from the cameras. Alongside her adventures with her mother, María spent four years in the army with the Four Shadows of Light, moving from one place to another. Her favorite base is the John F. Kennedy Special Warfare Center and School. Their military training began there, with Veda's authoritative voice leading their bootcamp exercises.

She questions whether wearing the locket would improve her shooting skills. María heads to the shooting range, where the sound of gunshots help drown out her stress. She shows her military UFE vendor clearance badge, grabs a gun, and sets up the target. She reacts to the whistles from the other cadets by firing five rounds, grouping them all within an inch of each other in the center of the target. Muttering under her breath, she ponders the possibility of possessing the same skill as Nicolaus— by closing her eyes and feeling the enemy, in this case, the metal target.

With her mind focused, she exhales and launches her arm forward, mimicking the motion of throwing a discus. The bullet strikes the dead center of the bullseye. The cadets jaws drop. She smiles. "Just another day at the office, boys."

She hears one cadet chatter as she's leaving. "I'm in love."

At around nine o'clock, she heads to the UFE building complex on the army campus. She approaches the front desk, where the representative greets her with a cheerful smile, "Good Morning. How can I help you?"

María fidgets with her badge. "Hi, my name is María Landowski-Jiménez. I work for Advanced Weaponry Discovery out of the McKinney location. My boss should have submitted for contractor access to the archives."

The front desk representative instructs her to use the kiosk to check in, and she'll let the archives department know that she is there.

María paces to the archives, passing through two security checkpoints. Sometimes she longs to emanate the same peacefulness Akari does in these instances. María's inclination is to abandon all the planning and kick everyone's ass in order to gain entry into the vault. "Finish it quick," she mutters to herself. Right away, a cadet stammers at her, "How, umm, how can I help you?"

"I'm reviewing some specific cases for the research and investigations department. The front desk said they would let you know I'm here."

"Yes. Ma'am, we have these two cases in the primary archival section."

María asks about the massive vault tucked away in the depths of the archives. The cadet informs her she needs executive permission to access it, and he can't grant her access. María nods in agreement while she glances at the two cameras facing the desk. She gazes into his eyes, trying to replicate Nicolaus's eye trick, but it fails.

"I'll retrieve the archives for you if you want to have a seat in the conference room, and I'll bring them in."

"I'd rather just go in and review."

"OK, I'll need you to hand over your phone, as we don't allow electronic devices in the archives." Upon giving him the phone, he escorts María into the primary vault. "If there's anything I can assist you with, please inform me."

"I will. Oh, what if I need to make copies?" María replies.

"You're allowed for a maximum of twenty pages." He stammers again. "If you would like, I can make the copies for you."

"Thank you so much. Give me some time, and I'll bring the documents to you."

He steps out of the gate. María's eyes shift upwards and fixate on three additional cameras mounted on the ceiling. She exhales and finds the first archival box, riffling through paperwork and glancing at notes. She pulls out four pages. While she scans for the next box, she peeks over her shoulder at the officer, who now has his back toward her while he sits at his desk. This was her chance to examine the high security vault. She hurries toward the steel vault, her gaze landing on the retinal scanner and the digital keypad. With her right hand, she reaches up to adjust her non-prescription glasses and clicks the brand logo on the side to capture a picture. Nicolaus created the mechanism and Dodge handpicked the frames to add design flare for each of their personalities.

With the documents from both cases in hand, María leaves the gated area and says, "All done. Thank you so much. Here are the documents that need copying. I'll probably be back several times in the following days to review more."

"No problem. You read those fast." The cadet smiles, looking forward to seeing her tomorrow and considering the possibility of asking her out for coffee. María opens the door and heads out the front entrance while she texts Dodge to pick her up.

Dodge pulls in and exits the vehicle as she enters the parking lot. María gets in the driver's seat, and Dodge gets in the passenger seat. She floors the battle beast vehicle out of the army base, and Dodge asks, "So, you got a plan going to get inside that vault?"

"I believe so, but I want to talk to Nicolas about it. Also, both cases I'm reviewing have GREC and UFE involvement. They have redacted ninety percent of the stuff."

Dodge nods. "Why are you taking these cases seriously? It's like it's work, but you seem intrigued by them. You're there to gather more information about the bad dudes."

"We noticed an advanced version of chemical warfare during some of our operations, right?" She recalls Nicolaus and Akari, baffled by the biological mixtures and the mechanical deployment. Akari discerned similarities to DaeChie's patents on diabetes. The GREC and UFE are way more technologically advanced than the Armed Forces. Nicolaus helped them with a couple of their drone improvements, and Akari assisted on the auto healer formula, reducing the amputations. Each person felt a responsibility to contribute, but María's intuition urged her to pause their progress, sensing that the Federation was exploiting their inventions.

On their drive back, Dodge reviews the GREC website. He skims through the introduction. "'The Global Reform Establishment Coalition formed right after World War II as a way for the world's strongest countries to reform communist regimes and mold them into democracies.' It's such garbage. They're just greed and power."

María understood her mom saw this transformation going from world protectors to elitist controllers. Thirteen years ago, the reduction in NATO and the United Nations started—like a slow march to death. They'd been using government lobbyists and corporations to further their globalist agenda. "The World Reform Protection Bill, my mamá feared the most."

"That crazy stupid. No borders, no oversight, and complete world dictatorship!"

María's latest intel she gathered indirectly shows GREC's intertwinement with the world's top twenty economic and military forces. Her analysis is they are dissembling the UN to institute new priorities and avoid the original intent. While GREC asserts, it aids emerging countries and fights against climate change, and in cunning fashion, deploys its influence to dominate the masses and exploit the poor for its own gain.

Dodge continues to skim the website. "So, the summary is the wealthiest individuals in the world manipulate the media narrative. It's bullshit when only the top five percent of people have access to the resources they need to thrive."

"Oh, and we can't ignore their ultimate dark side." She grips the steering wheel. "The Coalition relies on illegal shit like cybercrime, human exploitation, and drug trafficking to stay in control."

The team witnessed firsthand the chaos of the organizations. It wasn't until three weeks ago that the team began untangling UFE's involvement. Two years of frustration had passed, but then, as if someone had flipped a switch, the details started pouring in like water from a faucet.

Last week, Akari hacked into a couple of their servers and found they deploy psychological warfare through social justice, geopolitics, and trade, among other insights that contradicted their public message, like the two pandemic strains she traced to UFE laboratories. She also found the financial shell companies seem to trace back to Pierce Roosevelt and their partnerships with the other largest financial institutions. Nicolaus and Dodge's whole role at their work is in confirming Pierce Roosevelt backs UFE for monetary gains or what other institutions play a part too.

María drives fast, consumed by anger and grief. She recalls the day her mom died and the sight of Parsons's face, which had ignited a fire within her. She grips the steering and clenches her jaw. "Dodge, let's stop talking about them!"

"Sorry, didn't mean to get you riled up." Dodge glances at the speedometer. "Hey, speed demon, you are way over the limit."

María lets off the gas pedal, blows a strand of hair out of her face in annoyance, and they remain quiet for a while. They have evidence of UFE's dealings, but very little from GREC—they need iron clad proof, not assumptions or hypothesis. She feels like a conspiracist, trying to force something into what it's not, but what if the Coalition has the Federation just do all their dirty work? A text from Nicolaus disrupts the twenty-minute silence.

Dodge reads the text to María. "Nicolaus and Akari are making dinner for us at your townhouse instead of us heading to their house."

Around four o'clock, they pull up to her townhouse. The scent of delicious Hawaiian cuisine wafts through the air, signaling to Dodge that Akari is the chef for the night.

After opening the front door, Dodge bellows, "Hello, where y'all at?"

From upstairs comes Akari's voice, faint but audible, "Bastard, I can never win against you in this game."

Nicolaus responds, "Well, that's because sports are my thing."

María walks to the bottom of the stairs. "Get your gamer butts down here and serve us some good home-cooked Hawaiian delicacies." A moment later, they both ran down the stairs.

"How did it go?" Akari asks.

María hugs her, and they discuss the plans while eating dinner together. After they finish dinner and are on to dessert, Akari mentions, "GREC has sent countless proposals to our mom's company for purchasing the patents in the past couple of weeks. They've been very aggressive and threatened to have the courts intervene if we don't comply. It's wasting our resources meant for research and finding cures, which has been their plan. Strain our funds, and then we'd sell."

Akari knows they have the rights to them for another eight years, but GREC wants them now. Her mom sent a swarm of lawyers, led by Andrzej Kowalczyk, to deal with them. Ever since the beginning of DaeChie Pharmaceuticals, he's served as their family and business lawyer, protecting his nephews, Marcin and Magnar's interest. Mr. Kowalczyk's law firm finds itself immersed in a labyrinth of legal intricacies against the most powerful organization in the world.

María surveys Akari. "Your mom doesn't want to sell, does she? Because that is our family company."

"My mom gets very dramatic about it, saying they'd have to kill her before she'd sell, and of course, I have to calm her down because, honestly, it might be why our family has paid the price."

Dodge puts his hands in the air. "We'd all be worth a couple hundred million if you sold."

"My mom would turn into a zombie and come out of her grave and take me down if we did that." Nicolaus chimes in. "We can't let go of what our parents started, especially since the Divinity powers have helped." He tugs his earring. "Akari's daily battle with the cure solutions, and our investigation into medical industry's corruption, is all dependent on DaeChie."

"Are you prepared for tomorrow?" Dodge asks María.

"Yes, and you're going in with me this time."

"For sure, and that'll give me a full day of fun, maybe shooting like you did today, miss show off."

Akari eyes Nicolaus. "We have to succeed tomorrow. We are so close to the definitive answers." He nods his head. Nicolaus uncovered paperwork after his parents' death that Pierce Roosevelt Financials & Investments invested in DaeChie Pharmaceuticals. That's why Casey wanted him and Dodge to take positions there.

María opens an energy drink. "Now, we have some plans worked out. Friday is a massive day for the four of us. Dodge and I need to go work out and let off some fucking steam. Don't you two have martial arts practice? And what did you both do during the day?"

"We went to my work, and Nicolaus helped me review my notes on the cancer trials to see where we were going wrong. It was nice that we got to work together in the lab, and Seok was not there. She's really annoying me with her surveillance." Akari wishes she had more details from when Dae was still alive. The logs disappeared, and she's baffled at how Nicolaus's mom went about the scientific creation. The components she's extracted from the serums go against all known ways of creating cures, matching how they figured out the other cures. She assumes that's why GREC wants what the Divinities gave to their moms and are trying to force their hands in court.

They all get up and hug each other before Akari and Nicolaus head out. Before Nicolaus exits, María claps her hands, "Hey, I did your sensing the target thing today. I can't do the influence eye twitch, but it was fucking awesome to sense the enemy without aiming at the target."

He winks at her. "You're a better shot than me."

"Oh, totally, it was straight in the center. I don't know if it was the locket or just straight up confidence."

He kisses her on the cheek and whispers, "Confidence . . . and maybe a little luck from the locket." As he adds in the extra, she slaps him on the arm.

Seized
of
Access

(17)

Present

Friday morning arrives with an overcast sky and a muggy, clammy feeling as María and Dodge drive to the army base. He heads off to the shooting range first, then to check out the other activities like archery, bowling, and the museum. María walks into the UFE archive section wearing a stunning, formfitting camo top and sleek black leather pants.

"Good morning. I need to reaccess the archives," María informs the cadet.

Without hesitation, the cadet replies, "No problem." She engages in small talk while she activates Nicolaus's frequency disruptor in her pants pocket. The device overrides the visual signal with a regenerated thirty second loop to ensure the security office remains unaware of her mission. The disruptor's activation produces an audible sound that echoes in her mini left earbud. Any camera within a hundred-foot radius becomes entranced by the spell of the device.

Before entering the archive gate, she extracts what appears to be a lipstick container from her purse and drops it on the concrete ground. "Oh, how careless of me," she quips.

"I'll get that for you," the cadet offers, reaching down to pick up the container.

She removes the container from his grip and ensures that the tiny opening for the spray is directed straight toward the officer. She clicks the button, and the potent knockout mist discharges onto his unsuspecting face. He stumbles and wobbles, but she catches him before he falls, laying him on the ground.

María sinks into the cushioned chair at his computer desk, drawn to the glowing screen displaying the archive library, which was left logged in. Her eyes dart to the search bar, typing *Divinities* and locating the vault and container number. María surveys the work area and spots a mini biometric safe underneath the desk.

María lifts and maneuvers the cadet, feeling the weight of his body in her arms close to the safe. She presses his thumb against the digital keypad screen, and the key safe opens with a click. María leans in, reaches her hand and pulls the correct metal key and shuts the door as she flashes a quick smile.

She retrieves another Nicolaus invention from her purse. A smirk plays on her lips and ponders how he can bring any concept to life with the proper motivation. With her left hand, she lifts his eyelids and scans the portable retinal scanner with her right hand.

Her breath quickens and a rush of adrenaline propels her toward the massive, fortress-like ironclad vault. She places the retinal image device on the scanner, and it succeeds. The digital screens prompt her to enter an access code. She rubs her hands and inputs the code descrambler device, and within five seconds, the screen displays ACCESS GRANTED, and the heavy vault doors unlock and open with a deafening clang. María strides into the vault and goes straight to the box's location. She inserts the key and turns. With a metal clang, a metal cylinder pops out. She removes the tube and uses the code descrambler device again, and it opens, revealing a single sheet of paper at the bottom. She picks up the document and scans it, her eyes widening in shock and disbelief.

"Got you—Hamilton Parsons." She growls and throws the paper in the tube, places it back into the slot and rushes out of the vault.

She bolts from the archival room and makes it to the front receptionist desk where seven officers wearing the United Federation of Enforcement badges wait, their guns pointing at her.

"María Landowski-Jiménez, please follow us. We will place you in a holding cell and discuss the charges if you do not comply. We may use lethal force."

"Can you tell me what I did wrong?"

"We may not discuss it. Please hold out your arms."

María obeys, and the military officers place handcuffs around her wrists. They escort her down multiple gray hallways and into an elevator traveling down multiple floors. María panics as she passes the rooms, other cadets, and military personnel. She realizes they are taking her to see Parsons. After a fifteen-minute trek, the escorting cadets stop near the end of the hallway.

The officers open the thick black metal door and walk in with her. "Sir, Miss Landowski-Jiménez, as requested."

A man with a bald head sits in a chair, staring at the opposite wall with the back of the chair facing the door. A fluorescent light bulb dangles from the ceiling, and a table lamp on the desk provides a softer light. The strong residue of cigarettes permeates the environment.

"Thank you, gentlemen," says the man with a thick New Jersey accent. "Please stand outside the door, and I'll tell you when to return and retrieve the intruder."

"Yes, sir." The troops back out of the room, closing the door, leaving María standing and staring at the top of a bald head gleaming from the lights. Hearing the voice from her past makes her muscles tense and her hands clench into fists.

"María, I've been waiting a long time to talk to you. It's been about twelve years, I believe."

Her horror-struck face confirms that this man killed her mom.

Hamilton Parsons turns around in the chair to face her. María's blood boils with hatred, and she would love to jump over the desk and plant his head on a stake. "Wow, that's the murderous look I wanted to see. I know you want to kill me—maybe dismember me — but then you'll be in jail the rest of your life and never complete what your mom started." He stands and meets her eye. "You see, I got you the job at the UFE contractor to keep my eyes on you. I knew you all would go this route so soon. So predictable. I set you up to discredit you and tease you a little."

Face to face with her mortal enemy, María's animosity fills the room. Her eyes glisten with a wicked glint.

Parsons walks around the desk to the front and stands a foot away from María while she stares forward, not making eye contact. She would kill him with her bare hands, even with the handcuffs on.

"My, you have grown so model-like. Not a little girl anymore," he says, circling her like a hawk.

He reaches toward her upper arm.

"Touch me, and even your mother won't be able to recognize your face." She twists her mouth, contemplates he appears changed, but it is him.

Parsons drops his hand and sits on the front edge of the desk to scrutinize her. With a wicked smile, he says, "I approved your fast-track in special operations training. It was me who orchestrated your hundreds of missions. You thought you were doing the world justice?" He curtly nods at María. "Your missions helped the UFE remove those who opposed us or got in our way. I'm still pissed that with each mission you fucked over us somehow. You freed thousands of my trafficked slaves and burned at least fifty million dollars' worth of cocaine. Not to mention all the weapons you destroyed which were for the Federation, all in the name of righteousness. You're lucky the UFE has strong financial backing."

María's stomach roils. The Federation used the Four Shadows of Light as pawns. Their goal was to dismantle and eliminate the most nefarious individuals. In reality, they eliminated the adversaries that might pose problems for the Federation. They did their dirty work without even realizing it— the betrayal and misuse of what her mother intended.

María's forehead glistens with beads of sweat as Parsons scrapes her heart, his eyes fixed on her locket. The veins in his neck protrude like tight wound violin strings. "You're only here standing in front of me because I made it so. I allowed you into the UFE so I could watch you up close. You will deliver the Divine power. I have one locket and I'll find the other two. There's still time to partner with me in figuring out what the Divinities' full scope contains. My legion of loyal troops could be at your service to rule."

"We will never partner with you. I would rather drop a nuclear bomb on your ass than ever partner."

"That's a letdown. It's your fault that your aunt, uncle, and cousin are dead."

María fights the urge to kill his ass right now, but she won't be able to find the missing locket. She tightens both fists, holding herself back, channeling her best inner Akari. Then it occurs to her that Casey is right. Parsons doesn't know much about the

Divinities. The Four Shadows of Light don't know the full scope, but this means Parsons is acting like a lone wolf.

Hamilton clutches the desk. "I still owe Nicolaus for the scar on my chest when he shot me after I killed his family. I'm looking forward to repaying the favor. You're also lucky I kept Marcin alive, because his food is so good, and I enjoy eating at his restaurant. That Catalina is scorching hot for an older lady. She's doable. Her husband, Herculano, could have an unfortunate car accident."

Thoughts of revulsion and helplessness circulate through her mind.

"Once I find the other lockets, we'll have a nice little negotiation session. You're just a poker chip, here to solve the famous Divinity riddle your parents started."

As he extends his hand to grab the locket from María, a sudden bolt of lightning erupts from it and strikes his body. With a flash of light, the ethereal bolt sends him soaring over the desk and smacks his head on the back wall, leaving an indentation in the drywall. The officers outside the room thrust open the door, and María turns around while still emanating light. She knocks out two of the troops with their bodies thumping on the ground. She's able to smash to the door shut and lock it before the other troops can enter. María reaches down, grabs the handcuff keys, and frees her hands. Her body pulsates with a mixture of rage and shock as she vaults over the desk, fixes her gaze on Parsons. "I'll get that locket back and kill your sorry ass. You're going to pay for what you have done."

A charred Parsons squints at María, unable to speak.

"By the way, I quit." She throws her badge at his face.

The five UFE troops outside breach the door. They point their guns straight at María while Parsons staggers, standing up. "Escort her out."

"But sir, we must arrest her."

Parsons shakes his head and regains his composure, judging it's going to be more difficult to get the lockets once they put them on. "I said, escort her out now. Let her go."

"Sir—"

His eyes blaze orange with anger. "Don't question me."

The Federation troops nod their heads in fear and escort María out of the building to the sidewalk of the parking lot. An officer glares at her. "Where's your vehicle?"

María calms herself, rocking back and forth. Parsons's eyes glowed like Nicolaus said he did when he stopped the office shooting. "I need to text my ride."

"We will wait here and make sure you leave the premises. If you attempt to enter again, we will prosecute you or kill you on site."

María leers at the cadets. They didn't know what was happening. They were doing their jobs as cadets. Leadership rules the roost, and these are just their pawns. She exhales to calm her rage. "I understand. Let me text him."

María texts Dodge: *GYAHN* (get your ass here now.) She stares at her phone with no reply from Dodge.

A moment later, two more troops arrive with Dodge in handcuffs. "These fuckers grabbed me while I was in the museum and said we've been kicked off the property."

With a click, the officers release Dodge from the handcuffs and order him to fetch their vehicle. He sprints toward the parking lot and, before opening the vehicle door, tells himself a joke to steady himself. "What do you call a superhero who can't swim? — A hero in deep water." He jumps into the truck, wondering if this was all a UFE setup from the start, with María gaining access to the archives.

As Dodge pulls up next to the officers in the battle-ready SUV, the officers raise their guns, with a slight tremble in their arms, prepared for a confrontation. Dodge does his best to defuse the situation while adding some humor.

"Hey babe, we'll get some coffee on our long journey back home." He kisses María on the cheek. "Hey guys, why so serious?" Dodge cracks up with himself for his uncanny way of using movie quotes.

The officers lower their guns. "We have barred both of you from the premises. You must leave immediately."

"No problem. We've got some catching up to do with the latest romance novel, if you know what I mean." He winks.

María edges into the driver's seat while Dodge converses with the officers. "Dude, that was totally uncool with handcuffing me."

"It's our job. They ordered you to leave the premises."

"By the way, that's a pretty dope ride," the officer on the right says to Dodge while opening the door.

"Homemade, baby. We took the sweetness of stock and gave it some steroids." Dodge shuts the door and, through the darkest tinted windows allowed by law, gives them the peace sign, and María floors away from the facility.

After the UFE troops escorted María out of the base, Parsons calls his boss, Veda Devi. "We have issued the threat, and we are proceeding as planned."

She replies, "Good. stick to the plan. We must keep GREC oblivious to the Federation strategy."

He hangs up the phone and rubs the handle of his gun. *Fuck the world.* A UFE soldier enters the room, and Parsons draws his firearm, aims it at the soldier. "The entire world is my throne. Do you want to join me or go against me?"

The officer's body tenses up and stammers, "I'll—I'll join you, sir."

"Good answer." Parsons's face twists in rage. "Now leave before I pull the trigger." The officer backs out at a slow pace and shuts the door.

Parson's stands up waving the gun as he talks to himself. "Once I have the lockets, I will lead both UFE and GREC. I'm the only one who knows what the world needs. Only me. Yes— Only I know the best."

He points the gun at his head. "Wonder what would happen to me?" The UFE's master plan involves genetically enhancing soldiers to create super troopers. Parsons, despite being deemed mentally unfit by the lead scientist, Seok, was the first to step forward as a volunteer. According to Veda, only a special bullet can kill him if shot. *Only what happens if he's shot in the heart or the brain?* He contemplated just shooting himself to see for fun. "I just need to figure out how to remove that damn locket from around her neck."

Dodge knows something went as bad as it could as María stares straight ahead, not saying a word to him. Dodge texts Nicolaus. *How's it going on your side?* With no response, he realizes they are still in the middle of the plan at Pierce Roosevelt Financials & Investments.

Twenty minutes turns into fifty, then ninety minutes with no radio, no words spoken, just the sound of traffic. María pulls up to her townhouse. Dodge contemplates to himself, *What the fuck happened?* The entire drive. They've never gone over twenty minutes without talking to each other.

María stares straight ahead, eyes unblinking. She's frozen, which is something Dodge has never seen in all the years he's known her, and he hates it. A fist of emotions he doesn't want to identify clenches tight around his gut.

"Hey, baby. Hey . . ." He puts the car into park and turns off the ignition. She gives no response. The fist tightens, propelling him into action.

Dodge hops out of the car and hurries around to the driver's side. María doesn't turn her head, doesn't flinch when he opens the door.

He can name the emotions now—it's not just one. He's scared. This is the woman he loves, despite the constant friction in their relationship. And he's livid. He's going to kill the people who hurt her, and he's going to make them wish they'd never drawn breath.

"Let's go inside, okay?" He presses a soft kiss against her cheek before peeling her fingers off the steering wheel.

She peeks at him and the emptiness in her eyes makes that fist in his gut twist. She lets him pull her out of the car, though she's silent as he guides her into the house.

He escorts her to the couch in the living room and helps sit her down. She sobs and screeches while throwing the couch pillows across the room. Since Nicolaus's family died, Dodge has never seen this much pain, anger, and anguish in María. After a couple of minutes, she puts her face into her hands, sobbing, and Dodge puts his left arm around her shoulder, doing his best to comfort her.

She screams, "Get them over here NOW!"

He grabs his phone and texts Akari.

Shades of Finance

18

Present

Nicolaus scans his badge through the window of their vintage 1970s speeder, dressed in a sharp, dark green fitted suit. Akari appears stunning in her elegant orange spring dress, with a single barrette holding up her hair on the right and a hibiscus flower tucked behind her left ear. He backs the vehicle into a visitor's parking spot.

Just before they step out of the car, he hesitates and twiddles with the glitter bottle, praying that Wayne set up the camera device to avoid the security cameras recording Akari's task. As a financial institution, cameras are everywhere, literally every ten feet plastered to the ceilings.

Akari rubs down his arms. "Are you ready to do this and hopefully confirm the UFE's financial backing?"

"Absolutely, plus you're the lucky charm."

As they enter the building, a towering double-story sign and a waterfall sparkle in front of Pierce Roosevelt Financials & Investments atrium greets their view.

Nicolaus escorts Akari to the security desk. "Good morning, Wayne," Nicolaus says, smiling.

"Mr. Landowski, the hero of Texas." Wayne, an older African American, responds and winks. "How can I help you?"

"My girlfriend and I are here to visit Mr. Roosevelt."

"Sounds great. I see a raise in your future, Mr. Landowski." Wayne, a tall, grizzled veteran with gray cropped hair, stands up behind the security desk and nods at Akari. "I'll just need your driver's license."

Akari retrieves her license from her purse. "It's a pleasure to meet you, Mr. Irons. Nicolaus spoke highly of your kindness, mentioning that you, Dodge, and him sometimes have coffee together in the mornings."

Wayne prints out a visitor badge and hands it to Akari. "We do. It's very nice—we are all set. You both are ready." Wayne reaches his hand over the counter to shake Nicolaus's hand and whispers. "You have an hour window. Get it done." Wayne's return to his home in Rochester Hills, Michigan, hinges on completing the mission of obtaining concrete proof of Pierce Roosevelt Financials & Investments' involvement. He longs to return to flying for Casey, rather than being stuck in an office and missing out on time with his sons and grandchildren.

Nicolaus leans back. "Thanks for being so kind and looking forward to the future." They let go of each other's hands, nod and smile.

"All right, it's time to get this soirée rolling," Nicolaus says to Akari as they stroll toward the elevator.

Nicolaus and Akari exit the elevator and wander over to his office area. Before he can open the door, around ten coworkers come running up to him.

"Nicolaus, we bought you a thank-you cake and gifts. Thank you so much for saving us all!"

"That's super kind, everyone. Just give me a moment to settle in and ensure Akari is comfortable before I meet with Mr. Roosevelt," Nicolaus responds.

A recent college graduate who had gone through the internship program, with Nicolaus sponsoring her hiring, admires Akari. "Can I ask you what the flower means?"

With a smile and still holding on to Nicolaus, Akari responds to Jasmine. "In Hawaiian culture, a lady wears a flower behind her right ear if she is unmarried or unattached. Wearing it on the left means you're happily married or in a relationship."

"I love hearing about different cultures. Alight, I'll leave you two alone." She smiles and walks away. They disperse, and Nicolaus and Akari walk into his office and shut the door.

Akari peers at Nicolaus, incredulous. "No blinds?"

"The higher-ups don't want anyone to have privacy here." Nicolaus glances straight out the glass window and the camera aimed at his office. "Wayne has us covered." Nicolaus sets down his backpack containing his and Akari's laptops.

Walter Roosevelt shows up at the door and thrusts it open with his assistant, Amber. "Hey there, my rockstar future head of IT architecture. Nicolaus, let's talk in my office, and Amber, my assistant, will take Akari for breakfast while the two men chat."

Akari gapes at Nicolaus like their plans always go awry, and they must ad-lib to succeed.

"Sounds great, sir." Nicolaus turns to Akari so they can't see his face as he bulges his eyeballs as if to say, *You'll have to figure this out.*

Roosevelt asks Akari, "Do you mind adventuring with Amber? We'll go have a one-on-one discussion."

"No, I don't mind at all. We'll have a great breakfast downstairs. I think I saw a delicious muffin I'd like to try." Akari memorized the food she glanced at when they entered the building. If they run into such situations, Nicolaus and Akari are aware of their environment: closest exits, stairwells, fire alarms, pull switches, and casual banter fill-ins.

"Wonderful. Let's go chat, Nicolaus," Mr. Roosevelt says. With casual conversation, they walk down the marble hallway and then ride the elevator to the top floor.

Amber surveys Akari. "Hi, it's nice to meet you. Let's go downstairs and get the muffin you were looking at."

Akari nods in agreement and gets up from the desk. As they stroll down the hallway, Akari says, "Before we go down, I need to use the powder room."

"No problem. It's right down the hall. I'll take you there."

Akari gets the feeling Mr. Roosevelt doesn't want her alone. How would she shake this obnoxious tailgater? "Thank you, I'll be right out." Akari walks into the bathroom and paces for a moment in front of the mirror. The idea enters her mind, and she texts her mom. *Call me. We can review the studies from last week. Trust me, we need the time to review again.*

Chie calls Akari while a couple of women enter the bathroom. Akari blurts out as Amber opens the door, peering in, "I have time to review the last four studies now. Nicolaus is with his boss, and we must show them to the board this week." Akari walks to the door, speaking into her phone. "Mom, hold on." She squints at Amber. "I've got something I've got to go over with my mom. Can you lead me back to Nicolaus's office?"

Amber nods and they stride down the hallway.

Akari asks, "Could you grab me a coffee, please? My head will start splitting if I don't have one. Nicolaus didn't stop on the way. He was eager to talk with Mr. Roosevelt."

Amber understands as everyone relishes meeting with the CEO, her boss.

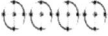

Nicolaus and Mr. Roosevelt exit the elevator to the seventeenth floor and walk past a conference room on the right and the café area on the left. Mr. Roosevelt opens his door using his thumbprint scan. Nicolaus sees a lavish setup with a wraparound couch, a pool table, and a full wet bar.

"Please have a seat. Let's chat." Mr. Roosevelt motions Nicolaus to sit on a plush chair in front of his grand desk. As Walter settles into his office chair, he says, "Let's discuss the future of digital solutions and architecture. I'm interested in replacing about forty percent of the workforce with artificial intelligence and automation. What suggestions do you have, Nicolaus?"

"Well, using AI or automation as a weapon to fire or replace humans is not only wrong, but also inhumane. The real question is how to make the company and employees more efficient. It's about intent." Nicolaus smirks.

"That's interesting." Roosevelt folds his hands. "I guess that makes sense coming from you. The person who stopped a worker from shooting up the place and creating an alternative algae energy source."

As Nicolaus and Mr. Roosevelt continue their technical conversation, Akari is busy devising a plan to gather the data they need to prove their hypothesis. She puts her phone on the desk and turns the speaker on. "Mom, I want you to behave as if this is all new, and we will review for the next twenty minutes. Trust me, I need you to win an award for this acting."

Over the phone, Chie says, "No problem. Let's review, and I'll go over the numbers."

Akari pulls out Nicolaus's laptop, which she has decorated with flower decals all over the back to match her laptop. She sets the computer on the desk, making sure the screen faces the blank wall for added secrecy. As it powers on, a faint glow illuminates the room. She enters Nicolaus's password and opens a typing application. Akari sees Amber walking up and then knocks on the door. She waves her in, and Amber sets the coffee beside her phone. Chie is spouting off the numbers and results of the last test. "Test 234b failed. The known reason is for a genetic loophole . . ."

She continues with the technical information, and Amber says, "That's some excruciating detail. I'll leave you to it; I'll be right outside." Akari nods, acting like she is taking notes on the computer.

As soon as Amber shuts the door, Akari pulls out a tiny flash drive, puts it in the port, picks up her phone, clicks the custom-made interference app she finished last night to avoid the installation process, and poof! Her pathway is untraceable. She signs into the vendor management system, which Nicolaus doesn't have access to the restricted clientele.

By opening a second app, she can reset the administration password on the single sign-on, and the application auto-generates a new password for her access. She gives a gleeful smirk and searches for the Global Reform Establishment Coalition, Parsons and Veda, with no results. *So does that mean Roosevelt does not sponsor GREC or is that on a different system?—that'll be for a later time.* She then searches for the Federation. The results show twenty thousand UFE transactions. Akari opens a third app on her phone, which captures the full details of the results table. She glances out through the glass window and sees Amber is gone.

"Akari, you there?" She almost forgets her mom is still on the phone.

"Yes, Mom, keep going, don't stop, keep going," Akari says with a sense of urgency.

"Got it. I'll go through the next case study," Chie replies.

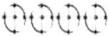

"Thank you for your perspective, Nicolaus. It's different from what I was going to tell the board. There's a way I can skim off twenty percent of the workforce by the end of the year to make the shareholders happy, and then you could present the digital product architecture implementation plan across the enterprise and subsidiaries," Mr. Roosevelt responds, glaring at Nicolaus.

Nicolaus clutches his fist with Mr. Roosevelt's callousness toward laying off humans to make rich people even more prosperous. "It would be an honor, sir. I relish the opportunity to showcase a roadmap to ensure profitability for the company and shareholders," Nicolaus replies, holding back his actual feelings.

"Here's some advice that will prove invaluable as you climb the corporate ladder. You've heard it before, but it's critical to keep your friends close and your enemies even closer." He fixes his piercing gaze on Nicolaus, searching for any hint of reaction, but Nicolaus doesn't give Mr. Roosevelt the satisfaction.

"I understand, sir. The best way to rise to the top is to focus on myself and my ambition."

"I knew you would grasp the concept. You have a very intelligent girlfriend and a bright future. Pun intended, if you know what I mean. Also, can you teach me that color changing eye trick?" Roosevelt pauses. Nicolaus grits his teeth with Roosevelt's confirmation he's definitely involved with in obtaining the Divine power. "Your mother possessed the same qualities as Akari." Mr. Roosevelt's grip on the armrest of his chair tightens as if holding himself back from a fit of intense jealousy. "If it weren't for her unwavering loyalty to your father, which I'm still trying to figure out, I might have been your father. That's one reason they promoted me to CEO. She was one of the biggest gambles I took, and it paid off. We became the angel investor in DaeChie Pharmaceuticals, thanks to her ingenuity."

Nicolaus feels a surge of anger. He moves his hand down to his pants pocket and clasps his keychain with the microchip from his dad's last invention. "My father was a simple man, but everything he did was for her. It taught me that working solo only gets you so far. But when two people work together as one entity, it's unstoppable."

Both men lock eyes, sizing each other up and engaging in a mental game of staring, which only ends when a beep sounds from the scanning device, and Amber enters. "Sir, I just want to let you know Akari has an important meeting with her mom, and we didn't get breakfast. Would you like anything?"

Mr. Roosevelt glares at Nicolaus. "No, thank you, Amber. That'll be all."

Amber turns around, opens the door, and walks out.

"Let's check in on your Akari and see how she's doing."

Neither Nicolaus nor Mr. Roosevelt break their eye contact. After a minute Nicolaus can't stand the deafening silence. "Sir, why are we staring at each other? Is this some sort of test of corporate fortitude? Because this is getting a little strange. I came here expecting a promotion and celebration with my future bride."

"This is a test—let's go see her," Mr. Roosevelt exclaims, rising from his chair and gesturing for Nicolaus to catch up.

Sensing the urgency of Amber's absence, Akari searches for her mother's pharmaceutical company. She downloads the content to her phone, opens the password reset app, clicks the revert button, and submits it. The screen displays a message: YOU NEED PROPER AUTHORIZATION TO VIEW THE RESULTS. She hurries to close the vendor management program and then clicks the shutdown computer button. Akari takes out the mini flash drive, puts it in the backpack, and removes the stickers from Nicolaus's computer. She puts the stickers in the bag, closes the laptop, and sets it away from her next to the monitor on the desk.

Akari grabs her laptop out of the bag and turns it on. "Mom, start over with the one you are on, please. I know it's annoying." Chie then, without asking why, starts from the beginning.

At that very moment, the CEO and Nicolaus stroll toward her. Mr. Roosevelt slings the door open and spins her laptop screen to his sight.

"What the hell are you doing?" Akari raises her voice while she spreads her arms wide.

"Akari, is something wrong? Do you want me to stop or continue?" her mom asks.

"Sit tight, Mom—ahh, never mind—we'll continue this case study review later tonight."

Mr. Roosevelt turns fiery red with frustration because he knows they are up to something. "I'm so sorry. I thought . . . I'm very sorry, and that was inappropriate."

Nicolaus taps his foot. "Sir, are you alright? You seem on edge. Maybe you should take a vacation or something."

"Maybe you're right." Mr. Roosevelt leers at Nicolaus. "You've been promoted to director of IT architecture with a two-hundred-thousand-dollar-a-year increase. I'll have an offer letter sent to you by human resources. Take the next two weeks and go celebrate." He then ogles at Akari. "If you want some financial advice or help with perhaps a joint venture with other pharmaceutical companies, let me know, and I can make arrangements?"

There is so much resentment emanating as Mr. Roosevelt let out a deep, angry breath, almost like a snarl.

Nicolaus shakes Mr. Roosevelt's hand with each other's grip hardening like they were in an arm-wrestling competition. "Thank you again, sir. We are grateful for the offer of a business partnership and enthusiastic about the promotion."

"Just remember, without me, your family would have nothing . . . Divinity." Mr. Roosevelt lets go of his hand, spins around, and storms off down the hall.

Akari peers at Nicolaus. "Let's get the hell out of here."

Nicolaus contemplates the quip about the Divinities, and the bright comment. *How much information does Mr. Roosevelt know?* They grab their belongings and leave the building as fast as possible, with several other worker interruptions thanking Nicolaus before they exit and leap into the muscle car.

"We got everything, and yes, they are the full backbone of the UFE. So, Mr. Roosevelt is buddy-buddy with Veda and Parsons. I found nothing, absolutely nothing on GREC. We'll review all the data later with María." She releases a long, audible breath as they exit the campus. "I need to shower to get rid of this, yuck," a shiver runs down her spine.

"I feel you. Let's get to our house and discuss."

"You're calm. Most of the time, it's the other way around," Akari says, with her eyebrows raised.

"It took everything in me not to punch that sorry ass, scum ball, and break his nose, arms, and legs, but for what we need to do, I didn't."

Akari laughs. "Keep it going. It is making me feel better."

Nicolaus replies, "I wonder how María and Dodge are doing? Their trip couldn't have been worse than our office visit with Mr. Elitist."

"When we get close to the house, I'll text them." Akari hears her texting sound in her purse. She pulls out her phone. "Shit. Dodge texted . . . *GYAHN.* I'll tell them ten minutes?"

"Maybe, then, their day was worse. If Dodge is texting you that."

As they arrive and enter the house, Nicolaus walks straight to his cousin. He bends down and presses a kiss on her forehead, grasping her hand. He gazes at her. "Please tell us what happened so we can help you."

María nods, lets go of his hand, and tells him to sit down. Her voice trembles as she shares the details, igniting a wave of anger in Akari, Dodge, and Nicolaus that they haven't experienced since their days in the military. A cold sweat makes Nicolaus's skin clammy and sticky. He fidgets with his keychain, with the encased microchip, and then moves to the glitter bottle. Akari's heart races and feels like it's about to burst out of her chest. She takes in deep breaths. Dodge's stomach churns with a knot, as if someone is gradually winding it into a tight ball.

The moment María finishes, Akari jolts up from her seat and rushes to embrace her best friend. Her hand strokes María's hair. Akari's voice booms in anger. "Parsons is an abomination."

Nicolaus smacks his right hand in his left palm. "I'm proud of you, María, for not taking out Parsons right then and there."

"Aamirah showed us in the vision. We have choices to make . . . to choose our path. We have to get the lockets and get this rolling. That was not the right time. I'm telling y'all he's royally fucked up. And Nicolaus, his eyes glowed orange."

María fidgets with the locket and eyes Dodge. "I love you. It was impossible for me to speak during the drive. Thank you for allowing me to get through this without attempting to fix it with your jokes. I needed the space."

"It had to feel good to zap that asshole with a Zeus bolt."

María chuckles. "Fuck ya, it did."

"Hey Nicolaus, write that down—María said she loves me."

María shakes her head and gazes at Akari with a hint of worry. "Now you know about my day with a narcistic psychopath. How did your day go?"

"We got all the financial records. From what I skimmed while downloading the files, it confirms that Pierce Roosevelt is the full financial backing for UFE. Nothing on GREC."

"So, let's take the head off the snake?" asks Dodge.

María replies, "GREC has to be involved. This shit is too big not to have them orchestrating this."

Nicolaus nods his head. *María's intuition is like ninety percent spot on, but it only seems the UFE is the rogue organization. That's why they killed his aunt. It appears like the UFE is running a coup against GREC.* "Akari and I will start the analysis tonight if you would like?"

"No, I got it. It'll calm my nerves down."

Just then, Nicolaus receives a text message from Casey. He replies with a thumbs-up emoji.

"Casey will be here in the morning and wants us to meet him at the restaurant at eight o'clock sharp." Nicolaus hugs María. "You get some rest. Don't stay up too late crunching the numbers, and we'll see you bright and early." Holding onto him tighter, she dwelled over Parsons' accusation that she played a major role in his family's death.

"Cousin, you're going to crush my ribs."

They separate and Akari hugs María. "At least we know that once the locket is on, a person cannot rip it off. Let us know if you need anything, call or text. We'll be right there for you."

Café
of
Invasion

19

Present

Nicolaus wakes up with Akari lying on his chest, her arm wrapped around his waist. Their eyes lock, and she reaches out to pat his stomach. "You fell asleep like a rock while looking at your family's scrapbook."

After María's encounter with Parsons, Nicolaus felt defenseless and vulnerable. His cousin confronted the devil with unwavering bravery. Could he have handled it like she did? That sensation is something he loathes. As quick as possible, he slams shut the door to his mind, refusing to let any self-doubt seep in. "I needed to see my family to stoke my fire."

Akari closes her eyes. "We will get retribution on the wicked."

More questions circle his brain. *How do the UFE and Roosevelt know so much about the Divinities? Do they have a special book or an insider with knowledge? But who? And what do they know?* Not even a week ago, they were making progress on the investigation, but Parsons, UFE, Roosevelt—it's like someone hit the fast-forward button on their life.

Akari feels his heart rate speeding up and puts her hand over his heart to ease his mind. With a gentle touch, he clasps her hand, his fingers gliding over hers.

An hour later, Akari and Nicolaus pull into the restaurant's parking lot at Julieta & Marcin's Café. A smile spreads across their faces as they spot Casey's and María's trucks parked outside. He reverses the rumbling '70s vehicle into a parking spot next to Casey's big rig.

As they walk to the front of the car, they hold each other's hands and share a passionate kiss. After their lips unlock, Akari says, "Let's get into the café and get you a churro. I'm sure María will have a field day with you over wanting a churro instead of an omelet." They both burst into laughter and stroll toward the café. Nicolaus holds the door open for a happy family exiting. Then Akari enters, greeted by the authentic aroma of Mexican seasoning wafting through the air. While he holds the door, Nicolaus feels a shiver up his back as his eyes glimpse three UFE trucks rolling down the road. He gives a piercing stare: *one he totally gets, two something is going on, but three—something is off.*

Casey, having recognized the distinct sound of their vehicle, greets the couple at the door. "Akari, your charisma continues to impress me, and I'm still trying to figure out why you're tagging along with this guy," Casey exclaims as he embraces Akari. "The family is waiting for you in the banquet area," he adds, pulling away from the embrace. "María's been anxiously waiting for you all morning and will pounce on you as soon as you enter."

Akari chuckles and navigates through the dining room tables before unlatching the door that leads to the forty-person banquet area at the back of the restaurant.

Casey shakes hands with Nicolaus and gives him a massive bear hug, with his huge pecs, and titan sized arms squeezing Nicolaus. As they pull away, Casey asks, "Nicolaus, you look like you just saw a ghost."

"I—I'm sure it's nothing. Paranoia. Never mind, it's all good."

Casey pats Nicolaus on the back as they stride toward the swinging back door. "Well, the past couple of days will do that to you."

Nicolaus pushes the door open. The hinges creak as they step inside. He views Dodge, María, Herculano, Catalina, and Akari all gathered at a table in the middle of the room.

Akari turns to Casey. "Thanks for the warning. María almost knocked me off my feet." Casey laughs as Nicolaus greets everyone with a warm hug.

Catalina nudges Herculano's arm as he hands Akari a piece of paper. She peruses the document. *Your mom and dad have gone off the grid. They'll contact us when it's safe.* She clutches the note and feels a sense of dread creeping up on her. Nicolaus and Akari's eyes lock and he mouths, *Trust*, as he places his hand over his heart.

Within five seconds of each other, Casey, Nicolaus, and Akari's phones ring.

Akari almost fumbles hers from the table, grabbing it before it hits the floor. Her voice carries a tinge of sadness as she mutters, "It's my cousin." Her heart aches for her parents' absence. Akari's cousin Keahi Iona and her four other cousins run the family farm back in Oahu.

Nicolaus grabs his phone from his pocket as Akari walks to one side of the banquet space. "It's Seok." He raises his eyebrows and regards Catalina. "She never calls me. It's always for Akari."

Casey snatches his phone from his side holster. "What's Gerald want now?"

"Spooky—this is like the Twilight Zone or something," Dodge says to María, waving his fingers in the air. "Three phones ring at the same time. Welcome to the fifth dimension—"

María shakes her head. A smile plays on her lips as she lets out a soft chuckle. She eyeballs Nicolaus deep in conversation as he scowls, walking in circles. When he arrived, he seemed on edge or preoccupied. When he gave her a hug, she felt his tenseness.

Akari answers the phone. Keahi whispers. "Forty military guys from the Federation are walking around the property, and they ask me when was the last time your parents were here. They slammed Lagi on the ground after he gave them his typical backtalk. Does this have to do with anything from your military days?"

Akari's heart sinks. "Tell your brothers to remain calm; don't antagonize the troops. Let them search and call the police."

"Already called them, and the police said this is official Federation business."

"Keahi, keep calm. I love you, and tell them everything will be okay."

"I don't know what you four are into, but this is not cool. They said they are staying until their boss gives them the green light to go."

Akari considers, *This has to be Veda or worse, Parsons.* She replies, in native Hawaiian, "I'll call you right back. Be safe." Akari hangs up.

Seok was Nicolaus's mom's best friend and partner at DaeChie Pharmaceuticals. Since the tragedy, he has felt an icy distance, a reluctance from her, as if he is to blame for his mother's death. "Hey, Seok. Is anything wrong?"

"The Federation is here. There are at least thirty troops standing in my lobby."

"What?" He grips the phone tighter. "Did they—"

Seok interrupts, "Their orders are to stay until a message is delivered to you four."

The three UFE trucks he observed outside weren't random but for them. Nicolaus's muscles tighten even more, and he didn't consider they could. He feels like one of those wind-up monkey toys, ready to burst its cymbals. If Parsons walks through that door, will he contain himself? He sees Akari's arms shiver, betraying the calmness in her voice. "Did they say what message?"

"No. They said it's being delivered to you. Nicolaus, all you ever do is create problems for me. Not only are you distracting Akari from her work, but you also haven't finished the projects I requested, and now this."

He wonders, *why is she such a bitch to me?* She used to play EpicBloxx with him and his sister. They'd make frozen popsicles or tubsicles in the lab for fun when they had to stay at DaeChie while the adults worked. She's the one who showed the differences between organic and GMOs. And it's not her lobby— it's their family's company. "When is the message supposed to arrive?"

Casey clicks the answer button. "Yes, Gerald—did the alarm go off again in the barn?"

Right after the parents purchased the ranch, Casey enlisted the local veterans to watch over the property. Gerald is an old friend and the head security officer. He's a former Navy Seal, and he owns Country Walsh Diner with his son Lawrence. His raspy voice replies. "There're about thirty ruthless thugs from the United Federation of Enforcement."

"What did they say or want?" Casey replies.

"This is some big brother government bullshit. They ain't coming on this property. No way no how."

"Do me a favor. Take three big, deep breaths, calm down, and focus. You're no good to anyone if you can't think clearly."

There is a slight pause in the conversation. Casey hears a couple of raspy breaths from Gerald. "Better?"

"Yes, better. The Federation is squatting at the entrance and said they ain't leaving until they deliver a message for the four of them. What the fuck did they do wrong?" Gerald harbors a strong disdain for the Federation, viewing them as bullies who use jurisdiction and government red tape to intimidate the local police and anyone who resembles a militia entity.

Casey hears shouts and commotions from the front of the restaurant. "Just stand down right now. I'll call you right back." His neck turns to the swinging door as fifteen combat-ready UFE troops and one black-suited, muscular man walk through.

Nicolaus's body feels a cold winter wind cut through his clothes to the bone. He responds to Seok, "Message received. I'll call you back." He hangs up the phone, staring at the bald man he presumes is Parsons. Nicolaus can't forget the cold-hearted eyes.

Hamilton Parsons struts to the table as the troops encircle the room with their guns aimed, ready to let loose. "Well, isn't this a happy family gathering?"

María feels the ragged rise and fall of her chest, like she's back in the dirt with her dying mother, reliving the worst day of her life. She jolts up. "I can take your ass, and all your little freaks, six feet under." She grabs both of her sidearms by her waist. Herculano motions his hands down to put her guns away. The soldiers point their guns at her, and she only realizes they are outnumbered when Dodge tugs on her pant leg.

"Feisty, love it." Parsons' eyes go from María to Casey. "Oh, look, it's the hotshot mover. You think you're so slick to keep tabs on the UFE, when in reality we have you under constant surveillance."

Parsons circles the family, stops and stares at Nicolaus, their noses three inches apart. Nicolaus's arms pressed by his side. He taps his fingers against his pants, doing his utmost not to react, but too late. He grabs Parsons's hands, and within milliseconds, Nicolaus has Parsons on his knees with a gun pointed at his head.

"I should have finished you that night." This man killed his parents and sister. He still hears their screams. "What's the message? Tell me or I'm going to enjoy watching your blood splatter across the floor."

Parsons laughs. "Do it. Come on, little Nicki. Kill me."

One troop squawks, "Sir, give me the order and I'll take him out."

"That won't be necessary." Nicolaus grips the gun harder as Parsons smirks. "You shoot me,"—he snaps his fingers—"everyone at the table dies, everyone at the ranch dies, everyone at the farm dies, everyone hiding dies." Parsons's phone rings in his coat pocket. "If I don't answer this, then Veda won't be happy and she'll give the orders."

Nicolaus contemplates just letting loose on the trigger as he leers at Parsons, and his hands shake. The Four Shadows of Light witnessed Veda's ruthless behavior on one of their last missions. She cut down an ambassador and his associates for deviating from the UFE's orders. They caught sight of her rage, and only then did María believe Veda had something to do with her mom's death.

Dodge clears his throat and edges up, nodding to the troops. "Yo, put the gun down, dude. The mobster is not worth it right now. They always get it before the end credits roll."

Nicolaus's finger twitches on the trigger. The sight of his sister crawling in a pool of blood reruns in his mind.

Akari speaks up. "Let's hear the message from Veda. Nicolaus, they have us surrounded." Her voice punctures his anger, and he pulls the gun away from Parsons's forehead, leaving a circle indentation from the barrel, and sets it on the table.

Parsons stands up and pulls out the phone. Before he answers, he howls at the ceiling. "Good little Nicki. A little bitch, just like your father." Nicolaus reaches for the gun he just set down, but stopped short, knowing they have the lower ground right now. After a moment, Parsons snarls at María, "It's for you." He sets down the phone on the table and pushes it across.

She takes hold of the phone and raises it to her ear to hear Veda's voice. "You have two days to find the lockets and unlock your abilities. I'm on your side. I want to see you reach your full potential."

"So you threaten us, turn your back on us." Veda, as their handler, orchestrated their missions and was her mom's protégé. María punches her fist on the table. "Why go through all of this?"

"Can't you feel the Divine power coursing through your veins? It's time. We thought, during the operations, you four would awaken the Divinities." While GREC had their own motives for harnessing the power, Veda's mission centered on awakening Medium, the anti-Divinity, which required activating four of the lockets. *Julieta would yammer on and on about waiting until Aamirah rose to be by their sides.* "Your moms were incredibly annoying by refusing to give you the lockets earlier. Look, there are multiple factions coming for you. I want you on the right side of this. Two days and I'll have Parsons give you Dodge's locket back. After you get the other two lockets, you can dispose of Parsons as a gift from me to you."

María's lip sneers. "What factions? And why didn't you come in person?"

"I thought getting him involved would quench your thirst for revenge and challenge you. So, just get moving."

"You didn't answer my question about the factions."

"You soon will find out. Give the phone back to Parsons."

María leans forward with squared shoulders and slides the phone across the table. "For you, fuckhead."

He grunts and winks at her while picking up the phone to speak with Veda. "They're so ripe for the taking."

"Execute the plan and don't fuck this up."

Parsons rolls his eyes and hangs up. As he backs away, glimpsing at the ceiling. "Shut up! Stop Talking!"

Nicolaus hears the same sinister voice echoing through his mind. "Listen to Veda or DIE!"

Parsons shakes his head and gestures outwardly. "In a matter of minutes, local police will raid your houses. I told them you're part of a drug smuggling ring. You won't be able to go to your homes, leaving you without your guns, clothes, inventions, vehicles, etcetera, etcetera, etcetera. We will call them off in a couple of hours." He turns on his heels and strides out the door. The sound of the troops' boots clatter behind him.

Motionless, the Four Shadows of Light's eyes stare at the banquet door.

Nicolaus scrutinizes the gun, pissed at himself for not pulling the trigger. *Would the UFE really kill their family and friends?* He let Parsons get away twice. *What about María?* Nicolaus glances up from the gun to his cousin.

Her blood boils and trembles like a fish out of water. Veda, their commander and trusted ally, is now toying with them. She reflects to when her mother, Veda, and she had competitions together. *They would shoot arrows from seven hundred feet away. Julieta and María hit the bullseye eight times in a row. Veda limit was four times. Veda never showed anger or jealousy. Then there's Parsons. Twice in two days she had the chance to kill him, but didn't. She dismantled an entire drug lord compound but couldn't exact revenge.*

Breaking the silence, Dodge quips, "Well, that was shitty as shitty can get." He pushes away his plate.

Nicolaus picks up his vibrating phone with a text from Seok: *UFE leaving.*

178

Akari texts her cousin back after receiving the *all clear* message. She then checks their house sensor and camera system to see if Parsons is lying. Akari flips between cameras and toggles from their house to Marcin's, the Vargas's, María's, and Dodge's homes. She grimaces. "They are swarming at your townhouses and our house. It seems Marcin and the Vargas's homes are secure."

After responding to Gerald, Casey's attention shifts to the rest of the group. "The ranch is clear. Here's the plan, you four, head there now. That'll be our base of operations. I'll join you soon." He glances at Catalina. "Stay strong. It appears they are playing with them and using us as bait. Get some rest tonight. You'll need it in the days ahead." Catalina gives a faint smile. Casey turns to Nicolaus. "Your Divinities locket is at the ranch. When you get there, seek the specific location your dad mentioned to me—where your spark ignites."

Upon hearing that phrase, most people imagine spark plugs or a lighter. However, it was Nicolaus's favorite thinking spot, where he often devised ideas and found peace.

"Nicolaus, before you go, we have churros waiting for you," Catalina says, while holding the bag. "Akari said you were craving them. Good luck and stay united."

Spark
of
Ranch

20

Present

Nicolaus taps his thumb on the top of the muscle car's stick shift, mulling over not having his truck. Metal and machines give him a sense of comfort and protection, like a warm blanket. He's a machinist at heart. Dodge poked fun at Nicolaus whenever they watched a horror movie, where a person puts the blanket over their head to protect them. He would have the real deal with iron clad vaulted protection with tech gear inside. Dodge expected a machine to come out of the walls and protect Akari and Nicolaus's bedroom.

Nicolaus chuckles, musing over María, trying to find weak points at his battle tank. She didn't want a repeat of her mom's death, so she went to extreme lengths for both of their vehicles by launching grenades and unloading rounds of ammunition at it. So far, they have found no weaknesses. Akari and he have been working on a living force field as added protection, and failed at every turn. He ponders—*what if the Divinity powers give them the ability to complete some of their progressive concepts?*

Akari observes the absence of conversation and the tense posture as Nicolaus drives. "We'll go retrieve your truck as soon as we can." Akari loves the hot rod—a gift to Nicolaus from his dad before he died. Together, they worked countless hours, upgrading the silver glittered exterior and the interior with modern technology and amenities.

On the hour drive, Nicolaus loosens up when Akari suggests they discuss the café intrusion over the communications device with Dodge and María. Halfway through the commute, the team changes the subject to strategize if the UFE or any other outside forces decide to attack. Akari designates María to come up with a tactical defense plan for the ranch.

The moment they arrive at the ranch, the mouthwatering smell of barbeque hits their nostrils, while a dozen jacked-up trucks and military-style vehicles greet their eyes by the barn. Nicolaus feels a wave of nostalgia wash over him. It feels like their army days at the bases.

María and Dodge pull up behind them and hop out of their pickup truck. María's voice booms. "Who's ready to deploy the ranch protection reserves? Follow us!"

They stride toward the water tower. Magnar erected a building at the bottom, which included an underground bunker with a wide selection of state-of-the-art guns, ammo, and accessories. María pushes aside multiple steel bookcases to reveal a solid metal door. Only the Four Shadows of Light and Gerald have access to the bunker. María presses her hand against the digital keypad, speaks her call sign, and the thick metal door opens. The pack of veterans follows her into the modern cavern and hauls out the massive inventory to the barn for prep and testing.

Standing by the barn, Akari glances at Dodge. "While they handle the weapons, you and Nicolaus head inside the house and retrieve the drones. You're going to train the veterans on how to fly your masterpieces. No one in the world is a better sniper than you, and we need your overwatch expertise."

Nicolaus nods to Dodge. "I second that. Your sniper statistics speak for themselves. You are second to none as our protector."

"Bro, I'm going to cry. You two are lathering me with compliments. I'm the greatest sniper the world has ever seen and will ever see."

Akari sighs. "Go get the drones."

Nicolaus runs his hand over the back of his neck. His gaze meets Akari's. "You know my spark. You know where to locate the locket."

She beams at him. To outsiders, Nicolaus may seem confident, but he keeps his vulnerability hidden. His closest friends and family are the only ones who grasp that his empathy is the core of his consciousness. Akari strides past Dodge and plants an enormous kiss on his lips.

"Nicolaus, I need you to focus on our flying birds, not your love birds," Dodge says with a wide grin.

He and Akari break apart with his knees weak and her cheeks blushing. "Dude, you ruined the moment."

"You can have a moment later. Let's get the drones flying because I have to train these guys. Stubborn military veterans." He chuckles because the four of them are obstinate as mules.

"Yeah, you can have your moment later." Akari giggles. "Because if it's there, then you will undoubtedly have your moment." Nicolaus's grin widens with a suggestive wink.

Akari struts toward the greenhouse, recalling their parents' delight when they bought the sprawling property. The kids, filled with excitement, played tag, perfected their martial arts techniques, and took part in games of cornhole, horseshoes, and go-carting. Her favorite location was the third greenhouse closest to the windmill. The spinning shadow, cast by the afternoon sun at one o'clock, transformed the tables and plants into a moving canvas, resembling a priceless choreographed art piece.

She brought Nicolaus to the greenhouse to teach him gardening. They spent hours watering and transplanting the plants or vegetables her parents had hauled to the ranch. With each scoop of dirt and gentle placement of roots into new pots, their hands brushed each other, giving her a fluttering sensation in her chest. Being around Nicolaus made her feel alive. They understood each other, and even at a young age, an unbreakable bond existed between them. Since they were fifteen, he prioritized her needs before his own—whether it was a simple gesture like opening the car door for her, or listening if she needed to vent, or having dinner ready if she had a stressful day at work.

As Akari steps into the greenhouse, she recounts Nicolaus telling her that when his dad took him to the ranch to work on cars, he would become bored or frustrated that he couldn't be with her. So halfway through the day, he would go to the spot, sit for twenty minutes, and reflect on her, then return with boundless energy. Magnar asked Nicolaus if he had consumed energy drinks or something the first few times he came back all fired up.

Nicolaus replied, "I haven't. You know mom would get mad at me because they have too much caffeine, and as Mi-Cha says, it would make me even more annoying. So, let's get rolling. I'm ready for whatever the next project is."

Magnar followed Nicolaus one day and observed him sitting on the spot. Magnar understood he just needed a thoughtful moment about Akari. It was Nicolaus's spark. Magnar understood because that's how he felt about his wife, Dae.

Akari stands where they told each other "I love you" for the first time. Around the wooden bench at the center of the greenhouse, she searches and sees nothing. While surveying the area, her eyes fixate on a couple of bricks on the floor with faded paint saying AKARI AND NICOLAUS FOREVER with a heart symbol. She bends down and examines the bricks. Her hand glides across the surface, and she discovers a cross-like symbol etched into the brick in the middle of the red heart. She and Nicolaus selected the brick because of the symbol. She extracts her pocketknife and slices the paver sand from the brick crevices. Getting to her feet, she examines around and grabs a small shovel. With a forceful pull and a loud grunt, she lifts the brick up and shoves the paver sand to the side to reveal a small metal box with the Divinity symbol. Akari's heart pounds as she opens the container, and the locket glimmers in her eyes. Overwhelmed, she rises to her feet with her skin tingling. She shakes her head to snap out of the trance and strides to deliver the box to her love.

Nicolaus opens the closet in the ranch house spare bedroom, and Dodge's jaw drops. "You took our blueprint and mass produced thirty drones? When the fuck did you do that?"

"I just rolled up my sleeves and cranked them out in the past year. Our design was flawless, so just sat down with the parts and it became an assembly line."

Dodge ogles at the stack of remote controls, admiring his design with some slight visual tweaks from María and Akari. He handled the look and feel, so he replicated the aesthetics to match a stealth bomber with the addition of two high-powered propellers. Nicolaus handled the blueprints. Dodge chuckles about Nicolaus getting frustrated, saying function over form as they battled over the original prototype. All María wanted was to have an overwhelming amount of firepower at her disposal. Akari had to intervene to prevent them from shouting at each other and refocus.

Dodge whistles shaking his head. "This shit is so dope. Can't wait to see this swarm flying."

"Shock and awe, for sure. Six months ago, Akari and I changed the kill switch to act as a dive bomber. Just mark a target.

She coded it to help with a quicker nosedive. I changed the gun chamber to slide forward to help gravity and get it quicker to the ground."

"I love it when you two work together. She gets you to finish your inventions." Dodge laughs.

Nicolaus sighs as he fiddles with a propeller. He knows that's an area that needs improvement—pushing himself. Everyone around Nicolaus had to challenge him to reach his potential from his mom to his sister, Asa, Akari, and so on. At some point, he has to assume responsibility without relying on others to motivate him. "I'm working on that, bro. Sometimes I just roll and get it done, but I get bored. Plus, I enjoy working as a team."

While they are moving the drones from the closet to the barn, Nicolaus wishes they hacked into the UFE facial recognition database. Akari tried a couple of different avenues over the past three years with no success. So, he devised another way to differentiate between the good and bad guys, and ensure the drones didn't shoot friendlies. The drones use heat sensors in combination with sensor patches that signal the drones. Before battle, they attach the patches to their skin. The drones won't shoot them. To make María happy, he included fifty rounds of ammunition with a gun barrel and six automatic grenades. In order to safeguard against hacking attempts, Akari installed a firewall and incorporated a kill switch as a fail-safe measure.

The original concept for the drones came from high school when they started the robotics team. They received a competition kit and had to obey the rules, though they found loopholes, like María's idea of using an EMP device to kill the other robots. The Four Shadows of Light recruited classmates to join the team, with DaeChie Pharmaceuticals as the primary sponsor. The team won seven regional competitions and the national championship their senior year.

Akari bursts through the back door just as they grab the last set of drones from the bedroom closet. "I love you, Nicolaus Vasili Landowski!" she exclaims, rushing toward him and leaps over the bed, their lips meet in a passionate kiss.

"Dude, it looks like she found your spark," Dodge says as he catches the drone slipping out of Nicolaus's hand.

Nicolaus caresses her hair as they part their lips. "I love you too, Akari Kanani Iona."

A slow smile builds on her face, and her attention draws to the box. Nicolaus's eyes grow wider. He hasn't seen his locket for sixteen years, since Shamrock Lake. Akari opens the box and reveals the locket. He reaches in and pulls the necklace out. *Tonight is his turn to activate the locket and see what Aamirah has crafted for his vision.*

"I'll put it on you right now." He nods as he turns around, and she takes the necklace, unclips the clasp, and places the chain around his neck, closing the clasp. Nicolaus turns around and they embrace for another kiss.

"Less kissing, more visioning from you both," Dodge cuts in, still holding a drone in his arms.

They chuckle, and Akari says, "Let's go review the strategy in the barn."

"Wait," Nicolaus says, shaking his head. "I have to help Dodge ensure the drones function correctly. If there's an issue, we might have to make modifications. I've only tested six to make sure they're battle ready."

"Dodge will figure it out. Can't you?" Akari suggests as they both turn their heads to face Dodge.

"Of course! Test all 30 drones. Train the vets who have tech skills. Next, you'll ask me to clean the toilet." A tinge of aggravation surges to Dodge's surface. There are moments when he perceives himself as the fourth wheel, someone who is not as important as the other three. "Sorry, just a little pissed that fucker

Parsons has my locket. I'll get the drones rolling while Nicolaus goes under the Divinity spell." He smiles and winks at Nicolaus.

Akari replies, "I didn't mean to upset you."

"All good in the neighborhood. Just want to see my vision, bury Parsons, and fuck up Veda's world."

"Dodge, we aren't a team without you. You know that, right?" Akari motions her arm out.

He bobs his head. "I know. Who would bring the humor in all the serious shit we've been through?"

After Nicolaus's family died, Dodge did a perfect reenactment of his sister teasing Nicolaus, skipping and boasting about how she beat him in EpicBloxx.

Nicolaus chuckles, "No one else can liven up the chaos."

After they drop off the last drones in the barn, Akari and Nicolaus clasp hands, standing next to María. The forty veterans gather to review the strategy for the ranch defense. Some veterans clean guns and prepare the reserves for an encounter with the UFE, while others sit on the ground in the stables or on the two tractors.

"What's the plan?" Nicolaus picks up a gun sitting on a haystack. "María, you got these guys ready to tango in a couple of days in case we need it?"

"All set and ready to roll."

Akari raises her voice. "If anyone has any suggestions, now's the time to speak up."

The veterans nod their heads, and María delves into the plan. "The water tower is Dodge's station. Nicolaus and Akari will attack from the right side, behind the RV graveyard. I'm with the guys in the front to avoid friendly crossfire. The drone operators will remote control from the greenhouses, and the drones will fly from the boathouse windmill. My assumption is Lawrence will lead the drone flyers once Dodge trains him up." She reviews the rest of the plan to the veterans, with a couple of questions and answers following. María glances at Nicolaus and observes the locket dangling from his neck. "Only two left, I see."

"Akari found it." Nicolaus smiles. "She can tell you during my expedition tonight."

Akari grabs his hand as he plops down the gun. "We should get the adventure started." She leans in and their lips meet.

María nods in agreement and chuckles. One veteran comments, "Dodge, you weren't kidding. Those two are like jackrabbits."

"Try being around them all the time. It's like one giant love fest," Dodge says with a snicker.

"You need to behave." María punches Dodge in the chest. "They are super cute."

Dodge rubs his chest because María's punch can knock many people out cold. "True, but I think they hold the world's record for most times in a year. And yo, we come in a close second."

"Agreed on both," María giggles while Akari and Nicolaus's lips separate. Akari's cheeks blush and the couple grip their hands and stride out of the barn.

As they approach the house, Akari stops near the door. "Ready?"

"Absolutely, and I feel better now that there are forty grown kids with guns in the barn." They chuckle while walking into the house.

Vision
of
Loss
(21)
Present

Akari accompanies Nicolaus into one of the ranch's three bedrooms. He sits down on the bed. "You'll be by my side all night?"

"Of course," Akari replies with a tender smile.

Nicolaus pokes his finger with his pocketknife. A drop of blood swells to the surface. He touches the locket. A flash of light swallows the room, pushing Akari's hair backwards. Nicolaus lets out a faint moan as the force thrusts him back into his pillow. "Damn, it feels like all my energy has drained out of my body."

Akari touches his forehead. "Just rest." She opens a bandage and places it on his finger.

Struggling to keep open his eyes, he glances down at his finger. "An anime bandage? Really?"

"Would you expect anything else? Now close your eyes and see what the Divinities will show you." He takes one last view of his love and falls into a vision.

ϙϙϙϙ

Nicolaus stands in a familiar yard, Akari's parents' yard, to be exact. He glances around the Iona's backyard, which follows the Japanese garden philosophy, but sees no one standing nearby. Only the birds fluttering around and the sound of the waterfall fountain greets him. After his family's death, Akari's dad, Keanu, became his mentor in gardening. He hears Keanu's voice in the distance. "The serenity of gardening instills patience and a way to ease the heart. You must find your inner peace within yourself and let go of the burden you feel upon you."

From behind him, he hears another voice whispering, "Nicolaus."

He spins around in alarm, only to be confronted by the breathtaking sight of a luminous figure that resembles an angel without wings radiating daylight. "I'm Aamirah."

His eyes scan the surroundings before settling on her striking blue eyes, fair skin, and flowing brunette hair. "Is this real or a dream?"

Her body adorned with jewelry, a graceful gown stretching to her ankles, and glitter spread across her cheeks. "Neither. It's a vision. A glimpse into your life. You have a Divine power that flows through your very blood. You must choose which way to travel, following the dark or the light. Your undying love for Akari is your guiding beacon."

"I know but—" Before Nicolaus responds, a blinding light flashes and Aamirah vanishes. Replacing her image is a memory from his life. He spots Chie, Akari's mom, and her dad standing on the patio at dusk watching them. As he turns his head, his younger self and Akari stand next to a lantern on a stone pedestal.

The unwavering compassion in Akari's eyes that, to this day, keeps him honest and eases the hate he endures for his family's murderer. Akari appeared nervous, and Nicolaus had never seen her anxious like this. She bit her bottom lip and pushed the hair behind her ear. "I've lit this, or its sister lamp, in Hawaii every night since I can remember. Tonight, I want to light it together with you."

Nicolaus focused on the moment, appreciating how much this meant to Akari, and his heartbeat faster than ever. He nodded, and they held each other's hands and lit the lantern. They sat on the cobblestone bench, their eyes locked, their bodies fidgeting, while the stars above cast a gentle glow on their youthful faces.

Their images evaporate, and Aamirah stands in front of Nicolaus. "You must assemble the chamber. You will create cures and inventions, but with that comes uncontrollable behavior. Without her, you won't complete the circle."

"This is frustrating. Just tell us what we need to do, and I'll do it."

"Your ego, if left unchecked, will be your undoing. The four of you were born in the four different seasons to derive the balance of nature."

Nicolaus reflects how they poke fun at each other with Vivaldi's *Four Seasons*. He was born in fall, when the plants are retreating and the harvest is in full tilt, two simultaneous events contradictory in nature: abundance through death.

Breaking into his consciousness, Aamirah says, "The Divinities turned to a sinful blackness when the chosen one of the chamber, my love, Medium, and the protector, Sinrye, defied the spiritual laws and destroyed our civilization. They now permeate and influence your world. You eight together must save the Divinities bloodline and face Sinrye's spiritual followers, The Accursed."

The scenery changes to a ranch field with Nicolaus surveying a man and a woman with four children running around. "Aamirah, is that Akari and I with four kids?"

"Soon, you will make a mortal choice, one that will define your world."

"Answer the question and stop the riddles."

"To make a difference in the world, you must learn to control your anger and make the tough decisions. Channel your energy into righteous intentions. Only you can choose to put your Divine armor on. If you do not, then love will fade away from this world. Faith is your binding agent to continue the quest your parents agreed to."

Nicolaus's vision dims to darkness, and he stands in a void of nothingness. "Why did you give Akari, María, and myself visions before we triggered the locket?"

"The Accursed are gathering strength while I lose mine. I've slumbered to preserve what little I have left." Aamirah's voice becomes distorted, cutting in and out with increasing frequency, and accompanied by a piercing screech as Nicolaus tries to catch the last of her message. "I had to send the locations of the chamber before the lockets activated to keep them away from Medium."

The sound of the familiar tone, which he had been longing to hear, fills his ears. An aura of his mom, faded yet luminescent, materializes before him in the blackness.

"My son. You know I will always be there for you in the valleys of despair and the peaks of joyfulness. Your dad and I prepared you the best we could, with no regrets for pushing your boundaries. Hold tight, and protect María, as you both know, the heart aches from loss. Stay close to Veton. When the time is right, marry Akari in a beautiful ceremony, peering over the water, and love her unconditionally. She's your one, and you're her one. I know you both encounter something beyond love, a sensation that defies explanation, *a Divine connection*."

Nicolaus bursts out. "Mom, I miss you, Dad, and Mi-Cha. Please, just tell me what to do."

"Nicolaus, destiny brought Julieta, Chie, and me together for something so great and powerful—we are the mothers of the Divine Nativity. It is up to you to choose the destiny you hold. The greed, corruption, vile power, and evil of a small group of elites want what we have and will kill everyone to get to it. You've trained fiercely and will become the elite warriors of faith in completing the Trials of Divinity. You are the future of this world. Without the four of you, the world is lost in chaos, bound with shackles and chains. No matter what, choose the Divine path in helping humanity. Don't let yourself fall prey to the self-righteousness of power."

Nicolaus shouts, his voice filled with frustration and confusion, "I get it, but I don't. I just want the answer!"

His dad materializes next to his mom. The warmth of their love cast over Nicolaus. Dae's silhouette spreads her arms outwards. "We love you so much and wish we could be there in the flesh with you. There is a balance of negativity and positivity in everything. Let nothing break your spirit. Stay strong. Akari will need you even more soon. Don't forget the wisdom your dad imparted about inventing, and my own teachings of finishing what you start, what needs to be done. The sanctuary awaits the four of you. The chamber's journey starts from there."

As he watches his parents' images approach, a rush of emotions sweeps over him. Their ethereal souls embrace, and he utters, "I love you both so much."

ↄↄↄↄ

Around two o'clock in the morning, María asks, sitting in a chair beside the bottom of the bed, "What do you think he means? We, together, will save the Divinities."

"I've been contemplating that since Nicolaus first moaned it." Akari sits up, massaging Nicolaus's side. "I can't help but think since we have the blood, then maybe our children will be a complete Divinity. Does that sound silly?"

"It's not silly at all. Maybe Aamirah is giving us powers that will benefit her, too? Everyone has an angle, right?"

"Do you think we are being used?" Akari raises her eyebrow. "I can't doubt her. It's frustrating to not have all the answers, but I guess it's up to her and maybe we're not supposed to comprehend her guidance completely. It's faith that she and the Divine power are working with us. Aamirah has given us a purpose, right?"

María grips the seat of the chair, reflecting about when they were Green Berets. *The Four Shadows of Light escaped many things that would've killed most people in the first five minutes. They can sense a punch, kick, or even guns firing before it happens. Even their academic scores were off the charts. Aamirah chose their parents, and the four of them, to do what was right for humanity.*

Droplets of sweat trickle down his forehead. María springs up from her seat. "I'll go get him another towel." She places her hand on Akari's leg. "You need to get some rest. Go sleep in the other room. It's my turn."

Akari shakes her head. "I'll lay down next to him. I'm not leaving his side."

María nods as Akari crawls next to Nicolaus. She leans against the door molding. María wishes she was ready to let go of her anger over mother's death and move on. Dodge makes her laugh and comforts her. He's adorable. But she can't let her guard down, not yet. She needs the chip on her shoulder with as little baggage as possible. María smiles at Akari and goes to get a towel from the kitchen.

Akari's eyelids grow heavy as she lies there, staring at the ceiling, her thoughts consumed by Nicolaus and the messages his vision may hold.

Capture
of
Love

22

Present

Around seven o'clock in the morning, Nicolaus opens his eyelids, turns his neck and sees the dimples that make his heart melt. He moves his hand and caresses Akari's cheek. Not wanting to wake her, he gets out of the bed, gets cleaned up and heads outside.

An hour later, Akari sits up, stretches her arms, views the windows wide open with a refreshing breeze filling the house. The sight of a baby's breath bouquet in a vase on the nightstand brings a smile to her face. Nicolaus let her sleep in. She searches the house, feels the coolness of the wooden floor, makes her way toward the back door, and flings it open.

Marcin and Casey are outside barbecuing; the veterans run mock drills with paintball guns; the drones fly overhead, and María practices her crazy car stunts in the field with an audience. Nicolaus strolls toward her with a grin and a slight hesitation. She wraps her arms around him, and for two minutes, they don't separate until a drone flies near their faces. Nicolaus reaches out to grab the drone, the sound of its propellers buzzing as it escapes his arm's length and rushes upward. They hear Dodge laughing over the flyers intercom while he operates the drone out of the greenhouse, jumping up and down after enjoying another energy drink.

Nicolaus turns his head back to view Akari. "Good morning, sunshine. I'm still jostling with a couple of things from the vision, but I believe it answered a couple more mysteries for us."

"What is that?"

"We will have four children together, two girls and two boys."

Akari caresses his face. For all of his faults, his sexy smile feels like the vibrant colors of the sunset, painting the sky in hues of pink, orange, and purple. His tenderness towards her, and yet his masculinity stays intact. He possesses both strength and weakness, as well as compassion and fierceness. "I love you so much."

Nicolaus, while their lips are an inch apart, responds. "I love you even more."

His eyes cast downward, fixated on the ground, as he taps his index finger against her hand.

Akari leans in as their foreheads touch. "What are you thinking?"

"Let's go inside. I'll tell you the full vision, but I have questions I think we can work through together."

The couple sits down at the kitchen table. Akari sips her brewed coffee. "Tell me everything."

He takes a large gulp of the Iona Family's home blend out of an army mug and then describes the vision. When he reaches the point where he mentions his parents, his hands shake and he cannot lift the cup. She places her hand over his, and Nicolaus finishes describing the rest of the vision.

Akari absorbs the details, takes a deep breath while she pats the top of his hand. *Aamirah chose their mothers for a reason. The Four Shadows of Light have a higher calling. Assemble the chamber and create the cures and inventions for the betterment of humankind. Could the chamber be too much information for a human to absorb? Is that why Aamirah told him he might lose his mind? Which location is the sanctuary—the Texas ranch, the Cascade mountains, or another location they still need to identify? The three of them must do everything in their power to prevent him from taking that wrong path. Which is what they do—support each other.*

They hear a knock, and María opens the door. "I just wanted to check on you two and see when you would like to leave to go to our places?"

"Give us twenty minutes," Akari replies.

Dodge pops his head in the doorway. "Crazy shit Aamirah delivered, huh?"

María pushes Dodge's head outside, and she shuts the door. Nicolaus runs his finger in a circle along the top of the mug, his eyes fixed on the abyss that fills it.

Before Akari speaks, he blurts. "My parents were there, but my sister wasn't. Is she an Accursed? Is she with Medium against us?" The realization hits him that Veda's eyes held a flicker—a brilliant orange—like fire raging in a hell storm. He gasps. *They are under siege by the Accursed. Sinrye will harness the power of the UFE to enslave the entire world.* His eyes start to widen and shine like a swirling emerald storm, morphing to orange in his pupils.

"Nicolaus—Nicolaus," Akari yells.

He snaps out of the trance as his eyes dart to hers. All he feels is rage, violence, yearning for answers and retribution. He springs up, soaring out of the chair. "We must be ready for what is coming for us. I must be ready, but I'm not strong enough."

Akari stands up, the steady thumping of his heart beneath her hand. "We are strong enough together. The four of us." She wraps her arms around him, feeling the heat radiating from his body. "Calm yourself. Tame the beast within."

ᘛ◌ᘚᘛ◌ᘚ

The Four Shadows of Light leave the ranch thirty minutes later and return to their homes.

Dodge pulls into María's townhouse parking lot. "Look at this. A couple of UFE officers chilling outside your home—standing in front of your door looking like some mannequins."

"Let's go see the damage, and what the hell those guys want?"

As they walk up to the front entrance, one officer glances down at a piece of paper with their picture. He raises his head up and surveys María. "Please state your full name to confirm."

"María Landowski-Jiménez."

"Great. We're instructed to hand you this envelope after searching the premises. You're permitted to enter the property."

"Thanks, shitheads. It is my property, and I don't need the UFE to give me fucking permission."

"Ma'am, we are just doing as we were told. Have a great rest of your day." The officers leave the porch and make their way to their vehicle.

"So y'all are like puppets." Dodge smirks smacking his fist into his hand. "Let me guess, your puppet master is Hamilton Parsons?"

The officers cast a stern glance behind them.

María and Dodge enter her townhouse. "Damn, man, they messed up everything," Dodge whines.

María squints at him and hands him the envelope. "Read it while I look around."

Dodge opens the envelope as she walks through her townhouse, considering to herself—*Could've been worse.*

"That prick," Dodge mutters.

María observes the kitchen with the utensils strewn about, smashed dishes, and the pantry food spread on the floor. "What does the note say?"

Dodge marches into the kitchen, and shakes his head. He passes the note to María. *Have fun! Call a cleaning service. I'll be in touch soon.—Hamilton Parsons.*

As Akari and Nicolaus made their way to their house, he replays the vision in his head. When he pulls into their suburban subdivision, the sight of his truck parked in the driveway jolts him back to reality. His straight face transforms into a smile, then fades into a frown as he realizes two UFE officers standing by the porch.

He glances at Akari. "Wonderful. The Federation rubbish is standing watch. I'll start the truck up to rattle them."

Akari advises, "Let's just find out what they want, then we can go inside and assess the damage."

Nicolaus nods and pulls into the driveway with the officers stepping down from the porch to the sidewalk. They exit the vehicle and head straight to the officers, who watch Nicolaus with a wide smile. "Please confirm your name."

"You know it's me because you're staring at my picture in your hands."

"Please confirm your name."

"Nicolaus Landowski."

The UFE officer passes Nicolaus an envelope. "You're permitted to enter the property. Have a great day."

He shakes his head in disgust. His eyes fall on the envelope in his hands. He opens the note. *Time is on my side, not yours. Get moving, unless you want your family and friends dead. —Hamilton Parsons.*

Akari intertwines her arm with his and scrutinizes the note. "Do your best not to let him fluster you." She gestures with her head toward the house. They enter their home, finding their belongings scattered everywhere.

Despite Akari's advice to Nicolaus to brush it off, she still feels violated. The UFE invaded their home, their personal haven, and destroyed their privacy. As her arm tightens, Nicolaus leans closer and kisses her on the forehead. She takes a deep breath and searches around and realizes her cat is not strutting about the house. She releases her grip on Nicolaus and ascends the stairs to their bedroom. The moment she walks in the room, Kaili darts toward her, meowing for attention.

As Akari walks back downstairs, her phone rings from Casey. She sits down on the couch. "Akari, put me on speaker so you both can hear." She clicks the speakerphone button. "Are you sitting down?"

"Yes."

Casey felt a burning sensation in his throat while he stares at a corkboard in his office. "Parsons abducted your parents this morning."

There's silence in the room. It's like someone took all the oxygen out of the room. A sharp pain in Akari's side, like a knife twisting in her gut. She can't breathe. Nicolaus's mouth opens, but no words come out.

Casey scrubs his hand over his face. "Parsons just messaged me that to the four of you are to meet him at the Frisco Fair later today. He'll text Nicolaus the details."

Akari recoils on the couch in a ball, her body trembles. Her parents are alive. Then why does she ache like they're dead? *Are they enduring physical or mental torture?* This pain brings home the worst kind of fear—fear itself. Nicolaus sits beside her on the sofa and wraps his arms around her. She turns around and buries her face in his chest.

"A-are you b-both still there?" Casey asks with a slight stutter.

Nicolaus kisses Akari on the top of her head and responds, "We're still here. Did Parsons say anything else?

"Just what I said. Akari—Parsons is messing with you all. Your parents will be okay." Casey takes a massive breath and sighs, "—Since he took your parents, Akari, it's just an assumption—but he has your locket, too." She grabs Nicolaus's shirt, not wanting to answer Casey about the locket. Her only worry was her parents.

Nicolaus replies, "Understood." He puts his cheek on her head while he rubs down her arm. *The note said they went into hiding. How did Parsons get them so quick? The UFE must have been waiting for a long time for the Four Shadows of Light to activate the lockets. The UFE has a ton of resources at their disposal, but this is too quick. Veda is playing a total game with them.* In their missions, she gave them the footprint of their enemies—their physiological traits, patterns, habits, but in his and María's blind rage, they knew nothing of Parsons. *How can you beat an enemy if you don't really know them?*

Fair of Chie

23

Present

Parsons speaks from his penthouse apartment. "Mr. Zhao, Veda knows what I'm doing. The time to strike is now and push them to the brink."

Mr. Roosevelt interrupts. "Do not kill them. We don't need another loss like Dae's daughter. They are the key, Parsons. As much as I would like to take down Nicolaus, that insulated piece of filth."

Parsons fidgets with his tie. Veda's directive eleven years ago was to kill the parents and Nicolaus and abduct Mi-Cha. His uncontrollable rage met a voice in his head. The voice got ahold of him, strangled his mind—*do not shoot Nicolaus, shoot her.* He shouts into the phone, "I know we need them, but there was nothing about saving the parents!"

Wei Zhao shifts in his seat. "Hamilton, have you got the two lockets?"

Parsons stares at his desk with the two lockets in front of him. He grabs one in his hands, encounters a shot of adrenaline with a sudden craving, a longing like a drug addiction. He growls, "Yes, both lockets are here."

"If you two are wrong about releasing the news, we risk the Divinities being exposed. We've already dealt with the fallout from your little stunt searching of their houses. Don't kill the parents until we have the lockets. Then bring the lockets to Roosevelt."

Parsons shakes his head and sets down the locket. He closes his eyes while his fingers drum on the table. *Why is GREC so worried about the media? Don't they control the words strewn about the internet with artificial intelligence? They can spin this whatever way they want.* "Isn't it true that we control the media?"

"We control the media narrative, and we'll create the leverage and distraction, but if you don't hold up your side of the bargain, Parsons, that's it, you're done. We will release the Iron Scepter upon you."

He thrusts himself out of the chair, slamming his fist on his desk, leaving an indentation. "Don't threaten me with your ridiculous assassin. What kind of name is that? It's just another bitch ass trash who can't stop me. Without me, you both are nothing. I *am* the Federation!"

There's a long pause as Zhao mutes the phone so Parsons can't hear the GREC board's discussion.

Zhao unmutes the microphone, "Parsons, you and Veda have twenty-four hours to get all four lockets. If you fail, then it's both of your heads."

Parsons hangs up and a ringing sensation buzzes in his ears. The sensation in his head is overwhelming, as if it's on the verge of exploding. He screams. "Get out of my head. Get the fuck out of my head now!"

The murmur of Medium dissipates. With labored breathing, he collapses into his chair. The voice began on the day he received the Divine serum injection from Seok. Though she didn't want him as the first experiment, with her saying he's too fucked up in the mind to sustain the blood of the Divinities. Veda stood at the laboratory door with a gun ready if Seok didn't. That day, all he recollected was killing Julieta. *Kill her*, the voice chanted. He leans back in his chair and calls Veda.

"Hello, Parsons. What did the board say this time?"

"Nothing of substance, like their bureaucracy always says. What do you want me to do with Roosevelt and Zhao?"

"We leave Zhao alone right now. As for Roosevelt, I think his time is winding down."

Veda recruited Buchanan and Genevieve, Walter Roosevelt's two children, to join the UFE. They harbored a deep-seated hatred for their father, who prioritized his job over spending time with them. He always said money makes the world go around. Behind Roosevelt's back, Veda brought them into the Federation and started their training as the next subjects for the injection. "Walter is running out of usefulness."

Parsons replies with a voice low and menacing, "Text me when you want that done."

"I'll be in touch, and stick to our plans for the parents." Veda hangs up the phone with a wicked smile, rotating a steel vial of the serum between her fingers.

ʘʘʘʘ

María bolts into Nicolaus and Akari's house, catching sight of them cuddled up on the couch with Nicolaus's arms wrapped around Akari. María moves in for a group hug. Nicolaus pats María on the back, releases from the hug, stands up to plant a gentle kiss on Akari's forehead. María plops down and Akari leans her head on María's shoulder.

Nicolaus eyes Dodge. "I need your help with something."

"Whatever you fucking need, bro, I'm here." Dodge follows Nicolaus upstairs to the invention room.

María drapes her arms around Akari. "We'll get them back safe."

After a brief pause, Akari replies, "I know we'll do the best we can to get them back unharmed." She pursed her lips and then took a couple of deep breaths. In the silence of their embrace, she hears Nicolaus's thoughts whispering in her ear. She repeats the line out loud for María to hear. "We know nothing about Parsons. Who he is or what he is?"

"We thought the fucker was dead. The Federation redacted any information we got on him. So no, we don't know shit about his bald ass."

"I have an idea." She pushes María's arms away, reaches underneath the couch and pulls out a laptop. She sets it on the coffee table. María chuckles, because Akari has like fifteen hidden laptops throughout the house for when an idea pops into her head.

Akari wonders why she didn't consider this before. Oh yeah, because she didn't want to betray Seok and use DaeChie's network to get in. But their company has a contract with the UFE. If she uses Seok's sign in, then she can get into the Federations system. She turns her head, narrows her eyes at María. "Go into the kitchen underneath the pots and pans. You'll need to lift the bottom board and there's a hatch door. I need you to grab the flash drive."

Akari has her custom hacking applications on multiple drives throughout the house. María heads over to the kitchen, and she tosses out the pots and pans in the cupboard, causing them to clang on the floor. She runs back to Akari and hands her the drive.

Nicolaus and Dodge walk into the invention room. "Dude, they took all your creations and smashed them up."

"That doesn't matter right now." Nicolaus eyes the corner of the room where his steel bookcase is still in position. "Help me move the bookcase out of the way."

"For reals. That ain't moving."

Nicolaus grins. The bookcase swivels out when you unlatch the door mechanism. He walks over to a picture of the four of them from the army and removes it from the wall. He takes out his pocketknife and cuts out some dry wall. Dodge swivels his head from Nicolaus to the hole in the wall, which has a push button, and laughs. Nicolaus presses the button, and the bookshelf unlatches.

"All our army tactical inventions are in the vault behind." They push the bookcase out from the wall, and Nicolaus uses the retinal scanner and digital keypad to open the vault door. "See, all of them are here."

Dodge slaps Nicolaus on the back. "Looks like more unfinished projects." Nicolaus walks into the vault the size of a closet and grabs the magnetizer similar in size to a paperback book. It never worked as intended, but his gut says to finish it. *Different metals require a different bonding formulation. By tweaking the device to pull the lockets from twenty yards, it should ensure they get the lockets back.* For an hour, Dodge helps Nicolaus with testing and reconfiguring the magnetic pulse per the locket materials. Each time, they pulled the locket from further distances.

Dodge sees the intensity in Nicolaus's eyes. "Did Akari tell you to finish this?"

"For once, no. My entire life I've depended on my mom, Asa, my dad, Akari, her parents, you, María, to push me. It's time I finally start growing up and think for myself." Nicolaus places the locket in the main bedroom, pushing aside the fallen decor. "Hit it, Dodge. This should be twenty yards." The locket flies from the bedroom and slices through the drywall of two rooms, missing the electrical and plumbing in the walls. The locket lands smack in the middle of the magnetizer.

Dodge shouts at the top of his lungs, "Shit yeah. That bugger flew." Nicolaus's fist pumps in the air. He gawks at the holes in the drywall and sees Dodge holding the locket.

María yells from the bottom of the stairs. "Get your asses down here. We got some recon on Parsons."

"I thought they were going to fucking yell at us for the noise." Dodge snickers.

Nicolaus moves his hand outwardly. "I guess not right now."

As they run down the stairs, Nicolaus's phone vibrates with a text message from Casey. *Turn on the news now!* Nicolaus sees Akari reviewing a piece of paper, with Dodge joining her side. Nicolaus turns on the television in the room, ignoring María waving him over to review the printout.

"Breaking News: Federal Agents have found a drug smuggling ring in our backyard in North Texas. With live details, we're sending you over to Victoria with the latest," a female television anchor says in a cheerful tone.

"Thanks, Janice. We're in front of Julieta & Marcin's Café in Frisco, where federal agents have raided and issued an arrest warrant for Marcin Landowski. We are told that he funneled millions of dollars' worth of drugs from South America and Southern Asia and spread them throughout the Dallas-Fort Worth metroplex. The federal agents working in partnership with the United Federation of Enforcement officers have found evidence of money laundering and illegal weapon sales, too. As you see, we have footage of the raid on the restaurant and his house earlier today. The raid followed two other property searches, both belonging to relatives. There is an ongoing manhunt to find Marcin Landowski and anyone with any information about his known whereabouts. Please call the number on the screen. They are working with federal agencies, including the United

Federation of Enforcement, to track him down. Once we have more information, we will let you know. Passing it back to you, Janice."

"Scary stuff there, Victoria. In other news, the sporting world is—" Dodge turns off the television. Nicolaus stares at the black television screen.

María screams and bolts to the workout room intended to be the library in the house. "I'm about to dismantle this shit!" María smashes her fist against the punching bag.

Dodge yells over María's grunts. "They are just fucking with us. Don't let it go to your head."

María continues smashing the bag. "I'm going to kill him ten times over, so he can never hurt us again."

Akari hands Nicolaus the printout, which details Parsons's exit from the military, his personality traits, and the last line Akari points to: *Approved for Project Medium.* He furrows his forehead. Akari grabs a hairband in her pocket and ties her hair up in a ponytail. "I got locked out of the system when I pushed too far. But Project Medium is a DaeChie partnership with the Federation." He studies the paper, understanding that Parsons is an experiment, and their company is part of this whole thing— the bad and the good.

"How did you get into the system?"

"I'll tell you on the way." Akari yells at María, "Save your energy! We might need it at the fair."

Dodge approaches the punching bag and as she prepares to swing again, he positions himself between her fist and the bag. "Get out of my way!" María roars.

"No, no, and no. You heard Akari. We got to mount up and leave in twenty minutes."

At seven o'clock, they leave in María's battle-ready vehicle, heading to the Frisco fair. María, doing her best to remain patient, creeps into the parking lot, hearing kids cheering and rides

208

swooshing. With their tickets ready on Dodge's phone, they leave their vehicle behind and make their way into the fair crowd.

Nicolaus receives a text message from Parsons. *Behind the wheel. You better not be packing any weapons.*

Amidst a sea of people and light displays, they head toward the meeting spot, their noses filled with the scent of hot dogs, funnel cakes, and cotton candy. As Akari stomps toward the location, her upper lip curls in anger, knowing that the scents would always remind her of Parsons. Then, out of her left eye, Akari sees her mom walking toward her. Nicolaus, Dodge, and María observe eight UFE troops surrounding their position. Akari and her mom, Chie, embrace.

"I have little time," Chie whispers while she pulls out an envelope. "Take this." She kisses Akari on the forehead. "We love you." Chie backs away as the four UFE troops approach. Akari's heart races as she watches her mom walk off, ready to scream and act, reaching for her gun.

Nicolaus grabs Akari's hand. "Not now, and especially not at the fair." His phone vibrates in his pocket and pulls out the phone. *If you do anything, they will die now.*

Feeling a sense of dread, she snarls and storms off toward their vehicle. They follow Akari at a distance. Next to María's camo truck, she comes to a halt, her jaw tight with tension as she reads the note. *Tomorrow will be an even exchange. Two lockets for three parents. —Hamilton Parsons.*

"Take us to the ranch. I need to go shoot some rounds off!" Akari snaps at Nicolaus. Her skin flushes red as she hands the letter to María to read. María crumples up the note out of anger and throws it at Nicolaus. He unfolds the note and discerns faint writing on it in pencil. *Focus on the lockets, stay on the path, otherwise this is all for naught.* He recognizes the handwriting as Akari's dads.

꩜꩜꩜꩜

Bullets fly from their guns, accompanied by loud grunts, creating a whirlwind of precision strikes in the practice target's center. Akari pieces the connections in her mind. Seok is involved with Parsons. *Did she order Nicolaus's family and Julieta's death? Or was it Veda or worse—Medium?*

In between reloads of the fourth round, María wipes sweat from her forehead. "How many sides do you believe are working against us? And who do you think is in alliance together?"

Akari finishes reloading, then fires the entire clip at the target and sets down the gun with smoke rising. "Veda has her clan, which includes Parsons. Roosevelt is funding the Federation. Seok, I can't wrap my head around her angle. Then there's Medium."

"I know GREC's involved somehow."

Akari directs her attention to her gun. *They don't have one shred of direct evidence against GREC; it all points back to the UFE. Is Medium the anti-Divinity? But with Seok involved, this makes things more complex. The Coalition wants the cures, and they are angling to leverage the Divinities for their own self greed based on the lawsuits. But everything points at Veda, Parsons, and the Federation.*

With a loud bang, María takes another shot at the target, jolting Akari. "Let's say…we have Nicolaus call Roosevelt to rattle his cage so we can take the fight to them. We take Parsons and Veda out and save our parents, along with getting all four of the lockets."

Akari lets another round rip into the target bag. "That sounds way too easy."

"I'm sure you, me, Dodge, and Nicolaus can strategize a plan."

"I'm willing to do what it takes to get my mom and dad back."

"Let's go fucking talk to them." María holsters her two sidearms.

Dodge stares out at the stars through the barn doors. "I've got to be honest with you. Like, you, María, and Akari have had visions, and have abilities, and I'm like the unnecessary fourth wheel on a tricycle. I'm not important to this, and María is right. I've never suffered like you two have."

Nicolaus replies, "We each suffer and succeed in different ways. Not every life is the same. Some are born into money, some are poor. It's what we make of it." Nicolaus cycles through his brain, searching for the right quote for the moment. "What lies behind you and what lies in front of you pales in comparison to what lies inside you."

"You had to bust out your corny quotes when I'm trying to be serious."

"Can't go wrong with Ralph Waldo Emerson." Nicolaus smirks. Dodge recollects Nicolaus's dad bought a quote book for Nicolaus, and he and Mi-Cha memorized the entire thing to help convey points. "Look, you have a purpose. You're the protector, and don't doubt yourself. We need you for sure. You're my bro."

"Now you sound like Akari."

"She brings the positivity to the plate. What can I say? She rubs off on us just like you. I'm too serious sometimes, and you liven up the conversations."

After a pause listening to the crickets, Dodge says, "I've been thinking about our army operations and how we helped build this Federation centralized power, just like all those Hollywood dystopian movies that have an overlord that rules the masses, and how we got played."

"We didn't get played," María yells, as she and Akari approach. "It bought us time. Whatever Aamirah's grand plan is, she knew we needed the time. Right? Without the army training and operations, we couldn't fight back. Which is exactly what we plan to do."

Akari stands by the barn door and peers at Nicolaus. "We need you to shake things up with the weakest link, Roosevelt." Nicolaus opens his mouth to speak, but Akari silences him with her palm outstretched. "Just listen. There's an alliance between Parsons, Veda, Roosevelt, Seok, and Zhao, but their exact roles we don't know. In order to gain the upper hand, we sever the alliances and deploy a strategy of divide and conquer. We'll have them join us at the ranch for the exchange. Dodge and a couple of other veterans shoot long range if it goes haywire."

María throws her shooting gloves on the ground. "We make sure our parents are out of harm's way, give them the lockets, and fucking take them out." With a loud thud, she slams her fist into her open palm.

"Like—I'm coming to get you," Dodge replies.

Nicolaus smirks and nods in agreement. If they can get the two lockets near him, he can use the magnetizer to grab the lockets after they complete the exchange. His smirk dissipates as he tightens his jaw and dials Roosevelt while Akari paces back and forth.

"Calling so soon for something? Maybe a deal for your family?"

"Project Medium—what is it?"

"Don't know what you're talking about."

"We know for a fact that the Federation, DaeChie, and your company created the monster of Parsons. He has two lockets, and we assume you have none."

Roosevelt takes off his glasses and sets them on his desk. If they truly know, then maybe he can break the alliance with the UFE, have the Four Shadows of Light kill Veda and Parsons, and then he can have leverage over GREC. The day Nicolaus's family died, he regrets not stopping Veda's and Seok's plan. "I never intended for your mom and sister to die. Yours and Mi-Cha's intelligence made Seok green with envy, or in this case, orange."

"Then what was your intent—Just my dad?"

Roosevelt huffs and taps on the temple of his glasses. "A long time ago, your mom and Seok had a plan to replicate some of the Divine bloodline as an extension to stop the true evilness that is coming. The problem was the serum they created would fail ninety percent of the time. When the serum would integrate with the blood, extreme changes occurred. Thus entered Parsons and your former commander, Veda."

Nicolaus fidgets with a piece of hay, "Why are you telling me this?"

"There's a hell storm brewing—The Iron Scepter is Seok's latest experiment and revelation." He glances at his underarm, tracing the scar left from the injection that failed to take effect. "I don't stand a chance without the four of you. So, what do you all have in mind?"

"We'll complete the exchange at the ranch."

"I'll do my best to convince them of the location. I do have two conditions—that Parsons and Veda must die. Keep Seok for now."

Without hesitation, Nicolaus rumbles, "Agreed."

"I will reach out to you after discussing with Zhao. And Nicolaus, if you double-cross us . . ."

"I got it. All the evil troops will swoop down from the magical sky and kill us."

Roosevelt clears his throat. "This question is for both of us. Who's the real evil—Those who decide, or those who act on those decisions?"

Nicolaus hangs up the phone and makes strong eye contact with Akari. "We will get your parents back." He glances at María. "And we'll get Marcin back safe, too."

Akari nods, "Let's get planning for the different scenarios."

❁❁❁❁

Roosevelt grapples with his conscience as he prepares to dial Zhao's number, burdened by the remorse of never telling Dae he loved her and not intervening when Veda orchestrated her demise.

Zhao answers his phone. "Yes. Any good news for me?"

Roosevelt rolls his eyes. "Nicolaus agreed to the exchange—two lockets for the three parents. And to meet them at the ranch."

"I set the location, not him. Such children."

"I think the ranch is the best location. It makes—"

Zhao scowls and interrupts Roosevelt. "Call Veda. She has a suitable place scouted. She's already informed Parsons to bring the lockets." If Zhao plays his cards right, then Veda's force will take out Parsons and his loyalist. He'll send the Iron Scepter to protect Roosevelt and kill Veda.

Roosevelt leans back in his chair. "Are we really going to let them walk away with the family?"

"Do you even have to ask? No. They all die. To ensure that everything goes as planned, I'm also sending the Iron Scepter."

"I don't think that's necessary." Roosevelt rubs his arm and deliberates about the assassin. He feels a shudder course through him. It's a shadow dragon that annihilates all it faces. He sits up in his chair. "Wait, that includes me being left out in the open?"

"Trust me, Roosevelt. I'd rather deal with the devil I know than the devil I don't. I'll provide the GREC security force for your protection."

After a heated exchange with Veda about her plan, Roosevelt gets the location and dials Nicolaus.

"It's Roosevelt. I'll put it on speaker." Nicolaus sets the phone down on a haystack so the four of them can listen. "Roosevelt, what time are we meeting?"

"Seven o'clock at Wynwood Park Peninsula."

"I said the ranch."

"My superiors said the Wynwood Park Peninsula if you want your family alive. Just the four of you unarmed. Some advice—they will have a barricade set up on the main road. There's a small walking trail on the right side. Bring that truck of yours into the woods and have it at the ready. I'll do what I can to delay." Roosevelt hangs up the phone.

"Was that some remorse we just heard from Roosevelt?" María loads a magazine into her automatic firearm.

Nicolaus nods his head. "We need all the help we can get." During their conversation at the bank, Roosevelt clarified he did not like his father. But Roosevelt's facial expressions revealed a love for his mom. *María is right. There's remorse in Roosevelt's voice.* He put his hand to his forehead. *Is the Iron Scepter an experiment twice as evil as Veda and Parsons?*

"So, pretty much, go to a secluded wood with no weapons and we promise to not hurt y'all? But bring your truck." Dodge says.

Akari replies. "Dodge, can you have some drones ready to fly in case we need air support?"

"I can do that and have Lawrence and two of his flyer buddies control the drones."

"Then let's load up the Slayer's trunk with a full supply and drive in." María affixes a scope on one of her handguns.

Dodge blurts, "I'll get that bugger loaded up right now. Nicolaus, you want to help?"

"I'm going to get some rest." Akari stands up.

After she walks out toward the ranch house, Nicolaus fidgets with a piece of hay.

"Dodge and I will load up the vehicle."

He nods to María and follows behind Akari.

Nicolaus knocks on the bedroom door and cracks it open. "Would you like some company?" Akari waves her arm at him through the crevice.

He opens the door and lays next to Akari in the bed. They don't exchange a single word for fifteen long minutes. Akari breaks the silence, staring at the ceiling. "I remember when we first met. I had just turned ten." Part of her parents' farm includes tours for tourists, to explore the fields and learn about the Hawaiian farming practices. "María smacked you in the back of your head as we stared at each other." This wasn't a normal tour, as the parents went into the house and talked for hours. María and Mi-Cha shared a sister-like bond with Akari, something pulling them towards each other. She glances at Nicolaus. "You picked me up when I slipped on the ground and my cousins teased me, saying I had a boyfriend. In that moment, I sensed something forming between us." A glistening tear rolls down her face. "Just hold me, Nicolaus."

Scepter of Seok

As they drive near the lake's edge, Walter Roosevelt, accompanied by three armored trucks, gazes out the window of his black limousine. He mutters to himself, "Dae, I failed you and your daughter, but I won't fail your son." He waits for the GREC operatives to get out first.

The operatives' uniforms are dark burgundy with a black stripe going down each arm. Adorned with badges, each one signifying their rank in the Coalition hierarchy. The operatives wear matte dark gray helmets with tinted burgundy visors.

After Roosevelt climbs out of the vehicle and joins the operatives, they walk inward through a sparsely timbered woodland. Roosevelt's dress shoes fill with mud and dirt. They come upon an entourage of seven duplicate black armored SUVs, twenty-four troops standing next to Hamilton Parsons with an enormous smirk.

"Did you bring the lockets like Veda and Zhao asked?" Roosevelt wipes mud from his shoes on a tree stump.

Parsons cracks his knuckles. "Don't you worry your little self about it. I don't trust your asses."

"Where are the parents?"

"In the truck, you dumbass. We're waiting for the four shitholes of lameness to get them out."

"Your time is coming, Parsons," Roosevelt warns, pointing his index finger.

"Is that a threat?" He barks and howls, jerking his neck as if he just tasted an imaginary meal. "Because your little, bitty security guards are no match for my troops." He bangs his fist on his chest.

While Parsons and Roosevelt wait, the Iron Scepter climbs up an evergreen with squirrels and birds scattering. The assassin sets up a perch getting a full vantage point from above and assembles the sniper gun and calibrates the scope. Then the Scepter opens a small steel lockbox the size of a small journal with nine serum injected bullets and three empty slots. Julieta and Dae created them to counter Veda and Seok's Divine super soldiers. The Scepter caresses a finger over the empty slots: one killed Julieta, and Veda took the other two. The assassin plucks two bullets and loads them into the dual-fire weapon.

The Four Shadows of Light drive across the peninsula wearing their high-tech, full-body, dark green suits with built-in armor plating. Their lightweight material is resistant to cuts, punctures, and other forms of damage. When they see the GREC vehicles parked by the lake, Dodge blurts out, "Hit the button. I want to play the tunes over the loudspeaker to announce our entrance."

"Don't you dare hit the button," says Akari in a stern voice.

Dodge chuckles. "Of course I wouldn't—It'll ruin our surprise party."

Nicolaus stops the truck and rubs his temple. *Roosevelt parked by the lake for an easy bug out. Maybe his plan is for the four of them to attack Parsons and Veda, and then Roosevelt can sneak out the back.*

María smirks. "There's the wannabe barricade."

Nicolaus speeds up the truck and maneuvers past the federation troops to the walking trail, fitting through a narrow opening of trees, but loses one side-view mirror in the process when it collides with a tree.

"We'll see the entourage of ugly ass black trucks." María pats Nicolaus on the shoulder.

They come to a stop near the location where the troops, Roosevelt, and Parsons are standing. After they exit the vehicle, Parsons bellows, "Well now, here're the little horseflies." Parsons grips his automatic assault rifle and glances at four of his officers. "Make sure they have no weapons on them." The officers pat them down.

"Touch anything you shouldn't, and I will kill you," says María.

"We have the two lockets." Nicolaus squints his eyes at Parsons. "Where's our family?"

Parsons nods to his officers, and they grab the three parents out and throw them on the ground with their mouths duct-taped and hands bound.

"Lay another hand on them and I'll slice you to pieces!" Akari blurts with her heart thumping.

Nicolaus extends his arms out to stop María from going to her dad. She scowls at him as twenty troops raise their guns at them. He mouths, *Patience.* He turns his attention to Parsons. "How do we know once we give you the lockets, you won't kill them or try to kill us?"

A convoy of three armored military vehicles arrives. "Who the hell is this? It's like a fucking car dealership out here." Parsons whines as his UFE troops turn their guns at the vehicles. Veda exits the truck with more troops.

"Hello, Parsons. Hello, Roosevelt. And hello, my Four Shadows of Light," she says, stretching her arms out wide, projecting her voice. Veda acknowledges the parents. "That's no way to treat them. Take the duct tape off." Parsons growls and nods to his troops to take off their restraints. "Your parents for the lockets," she says with a wink at Nicolaus.

They unfasten their lockets, and María passes hers into Nicolaus's waiting hand.

He walks toward Roosevelt as Veda pulls out her gun and points it at Marcin. "Roosevelt doesn't get the lockets. You keep them. Parsons, give them the two lockets you have."

"Fuck that," Hamilton Parsons blurts.

Veda then motions the gun at Parsons. "They will unlock the lockets, right here, right now." She points the gun back at Marcin. "Once Akari and Dodge do that—the four of you will go with me and the parents are free to go."

Parsons aims his gun at Nicolaus. "I'm taking them with me. I'll have the power." He screams as a piercing sound enters his ears. He points the gun at Veda. "I'm not giving them up." The sensation of nails on a chalkboard fades away. Medium enters his mind. *The lockets are the key to my freedom—listen to Veda or die.*

"Let them get into the truck and leave safely!" María pleads.

"We have a deal, Veda," says Nicolaus with his arms in the air, still holding the lockets.

"All four of you get on your knees," Parsons yells to the Four Shadows of Light, with Veda now pointing the gun at Parsons.

The Iron Scepter peers through the scope, ready to fire on Nicolaus. Zhao shouts over the intercom device, "Wound Nicolaus—kill Veda and then Parsons." With a slight hesitation, keeping the scope locked on Nicolaus's head, the Iron Scepter moves the gun's aim a little higher and pulls the trigger.

The blood splatters across the truck's windows, and Parsons's body smacks the ground. "Shit," Veda howls. "Zhao double-crossed me. He sent that killer."

Nicolaus, María, Akari, and Dodge bolt toward the parents, knocking them to their stomachs to protect them from the onslaught. The triangular battle between Parsons's UFE loyalists, Veda's UFE force, and the GREC security operatives blister the air with gunfire.

A loud distinctive shot, with an ear-piercing screech, rings through the air as Roosevelt hits the ground, crunching against the fallen branches.

Veda crouches next to her armored vehicle, shooting at Parsons's faction. Her two-way radio booms around her. "Ma'am, we have to pull back. GREC has an air raid of drones coming in."

"Fuck. Fuck. Fuck." She considers the Coalition operative mini drone quadcopter attack formation and the gruesome capability of those little devils.

Nicolaus sees a locket shining next to Parsons's body, and realizes the other is in his coat pocket. He hands María their two lockets.

"Don't worry about the other lockets, Nicolaus. We have to get our parents out of here."

He ignores her frantic request, shakes his head, and pulls out the magnetizer. The lockets land on the device faster than a drag racer crosses the finish line. Veda points her gun at María and fires. As Marcin leaps over María, he takes the brunt of the bullet's impact next to his heart. The piercing scream leaves a lasting evil echo in her ears.

Nicolaus grabs Parsons's gun and shoots Veda before she can pull the trigger again. The bullet enters her calf, and she howls. He fires more rounds in her direction, but she avoids another gunshot wound. Veda retreats behind one of the armored vehicles while the GREC operatives draw back away from chaos.

Akari shouts, "We have to get out of here! You heard what the troops said."

"I'm on it." Dodge bolts to their truck, getting inside and flooring it, stopping next to the family. While bullets ricochet off the vehicle, María, sobbing, lugs Marcin's body into the vehicle.

Veda's force annihilates Parson's remaining troops with bodies thudding on the ground every five seconds.

Akari pushes her mom into the vehicle, and Nicolaus hustles to get her dad when Veda seizes the opportunity and fires two shots, hitting both of Akari's parents with armor-piercing bullets. She laughs out loud, ignoring the pain in her leg. As she prepares to shoot at Nicolaus and Akari, a loud and piercing sound causes their ears to strain, while a bullet grazes Veda's arm. She yelps, and mutters to herself, "That fucking assassin!" She opens the door to the armored truck and flees the battleground.

The Iron Scepter says to Zhao, "Confirming Walter Roosevelt and Hamilton Parsons are dead."

"I gave you a direct order to kill Veda!"

"The directives changed." The Iron Scepter smirks, turns off the communication channel and climbs down from the tree perch. Leaving the scene with at least twenty drones unleashing bullets and clearing out the rest of the troops on the ground.

I'll have to cover the political trail on this, Zhao deliberates as he calls his secretary first and then Seok.

Seok taps on her tablet. "Zhao, what do you want?"

"Did you give the new directives?"

"Yes. Roosevelt and Parsons had to go."

"Why save Veda?"

"I have my reasons." She relaxes her shoulders. "Your lust for the power is clouding your judgement. You can't possibly ignite the Divinities and have the power of sight. They must unlock their full potential."

"You told me I can get the power once I have all the lockets."

"You still don't comprehend the magnitude and the intricacy of the Divine power." Dae never trusted Seok like she did with Julieta and Chie. She's had to piece together through research and hypothesis on how the Divine powers work. Seok's efforts to decipher Dae's journal, penned in the Divine language, provided some roadblocks. Her analysis concludes the lockets hold the key to their powers, and it is crucial to ignite them in order for the chamber to work. "Give them a five-hour window to unlock the abilities. Then have Veda launch an assault on the ranch."

"I give the orders to the Iron Scepter, not you!"

"You're a whiny bastard for being the CEO of the most powerful organization in the world. You got the World Health Organization and the World Economic Forum bent down at your knees, yet you act like a little child throwing a tantrum." She taps a checkbox on her tablet. "Do you want the chamber or not? Once they see the full visions, then you can attack. At that point, all we need is one alive to use their blood to start the device, and then it will reveal the chamber piece locations."

"So, then we can kill three of them and capture one? Why didn't you tell me that before?"

"Just shut up and do as I say. Now get off my phone and go do your cleanup work."

Seok recognizes that the Federation and the Coalition will falter in the attack once the Four Shadows of Light harness the power of the locket. She must continue dangling the carrot on a stick for Zhao. It's part of her plan.

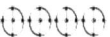

Dodge floors María's Slayer out of the forest, trailed by the clang of bullets. "It'll be like ten minutes tops before we get to the closest emergency room."

Akari and María attend to the parents in the middle row.

"Mom! Mom, stay with me. Please don't leave me."

"My daughter, my sweet Akari, remember what I said? You are my everything. Take care of Nicolaus, assemble the chamber, create the cures we've been working toward." Tears now flow like a river from Akari's eyes. "Only the chamber will give the ability to cure the diseases for good. Finish what we started," Chie says, and her eyes drift closed.

"Mom! Mom! No! I love you." She kisses her mom's forehead. "I promise we will create every cure for every disease."

Marcin eyes María. He extends his arm so his hand can touch her face. "Finish this—three pieces lie on the family land. Find them and fix this world."

His hands drop to her lap. María screams and grips her dad's body with bloody hands.

"Nicolaus—my son, Nicolaus—that sounds good. Chie never let me say that." Keanu chuckles, then a raspy cough. "Marry her. Take care of her. Love her."

"I will with all my heart and soul."

"You are the key to awakening the Divinity. You will lie in the chamber and solve all the inventions to ease the burdens of this world. Use the power of sight to harness the ancient abilities of the Divine." Keanu, struggling to breathe, mumbles, "There is no significant change without sacrifice." He closes his eyes and falls still.

Akari and María stare at their parents' lifeless bodies when Dodge flies into the emergency room driveway and slams on his brake.

"There's still time. Get them out." He races inside the hospital. "We need three stretchers now! We have three gunshot victims!"

The emergency attendants jet to the truck with three stretchers. They open the doors with María sobbing, and the medical personnel lift Marcin out.

"He's not breathing. None of them are."

Five more personnel run out to help, pulling Chie and Keanu out of the vehicle, and try to resuscitate them using all means necessary. They rush them inside, with Akari, Nicolaus, María, and Dodge running right behind them.

The receptionist yells, "You have to let them do their jobs. Stay here."

María and Akari sob on Dodge's and Nicolaus's shoulders. The next five minutes felt like five days while they wait for a word. A doctor walks around the corner into the lobby, his arms hanging on his side and tears swelling in his eyes. "I'm sorry. There's nothing more we can do."

María pushes Dodge away and smashes her fist through a wall as her body emanates light. He rushes to her side and grips her arms to stop her from glowing.

Sensing that María might burst, Nicolaus glances at the doctor with Akari still latched on to his shoulder.

"A huge shoot-out took place at the tip of the peninsula, and our family got caught in the middle."

Dodge calms María, and the faint light dissipates.

The doctor replies, "I'll call the police. You call your loved ones to let them know."

The TV in the lobby chimes. "We have breaking news regarding the reported massive shoot-out in Little Elm and the federal investigation surrounding Marcin Landowski. In a moment, we will have a virtual statement from the Federal Bureau of Investigation, followed by a press briefing from the

Global Reform Establishment Coalition. Please note, the footage you're about to see is graphic. Helicopters are circling the location where the devastation occurred. We don't know how many have died, as the authorities are just now reviewing the scene. We've just received word that the FBI is ready to make a statement and we're cutting to that feed."

A male FBI public relations director dressed in a blue suit appears on camera. "Thank you, everyone, for your undivided attention. Approximately one hour ago, a massive shoot-out occurred involving the Global Reform Establishment Coalition and the United Federation of Enforcement. We can only confirm that a rogue employee from the UFE used his authority to cause great harm to North Texas's citizens. We are conducting a full-scale investigation. Thank you again for your patience. The CEO, Mr. Wie Zhao from the Global Reform Establishment Coalition, will address the specifics."

Wei Zhao stands in the media room at GREC headquarters. "We will issue a brief yet definitive statement to ensure complete transparency to the public. All charges against Mr. Marcin Landowski have been dropped. He and his family will receive full compensation and a formal apology for this atrocious event. A twenty-year contractor for the Global Reform Establishment Coalition's subsidiary acted independently over the past couple of weeks. We can confirm he is now deceased. Having unique access to our classified data, he manipulated a host of internal employees in three agencies. He initially framed Mr. Landowski, but with the help of the FBI and through our partnership with the United Federation of Enforcement, we are arresting his collaborators for this horrific act of violence. As the FBI stated, a full-scale investigation began immediately. We apologize to all citizens of the United States of America, and we are in complete cooperation with all relevant federal agencies. The subsidiary, as of this moment, is shut down indefinitely pending the investigations. We have no further comment at this time." Mr. Zhao picks up his notes and walks back to the right of the podium.

"I'm so sorry. I don't know what else to say." The doctor's shoulders drop as he gazes at them.

Nicolaus's phone rings and regards the blocked number. He stares at Akari. "I'm assuming this is going to be Zhao."

He walks outside and answers the phone. "Is this Zhao?"

"Nicolaus. You made it out alive. Good. Very Good."

"Cut the noise. You murdered Chie, Keanu, and Marcin."

After a long pause, he says, "So, the parents are all dead. Along with Parsons and Roosevelt."

"We're going to fuck up your world, Zhao!"

"I assume you have the lockets?"

"We do."

"You better hurry and get those activated. Prepare for the Federation. Oh yes, I know a lot about what you are. Veda will burn you all down to the ground."

"Bring it!"

"Get those lockets activated, because you are going to need it." Zhao hangs up. He considers *they only need one alive*. He must let Veda know she needs to capture one at the ranch and the other three she can kill.

Vision
of Akari

(25)

Present

Nicolaus lurches into the waiting room. A gust of wind brushes against his back. He spins around and stumbles backwards in surprise. Asa, their martial arts instructor, a magus, stands before him.

Asa puts a hand on his shoulder. "Faith. Their spirit is still here. I'll see what is possible." Speechless, Nicolaus nods. "You have too much self-doubt and hide behind a wall of false confidence. Let your guard down, as that is the only way to learn." Asa strolls toward María with security and Dodge, trying to restrain her. Asa waves off everyone and bows at her. María's anger dissipates, her eyes widen. "María. Let go of the anger. Seek solace, for your mind needs peace."

As Akari steps into the lobby, she zeroes in on Asa. "This curse we call the Divinities took my parents."

Asa bows to her. "The blessing is not a curse." He waves his hand downwards. "Let us come together in prayer, for in prayer lies the hope we seek." He moves his arms outward. A lightning bolt strikes in the center of the lobby. The doctors and nurses remain still, without blinking. Even the buzzing of a fly comes to a halt as it floats with its wings motionless. The bolt whizzes through the lobby in a swirling tornado motion, wrapping around the Four Shadows of Light.

Aamirah gave her final Divine magus the ability of granting four Divinity life pulses, akin to a genie's wish or four lives in a video game. He used the first pulse to save Julieta at age 16, after Javier and the Mexican cartel shot her and her family. Aamirah saved Julieta to start the Divine mission on Earth, and Asa provided the training foundation for the Trials of the Divinity. He's using the second Divine life pulse, hoping to resurrect the three parents. Asa's energy fills the room, creating an atmosphere reminiscent of a scorching summer day with a gentle, warm breeze.

María drops to her knees. She hasn't found the strength to pray since their last army mission. "If it leads to my mamá and dad being together again, take my dad from this world. I regret the envy that I have towards Akari and wish for her parents to stay in this world."

Akari bows her head. "If my parents die today, give me the strength to move forward. Give María the strength if her dad dies. If their purpose is to stay here and assist us on our journey, please let them remain here to provide guidance."

Dodge bows his head. "My heart follows María's wish. I beg of you, answer her prayer. If it's not too much to ask, please protect my parents and sister from the wrath of the Accursed. My soul tells me that Melodi fights the spiritual demons in her head."

Nicolaus clasps his hands together. "I have faith in your decision. Given no other option, I choose to keep Akari's parents here so that they can guide us. We need one mother of the Divine Nativity here to help. The reunion of Marcin with his beloved Julieta, together with my parents, brings a sense of relief in the

229

face of a tough decision. We may not understand what's the purpose of the pain, but it strengthens us for the obstacles that await us."

Another lightning bolts strikes inside the hospital, and the ethereal glow dims around Asa. He staggers towards a wall to brace himself from falling. The aroma of a baby's breath fills the air. The medical staff blink repeatedly, shrug their shoulders, and carry on with their work duties, except for one nurse, who bustles to ask if Asa needs medical attention. He waves her off and points to Dodge, motioning to go to María.

The life support and patient monitors ping, and the vital signs for Chie and Keanu bounce to normal levels. With a quick nod of appreciation towards the sky, the nurse darts around the corner towards the lobby. "It's a miracle! Two of the parents woke up."

María buries her face in her hands as her shoulders shake with sobs. Dodge rubs her shoulders to keep her calm.

Akari runs into the room with her parents. Her voice shakes as she speaks. "Mom? Dad?" Both parents nod their heads and smile. She bolts to the middle of the two beds, kisses them on their foreheads, and holds their hands.

Nicolaus walks into the room. Akari turns her neck. "Asa saved them for a purpose."

"Go, my daughter." Chie tightens her grip. "Ignite the locket and take your anger out on the Federation and The Accursed."

"The Accursed will wish they never stepped in our world." Chie grips her hand tighter and then lets go. They walk out of the room with Akari taking one more glimpse at her parents.

Asa bends down and whispers in María's ear. "Despite my efforts, I could only save two. Your prayers directed which two." She let out a whimper. "Use that pain you feel. Use the anger you feel right now. Unleash it upon your foes, and only then can you heal."

"María, we need to leave," Nicolaus says. "Casey will take care of the arrangements. We have little time. We have to go."

"I'm going to kill—" María's words cut off when she realizes twenty staff members staring at her. "I need to see my dad's body before we go."

María trudges toward where her dad lies at peace.

Asa sits down in a lobby chair. "I will stay with the parents and call Casey. Nicolaus, go with María."

Nicolaus walks in to see María stroking her dad's forehead. He walks to the other side of Marcin's body. "He's now with your mom. Treating her to the most delicious meals. They finally reunite. I can see him teasing my dad and dueling in chess."

María kisses her dad on the forehead. "Sacrifices and choices for the greater good." She pauses, clenching her fist. "I don't care how many they bring. It won't be enough. They took my revenge against Parsons away from me. I will destroy them all."

Nicolaus nods as his chest tightens. "We have to go."

As the Four Shadows of Light travel to the ranch, Nicolaus breaks the icy silence by asking Akari, "What's the plan for the ranch defense and activating the lockets?"

"When we get there, Dodge, go straight in and activate." Akari replies while moving her legs in a Sukhasana or cross-legged meditation position in the passenger seat. "María, do you want to review the strategy together?"

"I've got this. The strategy works, and I need to break shit right now." María punches the back of the driver's seat as Nicolaus's body and cushion bounce forward.

Akari positions her hands with palms facing up in a yoga pose. "Then I'll activate the locket when we get there."

The hum of the tires on the pavement relaxes Nicolaus. "Dodge and Akari, I'll make sure you both are good." Dodge approves with a thumbs up while Akari offers a forced smile.

Once they reach the ranch, the forty veterans encircle them, expressing their condolences and sadness over the loss of Marcin.

After ten minutes, María stutters. "G-GREC and the UFE will be here later to-today." She rolls her shoulders backward while her hands tremble.

Akari puts her hand on María's shoulder blade and lifts her chin with her neck exposed. "We must be ready. Operation Guardian is a go." Casey gave the veterans with the nickname of Guardians, so it felt right to christen their first battle together as a united group with the same name. "María, fill in the details and review the strategy again. Dodge and I will be out of commission for the next five hours."

María's body stops trembling. She pulls in a deep breath, and her fevered stare from their operations days garners the veterans' attention. "Mount up!" She nods to Dodge for him to start his vision.

Akari moves toward Nicolaus and grabs his hand. They stare into each other's eyes as if to say she's ready for the vision. Before they march to the house, he raises his voice. "This we'll defend. We must protect the ranch at all costs."

Dodge, with the house door open, yells, "We are the force of one," and pumps his fist in the air.

ꝯꝯꝯꝯ

Akari walks down a pathway on her parents' farm in Oahu, gazes at the beautiful orchid garden, and grazes her hand across the flower petals. She sees her five boy cousins, Fetu, Haulani, Kai, Lagi, and Keahi, running around playing tag. Then she sees her dad, a well-known gardener on the island, talking with his landscaping company crew. Dropping to her knees, she peers to the right and sees her mom, a professor at the university, walking toward her with a book. It feels so real, and then she feels the soft touch of Nicolaus's hand on her shoulder. She stands up and then their bodies turn to ash like a volcano erupting around her, leaving nothing but a black and orange void as she screams her mom's name.

Aamirah appears in front of her with a blinding light. "We chose you. You four are our last hope of carrying the Divine. You must carry my bloodline. If you do not, then evil will rain down on you and your world. I am the queen and mother of the Divinities and the last remaining luminaries. You're the first and last of the Trials of Divinity. You will naturally carry our lifeline."

Akari replies, "What do you mean, the first and last? And what are the Trials of Divinity?"

"For many millennia, we gave civilizations across the vast universe options. We didn't interfere and allowed them to make their own choices. All civilizations we presented the gift to choose to insert the bloodline into beings without love or the attachment of being a parent. They chose political voting or instituted a hierarchy not based on faith, or emotion, or purity—but on the oldest, wisest, strongest, or wealthiest. I created the Trials of Divinity as my last hope. You must suffer the pain of true loss to understand true love. You must train through effort, perseverance, and collaboration, as nothing comes without practice. Last, you must choose light over dark, and not fall prey to the self-righteousness of power."

A blinding light flashes and Akari stands on a grassy field next to a steep cliff with the ocean water pounding the rocks below. She turns toward the land and notices Nicolaus surrounded by macadamia trees with four children running around him. "You must keep him from going into the darkness of the Accursed. It's your choice, even if that means engaging against him in battle."

A rush of violent wind lifts Akari off the ground and pushes her into the ocean. She gasps for air, struggling to stay above the water, and then a violent tug pulls her underwater. All goes to complete darkness. She opens her eyes to see a blinking light in the distance and runs toward it, yet never reaches the destination. The light breaks into four parts, like stars forming a cross. A bright circle connects the lights forming the Divinity symbol.

Aamirah's radiant glow increases. "Only the lockets can open the entrances to the chamber." Akari rushes toward the four lights, and then, with a bright flash, everything goes dark as she trips and falls. She pounds the ground with her fist, and a heart wrenching pain surges through her body.

Akari hears her mom's voice, and a vaporous image of Chie appears in front of her.

"Our sweet daughter. We have been fortunate to watch you grow into a bright, intelligent, hard-working, beautiful woman. Julieta and Dae didn't have that chance for their children. Aamirah heard the prayers and granted us more time to help in your journey." Akari cannot speak as the Divine outline of her mom raises her hand. "As you know by now, a higher calling chose you. The Divinities blessed us to have our children, and you all have their blood running through your veins."

The spectral silhouette of her mom dissipates, with Akari's screams echoing through the vastness. "Mom, come back to me. Mom, come back to me."

A wicked laugh from Medium blankets her ears. "I'm almost free! The other four will be the instruments of death for the four of you."

Aamirah's voice breaks through the noise on Medium. "Be strong, Akari, and vanquish the false prophets."

Nicolaus watches her facial expressions with a tormented gaze. Her body tenses up every minute and sweat pours down her face. María enters the other bedroom to check on Dodge. Three minutes later, they're in the doorway, staring at Nicolaus and Akari.

"Nicolaus—Dodge texted me and said he woke up. Is she okay?"

"She's jostling, tensing up the entire time, like she's being tortured." He shuffles his feet across the ground. "How are you are holding up, María?"

"Like I want to smash a bunch of bad guys, like, hundreds of them."

"I'm fine by the way. You know all I did was go through the visions, too, you know, like finally meeting that chick Aamirah," interjects Dodge.

María huffs. "You never quit with your antics."

"Nope, wouldn't be me if I did. So, would you like the short and sweet version?"

Nicolaus holds Akari's hand. "Go ahead, Dodge. Summarize it as only you can."

"Aamirah, or her nickname, so to speak, is Baby's Breath, because it's her calling card. The Divinities entrust me to help you three complete the circle. When I'm in proximity of you three, which my guess is a couple of miles, my protective powers are at their peak. I'm only the second protector with the blood, too. There's this blessing ceremony conducted like millions of years ago by the original Divinities. It's a distortion, but the gist is the protector keeps the balance for the team. The first protector, Sinrye, caused the near destruction of the Divinities in the Condemned War. He went bad, like super bad, like evil to the tenth-degree bad. He desired to be in Medium's place beside Aamirah. Sinrye tricked Medium, saying Aamirah was in love with him. In a fit of anger, he cast Sinrye out for his lies. Sinrye struck back with an army he assembled through the Divinity worlds they created, the Accursed. Medium, entranced by the power of not having to follow Aamirah, went to war against the good side. We are the last hope. Which means Medium and Sinrye want us evaporated."

Akari wakes up shouting, "Nicolaus!"

He drops to his knees beside the bed.

"I have to get up—I'm so angry right now." Akari struggles to her feet and stumbles. Nicolaus holds her up.

"Akari, take it easy. Your vision from my vantage point looked very intense."

"I don't want to take it easy!"

Nicolaus embraces her. "I love you."

"Never betray me, María, or Dodge."

He stares into her eyes. "I would never, ever betray any of you."

The door to the house crashes open and Casey races inside, out of breath. "The party is coming. Are you all ready? Is everything on point? I mean the visions . . . are you able to battle? I know it's a lot to ask right now, but we don't have a choice."

"Of course we are ready," María says with a harsh squint.

"Good. The veterans are getting into positions right now. Nicolaus, your paintball buddies came too."

Akari pores over Casey. "What about my parents and Marcin?"

"I've talked with Asa. He's taken your parents to the dojo for protection." He sighs. "Catalina and Herculano are taking care of the church and funeral arrangements for Marcin."

Akari nods as she and Nicolaus embrace. "We'll discuss the vision after we win this battle."

"How'd you know they were coming, Casey?" Nicolaus asks.

"Ricky." Nicolaus chuckles about the town sheriff who gave him his first model car toy—a police cruiser. "He said there's around ten military grade trucks and twenty armored SUVs. If you estimate, probably three hundred troops."

"I'm guessing someone gave the police an order not to intervene?"

"Correct. They are at the ready if we win—"

"We are winning—and winning without a mercy rule." María says as they march out of the house. "Let's go exterminate those dicks."

Ranch
Destruction
of

(26)

Present

Lawrence joins five veterans at the greenhouse preparing to unleash a drone aerial assault. His dad, Gerald, readies the older veterans to the reinforced windmill on the right edge of the property situated beyond the paintball field. A fortification made of sheet metal salvaged from a nearby scrapyard strengthens their protection with slits to provide firing positions for their assault rifles.

Johnny and Frankie guide the group of five snipers to the open field on the rear left side of the property, where Frankie's cousin takes over Dodge's position at the water tower. María shifted Dodge's responsibility to keep him close during Operation Guardian.

Additional troops storm into the house with guns pointing out the windows while others make their way to the horse stables near the barn. Vincent and other veterans from their marine paintball expeditions rush toward the small lake and boathouse. Some soldiers dive into the water to deploy their knife skills.

Following Akari's orders, the rest of the guardians stay in the barn as a backup.

The Four Shadows of Light grab two military grade assault rifles, one in hand and one strapped around their back, two sidearms secured to their thighs, a knife strapped to their ankle, and six shuriken ninja stars on their chest harness. Nicolaus pulls out his phone to select a music track on loop.

"Ah, yeah. Great call Nicolaus," says Dodge, bobbing his head.

In unison, they leave the barn at the back right of the property and make their way toward the entrance of the ranch. "This feels like our third mission in Myanmar, so fucking resolute on shitting on their parade," Nicolaus says.

Akari replies in a reckoning tone with her lip sneering, "For our families—the balance today shades to darkness."

"Don't leave anyone alive. Take no prisoners. Let it rip. Wipe those fuckers out like a plague," María says, baring her teeth.

Eight UFE military grade trucks roar into the ranch and park near the entrance with ten going to the right by Gerald, the RV junkyard, and the paintball field. The other ten trucks pull into the house driveway next to the water and boathouse on the left side of the property.

"They've sent in the front line for distraction. Keep your eyes on those eight by the entrance," Akari says, eyeing the tactic.

María grips her gun. "Our plan remains the same?" Akari nods.

Nicolaus's phone rings. "Veda or Zhao?"

"Give yourself up, Nicolaus," Veda says into the phone. She leans against the wall of a laboratory positioned away from the battlefield. "I'll spare the slaughter of the vets. I have no intention of getting involved with the other three—all I want is you." She focuses her laptop video display on his face.

"Once we're done with the eradication Veda, you're next," Nicolaus replies and clicks the end call button.

Akari winces in pain and puts her hand to her temple. The reverberation of Medium's laugh shakes her mind. She breathes out, relaxing her body. Nicolaus touches her hand, and a warmness rushes through her body.

"So, how do we, like, call our powers? Is there like a light switch? Or maybe saying out loud, 'Release our Divinities?'" Dodge wiggles his eyebrows.

María exhales. "I bet it works when we run straight at them, unleashing fucking hell."

"There's probably some automatic enabler on the lockets," Nicolaus adds.

Akari lets out a heavy sigh. "They will work we when need it the most. Trust in the Divine."

Nicolaus peeks at Dodge and nods. Dodge puts his right arm in the air with a flare gun. "I guess we'll find out. I just want to glow."

Nicolaus huffs, and then nods again to Dodge, who fires the green flare.

The buzzing sounds of drones overhead fill the sky. Nicolaus's automatic detection system unleashes a barrage of bullets from the water tower, taking down the UFE drones.

Lawrence's team of flyers redirects their focus toward the trucks in front of the house. In a calculated air raid, they eliminate ten Federation troops. The tables turn, however, when the enemy squad unleashes their own detection system, bringing down Nicolaus and Dodge's handmade drones.

Amidst the erupting gunfire, the sounds of birds and a rumbling train rolling down the tracks fade away. With their military camouflage blending into the field, the veteran snipers take aim and eliminate the Federation's troops. The UFE trucks unleash a barrage of automatic machine gun fire from their rooftops, engulfing the ranch in a storm of destruction.

The Four Shadows of Light emit a glow as they unload their assault rifles, maneuvering through the RV field on the right side of the trucks.

"Kill count?" Dodge asks María.

"Twenty-one, and you?"

"Nineteen. Plus, look at me. I kind of look like a ghost."

"Shut up and keep shooting."

Nicolaus and Akari bolt past his dad's old RV and grab two army grenade launchers with six rounds. The modified weapons they took as souvenirs from a mission that killed a top Iranian commander. The mission helped Israel in their fight against those seeking nuclear capabilities in the Middle East. Despite defying Veda's orders, their focus was on protecting the world. "Glad María left us presents," he says, excitement clear in his voice as he grabs one with both hands.

"I'll cover you. I have to reload, then let it rip," Akari replies.

In a split second, a flash emanates from one of the eight reinforcement trucks at the gate, triggering an explosion at the greenhouse. Glass shards and metal remnants fly, taking down a couple of Federation troops and two Guardians.

Nicolaus clenches the launcher, and stares at the fiery blaze, his mind fills with memories of Lawrence.

After Akari finishes reloading, she gives a two-finger salute to where Lawrence died. She growls, jumps up, and provides a flurry of cover.

"This is for Lawrence!" Nicolaus snarls. He launches grenade fire on four trucks as twenty Federation troops perish.

While screaming his son's name, Gerald sprints from the windmill. He unleashes a storm of bullets from his two assault rifles. Unfazed by the gunshot wounds, he presses on, fueled by adrenaline. He tosses aside his guns, brandishes a knife, and advances toward the Federation trucks, absorbing two more bullets. The former Navy Seal leaps at the troops and slits two throats before he collapses to his death with a torrent of bullets in his chest.

Another rocket collides with the ranch house, unleashing a deafening explosion that claims the lives of five more veterans. As the Guardians surface from the water next to the boathouse, droplets cascade off their bodies, creating a rhythmic sound that blends with their battle cries. They lay waste to more Federation troops until a thunderous boom signals their end, decimated by a rocket.

The Four Shadows of Light witness the death toll rising, and their anger seethes.

Seok clicks the microphone button. "The Federation seems on the losing end."

The Iron Scepter replies, "The losses are climbing on both sides. Another ten minutes, and they might be the only four remaining."

"Why haven't they released their full powers yet?"

"No one has challenged them."

"Hit Akari only to wound her. That should give her and Nicolaus a nudge."

"Understood." The Iron Scepter calibrates her rifle and lines up the shot in her scope. Before she fires, Medium enters her mind.

"We don't need them anymore. Kill them all!" The Scepter's hand moves towards the Divine bullets.

The soothing tone of Aamirah. *"My child. Don't let hate come into your spirit."* The Scepter moves away from the bullets, grips the gun, and fires twice.

Akari screams and falls backward with the UFE trucks by the gate, shooting at their location. Nicolaus and Akari gaze at each other's eyes with fear, angst, anguish, and rage as bullets whip past them and clank on the scrapyard. Nicolaus touches the first wound on her thigh and then a bright, blinding light shoots in the sky. Akari's body tingles with a surge of energy as she moves her left hand, witnessing a luminous trail following its path, reminiscent of an ethereal electrical display. As Nicolaus stares at her, she observes a mesmerizing, electric aura surrounding his body and face. Her pain dissipates.

"In a time of need, the Divinities are with us."

Nicolaus nods. They let out a primal scream and move toward their adversaries. Their body's graceful motion, reminiscent of tree branches swaying in the wind. Their aim and bullets lock on with precise strikes.

Johnny and Frankie load exploding bullets that Nicolaus created on a mission. When the bullets' impact the target, it includes a five second delay and then boom. They fire two long-range shots with the bullets, lighting up the trucks by the entrance as if someone planted two bombs on board.

"What do you know? Shots from the grassy knoll," Johnny says with a satirical smile.

"Dude, are you seeing this?" Frankie says, peering through their scopes.

"They're like death angels."

As the gunshots ring out, time seems to slow, allowing Nicolaus and Akari's bodies to maneuver around the projectiles. With incredible speed, they dismantle the troops. Each enemy sees a blinding flash of light before meeting their demise.

María and Dodge fire at will, eliminating the last troops on the ranch. After twenty minutes of insanity, gunfire ricocheting through the air, silence falls. The glowing of the full Divinity dims out of sight for the couple. Akari collapses onto the ground, and Nicolaus kneels beside her.

"It fucking hurts," Akari says. "In all our missions, only some bullet grazes. We get the power, and I get shot. What the fuck?"

Nicolaus kisses her lips.

"Even when she's shot, you two are kissing," Dodge hollers.

"How bad is it?" María asks Akari.

"I'll live. One in my thigh and one in my shoulder."

Seok grins with her laptop and the camera feed in view. "I got what I wanted to see; the full Divinity. I need you to report back to New York."

The Iron Scepter replies, "Understood. Leaving now."

Medium shrieks: *Your flesh and blood shall be mine and soul shall be devoured by the Accursed.* The eyes of the Scepter shimmer in a radiant orange hue, while the assassin's body engulfs in flames. The fire subsides from an invisible torrential rainstorm, and the Scepter's eyes revert to their emerald, green color.

Joining the Four Shadows of Light is the surviving veterans. "That was some shit. The last ride for me," one vet says.

Dodge smirks as Frankie and Johnny approach, almost out of breath. "Thank you, boys, for sniping their asses."

"Our honor, sir. This is our property. This is Sparta!" Johnny says, cackling.

Dodge drops the gun and turns around as María walks toward him. "You earned this." Their lips embrace.

"Help me up. I can't stand lying on the ground like this," Akari asks with a grumble. Nicolaus reaches out both arms and picks her up.

"I'll take Akari to the barn," María says. "Call the police and fire departments." She puts her arms around Akari's shoulder.

Nicolaus surveys the damage to the ranch, noticing the barn is one of the remaining three standing structures. A feeling of satisfaction washes over him. They defeated over three hundred troops from the United Federation of Enforcement. He then eyeballs Dodge. "Go help the wounded and get a damage count on our side. I'll call Veda."

His phone rings.

"I guess she has a couple of birds in the sky looking down." He picks up the call.

"Nicolaus, looks like you won this round." Zhao clicks his gold pen.

"Hmm—we can do this all day if you'd like?"

"You've won the battle, not the war."

Nicolaus loads a magazine into his gun. "It seems you'll have to do another press event to explain why the Federation attacked civilians on United States soil."

"That won't be a problem. Sure, the government is a little unhappy with the Federation and Coalition, but who cares? There won't be any press on the Divine powers. I'll dispatch the units down the road to remove the bodies. Nicolaus, we should talk about a truce. You'll keep losing friends and family, and we'll keep losing troops. The people of this country will believe anything we say to a point, so I think we should come to an accord. Thoughts?"

Nicolaus shoots a bullet right into the middle of the Federation truck's logo. Their top priority is to keep their family and friends alive while they pursue the chamber before Medium, Sinrye, the Coalition, or the Federation finds it for themselves. "Agreed."

"Great. I'll schedule a meeting, and we can discuss terms in New York at my headquarters."

"Invite your pharmaceutical and robotic comrades so that we can be done with this. Tell the UFE and to stand down. If I see one Federation troop, this next week—" He fires another round at the truck.

"There won't be. Mourn, and then we'll meet."

Nicolaus drops the gun and grips the phone. "Last request, tell Jezebel that if I see her, she's dead on arrival."

"You mean Veda?"

"That's what I said, Jezebel." Nicolaus smacks the end call button.

Wei Zhao finds it amusing that they now understand the Coalition's aim — solely the inventions and the cures. Instead of destroying them, this partnership might be more helpful for GREC in the long run. He calls Veda Devi. "Both sides lost. I'm going to parlay with the Divinities. If either of us attack, we'll continue losing and not get into the chamber."

"You betrayed the Federation, and we won't forget that." Veda slams her fist on the desk.

"I don't have to explain anything. The Federation works for the Coalition. You are just a paper pusher with Seok's serum. You'll never live up to what Julieta was and what those four will become."

"We shall see, Zhao." Veda throws down her phone in disgust. She's lived in Julieta's shadow for so long. Now she's deeper in the depths behind the Four Shadows of Light.

The voice of Medium rattles the room. *My darling Veda. Your time will come.*

An ethereal orange flame grows around her. The flames reflect off the laboratory walls and glisten off the glass beakers and tubes. She grunts and inserts the healing serum needle into her leg. The sound of Medium fades away. Her breath hitches as she huffs, consumed by an insatiable craving for Nicolaus.

With an irritated sigh, Zhao calls Seok. "Why didn't you pick up my calls? And where is the Iron Scepter? The assassin was the only way we could have killed them."

"You saw what they are capable of. My mission was to see the full abilities so we can continue running experiments on the fifth locket." Seok replays the ranch battle, analyzing it from multiple camera angles. "Trust me. I've been working on this for over ten years, and we are close." She fixates on Akari getting shot. "Sending you the coordinates and pictures. I need the blood samples."

Healing
of
Divine

27

Present

With a symphony of blaring sirens and flashing lights, multiple fire trucks, police cruisers, and ambulances storm the ranch. Shortly after, a convoy of United Federation of Enforcement vehicles arrives. Their engines roar as troops disembark and start collecting the lifeless bodies.

"What the hell are you doing?" A young police officer yells at the troops. A stocky man dressed in all-black camouflage walks to the officer, clicks a button to retract the dark orange visor on his helmet. "My name is Carver, and we have federal authority to remove these Federation troops. Here's my card, and you can have your captain call me. Flatbed transport trucks are also coming in to take all the vehicles away. The other men, we will not touch, as they should have proper burials."

Ricky, the captain of the police force, walks over. "We all lost friends and family tonight. Get your vermin out of here, and if I ever see those troops in this area again, I won't stop our true

American heroes from cutting your hearts out and feeding them to the coyotes."

"Understood. We should take about ten more minutes, and then we will leave." Carver reaches out for a handshake as Ricky marches away.

The paramedics put Akari on a stretcher while she watches other paramedics drape black blankets over the other veterans' bodies.

Nicolaus peeks to his right. "Dodge, did you check on the injured? How many fallen are there?"

"It looks like we lost twenty-seven."

"María, use our joint bank account and get their accommodations taken care of." She nods.

Casey walks into the barn. "Dodge and I will answer the questions from the cops and any investigators. You go with Akari."

Nicolaus sprints to the ambulance and leaps in. Akari attempts to speak, and he can't hear muffled speech through the oxygen mask. He peers at one paramedic, smiles, and says, "One word of advice: let her talk or she's going to rip it off."

"Only for a moment. She needs oxygen and rest. We had to secure her arms with restraints to prevent her from getting up."

"That's my feisty girl. You can't hold her back." Nicolaus smirks.

The ambulance driver shuts the back door while the paramedic removes the mask.

"Thank you. Give me a kiss since I'm locked in this tin can and it's making me lightheaded." Nicolaus kisses her, and they lock eyes until the paramedics insist on putting the mask back on.

Nicolaus stays with her throughout the journey to the local hospital's emergency room. Akari's hands latch on to the nurse when she attempts to take off the necklace.

"Please keep that on," Nicolaus pleads with the nurse as he points to his necklace. "Per our religious beliefs, it must remain on." She nods and instructs Nicolaus to leave the room.

As Nicolaus sits in the waiting area, the smell of antiseptic mixed with the bitter scent of burned coffee assaults his senses, causing a nauseating sensation and a faint shiver to run down his back. María walks in, they exchange hugs, and then they both sit down. They watch the emergency room burst with other fellow veterans involved in the battle, with the paramedics darting back and forth. As the veterans arrive, María and Nicolaus take turns asking for their statuses from nurses or doctors and, sometimes, receiving faint high fives from his war colleagues. They text Casey, Dodge, and Herculano the status of the veterans and Akari.

Nicolaus tilts his head. "Cousin, it was a risky move not to position Dodge on his perch for overwatch."

"I wanted him close to me." María grips the armrest of the chair and purses her lips. She misses her dad, and she can't lose Dodge. He needs her and she needs him. "I'm going to ask him to move in together." For the first time, she feels an aching feeling in her heart for companionship, love.

"About time." Nicolaus reaches his hand out for a fist bump. María grins and laughs as their fists meet.

Out of the corner of Nicolaus's eye, he spots fifteen doctors scurrying to a group huddle through the glass panel receptionist area. Nicolaus stands up and marches to the front desk representative, "Ma'am, I think those doctors are discussing my girlfriend. Can I go in and talk to them? That's the nurse and the surgeon."

"Sir, as much as I would like to, I can't when they are meeting. You'll have to wait." With a nod, he observes the grouping.

María catches the attention of the nurses by snapping her fingers in the air behind him as he stares in their direction. The nurse walks through the push doors. "I was just going to get you." The nurse turns to María. "And you are?"

"His cousin and her best friend."

"Okay. Come with me." They follow the nurse into the room and find Akari lying on the hospital bed with a warm smile on her face, engrossed in the television show playing on the screen while the monitors beside her chirp.

Nicolaus lets out a gasp of surprise. "How is she awake, alert, smiling, looking like nothing is wrong?"

Akari clutches her locket. "Honey, almost healed."

María strolls next to Akari and inspects what's left of the bullet hole in her thigh. "Fucking Divine in action, for sure."

"They want to run tests on me, but I want to go home."

María backs away toward the nurse while Nicolaus walks over to Akari, his touch gentle as he caresses her hand and plants a tender kiss on the top of her head.

The nurse clears her throat. "While she's resting, please follow me. The doctors want to speak with you."

Their smiles make each other's heart skip a beat. He nods, "Rest up."

Nicolaus and María follow the nurse to a conference room full of doctors and nurses. She shuts the door behind them.

"How is this possible?" The surgeon's booming voice breaks the silence. "There's not a drug on Earth that heals a human from a gunshot wound or any wound in that matter."

A doctor interrupts before Nicolaus can respond. "I mean, right down to the bullets dribbling out of her body. The regenerated tissues, cells, clotting—"

"I must be dreaming. This can't be real—my whole life." Another doctor responds.

Nicolaus attempts to speak, but another interrupts. "Unless this is some government Area 51 concoction."

"Shut up, everyone!" María's sharp bark silences the room, leaving only the sound of the air-conditioning vent. "Thank you." She smiles and nods to Nicolaus to speak.

"We own DaeChie Pharmaceuticals. You're seeing a live version of an experimental drug and future patent."

The surgeon raises his hand and peeks at María for approval to speak. She laughs and shakes her head. "Then patent it and release it to the public. This drug can save lives."

"We can't at this moment." Nicolaus taps on his pants pocket. "We're still trying to figure out how it works."

"Definitely Area 51 shit," says a younger doctor.

María chuckles and peers around two audience members. "You remind me of my boyfriend."

"The Global Reform Establishment Coalition,"—Nicolaus takes a contemplative pause—"They want the foundation for the drug—"

Akari shuffles towards the door and opens it as Nicolaus exhales. "You need the rest."

"I don't want to rest." She limps into the room, slogging the IV pole behind her.

María shuts the door. "Nicolaus is trying to describe," she nudges Akari's arm, "that DaeChie created a drug that heals wounds."

"I'm the lead scientist for DaeChie." Akari places a hand on a chair. "If word gets out, GREC and the UFE will snatch it away, ensuring it remains hidden and unreleased, solely for their benefit."

Nicolaus taps on the cold, metallic IV poll, his eyes narrow. "To ensure everyone's safety, it is imperative that nobody in this room speaks about this."

The surgeon bows his head with his hands in a praying position as his mouth goes dry. DaeChie Pharmaceuticals made the impossible possible by finding a cure for diabetes. Ever since the tragic murder of Dae, the most inventive mind of his generation, DaeChie's involvement in new cures is nonexistent. Witnessing the miracle of Akari's wounds, the surgeon finds himself in a room with the children of the founders. He didn't recognize Nicolaus at first.

He waves his hands outward. "Nicolaus, you've grown up. Your mom meant so much to the medical industry. I've read every article she published." He licks his lips. "Just go, do whatever you need to do, and let's pretend this conversation never happened."

A moment passes with total silence. A doctor in her mid-thirties chimes in, "We will be here to support you, but the safety of our families is nonnegotiable."

Akari's eyes scan the audience. "Thank you for understanding."

"Please do me a favor and have security wipe that camera's feed." Nicolaus points to the ceiling corner.

The surgeon replies, "I'll take care of the recording. We'll release her now. Let's update the reports to bullet grazes. Let's keep it that way." Everyone in the room concurs with head bobs. "Do y'all need a ride?"

María smirks, "No, I've got that handled."

"Can I disconnect this thing now? I'm a little over it." Akari grimaces at the IV bag.

After receiving official discharge papers, Akari gathers her belongings and they head out to the parking lot. Her elbow bumps into María's arm. "That's our ride? Figures." Parked is a Kazanowski Moving Forces big rig with no trailer.

Wayne shouts out the window, "Let's go! You're my last stop before I head out to Michigan."

Nicolaus's hands clutch together. "Excellent!"

They help Akari into the mega cab semi-truck, with her sitting in the front.

After dropping off them at their homes, Wayne waves goodbye and shouts congrats on another victory.

Akari and Nicolaus clean themselves up and climb into bed. Before they fall asleep, they gawk at each other. Nicolaus brushes her silky hair away from her eyes. "This week is going to be very tough. We lost a lot of good friends." María and he are now grieving the loss of their parents together.

Akari shifts her body. *How is María handling it so well? I almost lost my parents. Without Asa, there was a moment I did.* After sharing a kiss, Akari leans against his shoulder. She closes her eyes and says a prayer. "I bless María, who mourns the loss of both of her parents, comfort her in this time of affliction."

Just before they drift off to sleep, Nicolaus whispers, "No weapon that is formed against us will triumph. Every seed that shall rise against us in judgment will meet their day of reckoning."

Later that night in Dodge's townhome, he asks María. "Why are they so inconsistent? Like they go away and then randomly the same vision comes back."

"I've been asking that since my mom died. It's whatever Aamirah decides. That's why it's a vision from her. She's guiding us with parts of the story. We must walk the path ourselves."

"So, it's not the evolution of visions. It's one vision being told to us."

"Pretty much. Now go to sleep."

Dodge closes his eyes and falls into a dream of his Albanian superhero, Skanderbeg, the Warrior King, who protected Christianity from annihilation against the Ottoman Sultan, Mehmed the Conqueror. The dream morphs into a vision.

He sees his parents, Kreshnik and Dior, leaving communism in Albania as teenagers. His mother's words resonate with him as a Catholic. She speaks of how the United States eradicates the fear of religious persecution.

The image distorts, showing Melodi, his sister, firing round after round from a gun and enemies falling to the ground. Medium laughs as Melodi stands over Dodge with a gun pointed at his head.

Aamirah speaks, "Calm your mind." Melodi places the gun in her holster and reaches her arm out to help him to his feet. Her appearance fades away, and Aamirah materializes in front of him. "Let me show you what will happen if you don't listen to the righteous."

Aamirah hands Dodge a red poppy and the flower bursts into flames. He stands on a mountaintop over the Divinity home and grips a boulder next to him as explosions burst around him. A blue vortex surrounds his apparition's body and now stands next to Aamirah in a massive chapel as Medium and Sinrye strut toward her throne. Dodge's eyes are red and swollen from the burning of the buildings.

Sinrye, with a harsh, cutting tone, shouts, "It's over!"

Aamirah turns her head towards Dodge. "Medium, Sinrye, and the Accursed will bring about the destruction of all civilizations." In the Divine language, Aamirah raises her arms. "With my sword, I unleash a torrent of blood and fury, serving as the final judgment." A blinding white light vanquishes all life on the planet.

ꙮꙮꙮꙮ

As the week unfolds, a sense of anguish and sorrow settles over everyone who had lost their loved. Nicolaus and María agreed on the funeral home, as well as the church service and burial in the cemetery in the Catholic tradition for Marcin.

Catalina and Herculano made sure that the church service incorporated Mexico and Poland's funeral themes, reflecting their family roots.

Casey read Marcin's eulogy, holding hands with María. She felt a lump in her throat as she watched Marcin's coffin descend into the ground. Their closest friends and allies surrounded them as the tears flowed like the Rio Grande River. Even Herculano, the Venezuelan born chef, bears a trimmed beard and rugged charm and known for his impassive expressions, couldn't conceal the flood of emotions overwhelming him. His wiry frame, weathered deep brown eyes, framed by crow's feet, weeps.

Following the funerals, they found comfort by gathering for a brunch celebration at Julieta & Marcin's Café. Nicolaus recognizes a gentleman standing next to Casey, who introduces them to the family lawyer, Andrzej Kowalczyk. He reminds Nicolaus and Akari of Santa Claus with a jovial smile, a round belly, and slicked back gray hair. They pull Mr. Kowalczyk aside to discuss the upcoming GREC meeting and understand the legal aspects of their patents.

During the week, they attend the rest of the funeral services for the veterans who fought at their side. In between the funerals, showings, and burials, the Four Shadows of Light visit the destroyed ranch and begin game-planning the revitalization of the family property.

Johnny and Frankie pester Nicolaus where the source of glowing powers comes from. "Man, you two were like war angels," Johnny remarks.

Frankie follows up. "Except no wings, and I've never seen angels with sidearms in any pictures or stained glasses in churches."

Nicolaus responds, "Frankie, it's in the spirit's realm." He gives Frankie a handshake. "I'll leave it at that."

"I got it...the Transcendent Foursome or the Faith Warriors."

"Frankie and Johnny." Akari glares at them. "Enough with the questions and nicknames. If you must call us anything, go with the Four Shadows of Light. Now, go into the church and pay respects to Gerald and Lawrence." They nod and head into the church. She holds tight onto Nicolaus's hand. "This is our last service, and then we can go home and maybe let off some steam in a combat match."

"As long as you don't break my bo staff in half again."

While laughing, Akari says, "I'll break two instead."

After they sat down in a pew, a nagging sensation swirls around Akari. *Seok didn't show up for Marcin's funeral.* She shifts in her seat. Akari sent her multiple texts with no reply. Even when they went to the DaeChie Pharmaceuticals laboratory, Seok's office remained empty, her notebooks undisturbed. Akari bypassed the encryption for the company sign-in records and discovered that Seok had signed in from GREC and the UFE headquarters. Seok defected to their side. *Did she undermine them as soon as they were born?*

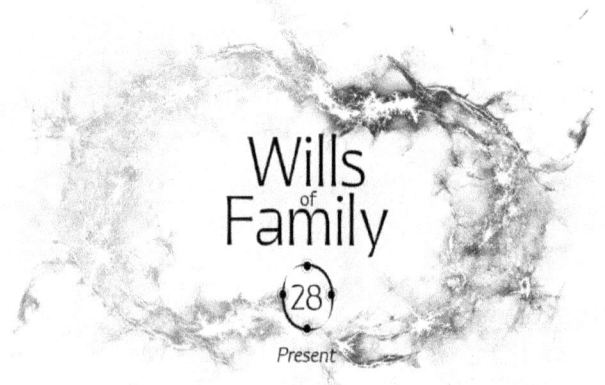

Wills of Family

28

Present

After leaving the last funeral viewing on Friday, the Four Shadows of Light travel to Kowalczyk Law Firm in Plano for their appointment to review Marcin's will and inheritance.

As they enter the building, Andrzej Kowalczyk strolls around the corner. "Hello, we meet again."

A couple of days ago, they observed him talking with Casey at the ranch, discussing the damage and working on a civil suit against the UFE and GREC as part of their negotiations during their trip to New York. He shakes their hands and then motions to his office.

Dodge strolls into the office, whistles at the high ceilings adorned with Christian frescoes and intricate moldings, and large windows that let in ample natural light. He fixates on a foot-by-foot sized Christmas snow globe on a column pedestal near the back. "It's the mighty orb of angel lawyers."

Nicolaus chuckles, María and Akari shake their heads. Andrzej moves around his mahogany desk with gilded accents and carvings. "Please have a seat. We have much to discuss, but little time to waste."

He waits for Akari, Dodge, and Nicolaus to sit before lowering himself into his leather executive chair. María leans on a baroque pillar and waves her hand, refusing to have a seat.

Andrzej is Magnar and Marcin's uncle. They forged a business partnership when DaeChie Pharmaceuticals started. "I've gone through all the paperwork, crossed the Ts and dotted the Is. These are your copies. Review them and let me know if you have questions. The top paper is a simple form for quick reading."

Akari took a deep breath and exhaled. "How can we trust you?"

"Your parents taught you to trust family, and I'm family. I don't blame you for the trepidation, especially with everything that has occurred." Andrzej points to the opposite side of the room with classic thick framed pictures. "Please see the back wall. It's my prized historical wall of family. You'll see quite a few photos with your parents and even some with all of you."

María's grabs a picture frame from a bookcase shelf. The glossy surface reflects the image of a joyful toddler nestled between her beaming parents. She rubs two fingers across the glass.

"I have six offices, one in Michigan. That one is now run by Melodi Markus, my apprentice." Noticing the others' surprised expressions, Andrzej peers at Dodge over his glasses. "You didn't mention that to them?"

Akari frowns at Dodge. "Why didn't you tell us your sister works for Mr. Kowalczyk?"

"I never ask her the specifics. She said she's working with a lawyer, and she babbled on and on. Kind of annoying."

Andrzej smiles. "Melodi always keeps up with the laws, policies, and rulings. She's like a web search of law knowledge.

Now, let's get reorientated and turn your attention to the first page."

"First, Julieta & Marcin's Café transfers to María and Dodge. The secondaries are Herculano and Catalina Vargas for the Texas Location. Kreshnik and Dior Markus for the Michigan location." He shifts a little in his chair, reading the next bullet point.

"Second, Marcin Landowski's house transfers to María. Third, the Snoqualmie cabin and property outside of Seattle transfer equally to Nicholas, Akari, María, and Dodge. Fourth, the Michigan Upper Peninsula cabin and property transfer equally to Nicholas, Akari, María, and Dodge." Upon hearing numbers three and four, Nicolaus pauses; he does not recall them owning those properties.

"Now that the properties are all set, before I get to the last aspect, do you have questions?"

Akari raises her voice. "I do. Seok—" She grimaces toward Nicolaus. "We believe she aligned herself with GREC and UFE."

Andrzej replies, "I see." He takes off his glasses and sets them on his desk. "I'll look into it."

If an insider betrayed them or fell under the influence of Medium, Sinrye or the Accursed, the three mothers had a contingency plan ready. He was to block any aggressive takeover or handover of DaeChie. Nicolaus and Akari are the only ones who can consent to any agreements.

He rubs his hands over his beard. "She called me today to prepare exclusive, non-exclusive, and partially exclusive licenses for your meeting with GREC." He leans his head back. "Seok's changed."

Akari huffs. "She's one step ahead of us. It's like she can read our minds or guess our moves."

Dodge pipes up, "She's the traitor in our midst—Mr. K. It's always the number two—always."

Nicolaus stares down at the ground. Akari hacked the UFE servers and downloaded the rest of the documentation from the DaeChie partnership with the UFE. Seok's experiments, though heavily redacted, appear to be at the heart of the Federation's Divine knowledge. She betrayed them; she betrayed her best friend, Dae. He lowers his brow, and his blood pressure rises.

For the past week, the Four Shadows of Light experienced haunting visions of Aamirah and Medium clashing in front of the Divine library. Her strength held back the 100,000 troops of the Accursed and Sinrye while battling her love. Nicolaus sees the same strength in Akari. She's unyielding, calculative, and above all else, her intent is that of righteousness.

Andrzej slumps his shoulders. "Akari, you'll find what you're looking for in the snow globe bottom. There's a document that your mom asked me to keep hidden after Dae died."

Akari bits her lip and furrows her brow, ambles to the pedestal. She inspects the globe and then waves Nicolaus over to help. She puts the globe on the side and sees a compartment. Nicolaus holds the globe, and she unscrews the compartment with her multipurpose pocketknife. The cover falls to the ground. She eyes a manilla folder, folded and wrapped around the wooden cherry wood base. She pulls out the folder and Nicolaus screws the cover back on and places the globe in its original display location.

Akari gasps. "Are you kidding me?" She removes the stack of papers and sees the breast cancer analysis and patents. "I've been working to solve this forever." She closes her eyes, raising her voice. The smell of baby's breath wasps through her nose; she lets out a gleeful whoop and pumps her fist in the air. She jumps at Nicolaus, and he catches her in his arms with her legs wrapped around his body.

"Alright, put those documents in a safe place, and keep them as a backup plan for your negotiations." Andrzej stands up.

Akari hops off Nicolaus, gapes at María, and raises her arm high with the papers. "We finally can cure breast cancer!"

María sets down the picture and hugs Akari. "Go put it in your vaults and then let's meet at the café." She kisses Akari on the cheek. "This is worth the fucking sacrifices. Doing what is right for humanity."

Dodge strolls next to Nicolaus. "Dude, your mom is, like, a genius."

A big smile spreads across Nicolaus's face, and they embrace Akari and María in a group hug.

☽☽☽☽

The Four Shadows of Light march closer to Julieta & Marcin's Café. They can smell the sweetness of cabbage rolls and kielbasa with a hint of baked tortillas. The Texas location features two distinct cultural flavors, marrying Julieta and Marcin's ethnic styles to create a warm, homemade, irresistible collection of newfound entrees.

María holds the deed and paperwork for the café tight in her hand. The crew's decision for the future of the Frisco location brought her happiness, with a gentle hum escaping her lips. Nicolaus opens the door, conveying his loyalty to Southern hospitality. Catalina Vargas, with her Argentinian silver-streaked hair in a loose bun, sprints to María, arms outstretched for a tight embrace.

As Catalina's high cheekbones that give her face a timeless elegance, and her dark, expressive brown eyes, framed by deep laugh lines gazes into María's eyes, she whispers, "María Valkyrie Landowski-Jiménez, we already miss Marcin, but looking at you brings a level of comfort."

Catalina's husband, Herculano, arranges the table, setting down four cups of coffee. The rich, earthy aroma fills the air. He turns around, his hand raises in a wave, signaling for them to sit down.

Nicolaus, Akari, and Dodge approach the table while María follows Catalina toward the kitchen-dining room junction.

María grasps Catalina's left hand. Catalina hears a faint rustle of papers. "Without you two, this restaurant wouldn't exist." Marcin spiraled into a year-long period of excessive drinking following the death of her mother. "You two kept it going and flourishing. We want you to have it, and then you can pass it down to your daughter. And we won't take no for an answer." María gives Catalina the paperwork and they embrace.

Catalina's lips quiver. "Thank you. We will keep your parents' legacy thriving."

While still in each other's arms, María replies, "There's only one condition. You must let Dodge add an entrée to the menu. Otherwise, the twit won't agree."

Catalina couldn't help but burst into laughter. "Naturally, he's the only one making a request."

María walks over to the table, nudges Dodge to move farther into the booth. "We'll head over to the ranch in the morning before we leave for New York."

Nicolaus nods and asks Akari. "What patents are we planning to lend?" He taps on the top of the coffee mug.

"We only lend them four patents. The two diabetes cures, the spinal synthesis infusion cure, and your patent for precision heart surgery." Nicolaus invented robotic arms that perform the surgery quicker with a 99 percent success rate. Akari programmed the application, and Dodge ensured the visual aesthetics helped the marketing. Their goal was to make the surgery more accessible to those who were less fortunate.

"We keep the breast cancer cure for us. We can't let Seok get her hands on it until we release it for the public."

Nicolaus and María grab their temples as a screeching howl enters their mind. She throws her head back, and Nicolaus grips Akari's hand on the table. Both Dodge's and Akari's muscles tighten with a sudden surge of fear. Nicolaus and María yell, "Stop!" The pain rushes away, and the entire café stares at them.

Herculano and Catalina bolt towards them, asking if they are okay.

"We should go," Akari says to Nicolaus.

Herculano addresses the café's patrons with a bright smile and his hands outstretched. "Sorry for the interruption, y'all."

Dodge reaches out for María's hand. Akari grabs Nicolaus's arm. They exchange hugs with Herculano and Catalina, and then they exit the café. María and Nicolaus, while next to their cars, share Veda's message from Medium.

Sanctuary
of
Parents

(29)

Present

Seven days and no progress. I made a mistake. I need all of their blood. Seok holds a vial with the last drops of Akari's sample from the ranch battlefield. The Iron Scepter lies on a metal laboratory table in a stasis state with two IVs corded to a centrifuge. Seok adjusts her bright white lab coat with dark burgundy stripes and pushes the stop button. She strums her fingers on the counter and shouts. *She can't get the location device to work, or replicate the bullets, or control the Iron Scepter longer than two hours.*

Wei Zhao enters his code, and the door slides open. "Miscalculated your hypothesis?" She grits her teeth, not answering. "Fine. How's Veda doing? And where is she?"

"There's loyalty in the blood. It moves against my will."

Zhao folds his arms, sneering down at Seok. "Where is Veda?"

"She is safe—where you cannot find her."

"You're playing a dangerous game." He growls. "One that if you don't deliver the chamber and Aamirah—you will die." He reaches his hand out and places it on her shoulder. Zhao's eyes blaze orange. "You will watch as I torture Nicolaus, then Akari . . ."

She sucks in a sharp breath as a stabbing pain shoots through her spine and spreads to her heart. She collapses on the ground, writhing in pain. He touches the arm of the Iron Scepter. Like a gunshot to his head, his body blasts backward, smashing through the laboratory glass window.

The pain subsides in Seok, and she climbs up and places her hand on the Iron Scepter's. The rhythm of her breathing slows to a normal pace. Zhao stands, brushing off the glass and metal, with the orange glow aura dissipating. "Remember whose side you're on." He thrusts his shoulders forward, spins around, and storms out of her sight.

Zhao stumbles down the hallway in the laboratory. He screeches to a halt as a searing pain reverberates throughout his head. With each twitch of his neck, he gasps for air, on the verge of fainting. He places his hand on the wall for balance and creeps into the bathroom. His legs weak, he staggers to the porcelain sink and his arms push downward. A small crack appears between the sink and the wall. He stares at the mirror; the spirit of Sinrye reflects on him. Every physical feature he possessed was a work of art, as if sculpted by a deranged artist with a penchant for perfection. Zhao closes his eyes, the pain dissipates, turns on the faucet and scoops water and splashes it on his face. Opening his eyes, he sees the reflection of Sinrye gone, leaving only his own reflection behind.

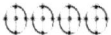

"Send them the message now!" Medium's spirit hovers in front of Veda, flames bursting around him for her to send his threat to María and Nicolaus.

Veda screams, "The Accursed will reap this world! His awakening is Aamirah's mistake. She will die if the four of you fail!" She crouches in a corner, shivering. Her skin turns red, with blisters rolling over her body. He releases his hand from her forehead. With the message delivered, the telepathic link between her, Nicolaus, and María breaks. Her skin heals with a cooling sensation of jumping in a lake in the middle of winter.

"Aamirah doesn't have enough strength to keep me in this form." He moves away from Veda. Aamirah can't fight Sinrye and the Accursed alone. Her champions, her Divine children, must assemble the chamber. Only then can he slay Sinrye and take the place by her side and earn her loyalty back to avenge his sinful alliance. "Veda, you will be my hand and sword to help the Divine children." He pauses, folding his hands into a fist. *My love is the source of my power. If Aamirah dies, then her selections become the Holy Divine, and I will cease to exist.* "Once they assemble the chamber, then we will strike them down from their heavenly perch."

After the battle on the peninsula, Seok used the Iron Scepter to infuse Veda with additional Divine blood. Her bullet wounds healed within a day. *Is she capable of pulling the trigger on María again?* She regrets her last attempt. Marcin was a good man. He loved Julieta. He would cook them mouthwatering dishes after training sessions. Veda visualizes Julieta, instructing how to aim and execute a precise strike on a target using different firearms, with a young María observing.

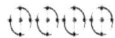

The Four Shadows of Light arrive at the ranch, as the heavy-duty machinery continues the cleanup work, and mountains of rubbish stand ready for removal. A fleet of eight drones that Nicolaus and Dodge built in the past week mount a surveillance parameter to ensure GREC and the UFE stay clear of the ranch airspace. Casey sits in his truck with a firearm in hand. They pull up next to his vehicle; the tires crunching against the gravel as they come to a stop.

With the finesse of a cowboy in a vintage western flick, Casey opens the door, spins the sidearm on his index finger, and slips it into his side holster. Nicolaus scans the property. *It's an empty pallet for them to build a next generation technology driven home base.* He grins at the ranch's railroad tracks. Casey, his dad, and Nicolaus converted Casey's guest house into a model train city. His childhood dream was to create a modernized life-sized replica.

"Follow me. The sanctuary awaits the four of you." When the parents purchased the property, they discovered a hidden underground tunnel system built for tornado and bomb shelters. The tunnels provide access to all the buildings on the property. Or at least they did before the battle against the Federation.

They walk past random small rubble strewn on the ground and black spots from the explosions to the tornado shelter next to the barn. Casey opens the door. "Asa is waiting for you all down below." They descend into the ten-foot square open room filled with emergency food, water, and medical supplies. There are two sets of bunk beds and plastic storage tubs on metal racks. María smiles and reflects on the times they stayed in the room when the tornado sirens blared. The smell of damp earth fills the air. Nicolaus, being the last one down, locks the door inside as he joins the rest of the team.

Asa smiles and bows. "Time to enter the sanctuary and continue with what your parents started."

Casey turns to Dodge to help unlatch the sliding metal door opposite the entrance. Akari asked about the door a couple of years ago, and Casey said there was a cave in, and they hadn't had the time to repair it. They slide the dual massive steel rough textured door into a slit in the wall with a loud clang.

A solitary LED ceiling light dimly illuminates the next room, casting faint shadows on the walls and shining off the metallic finish on the back wall. This room is two feet bigger, with two maroon brick walls on the left and right.

Dodge glances at the thick steel wall. "Talk about some déjà vu."

Akari walks to the back wall and runs three fingers against the cool Divinity emblem in the middle as it warms with her touch.

María steps back to review the wall. There is a large circle with four smaller circles at each side, signaling north, south, east, and west, creating a cross formation—a large version of the Divinity symbol.

Aamirah's vision from the previous night lingers in their minds. The four stood on Lake Michigan's shoreline as her body floated above the water. Her glowing aura and moonlight glistened off the slow, rolling waves. "One Divinity cannot open and see what's inside. Two Divinities can unlock the door. Three Divinities can open the door but cannot enter. Four Divinities can proceed." The lake and dune surroundings disappeared with a flash of light and then they stood in the same room. "Each of you can enter without the others once you've activated the sanctuary."

Nicolaus taps on his locket and ask Casey, "Who built the chamber rooms?"

"I helped build this sanctuary and the Shamrock Lake ones, but the others I don't know. Your dad was the only one who knew all the locations—and that knowledge died with him."

Akari turns to Asa. "What slots did our parent place their lockets?"

Asa replies, "Julieta on the left, Dae on the right, Chie on the bottom, and myself on the top."

María takes off her locket. "Let's give it a shot. We'll see if the same pattern works?"

"The lockets not only have to be positioned in the right slot, but must be placed in the correct order. Ours started counterclockwise with myself first."

María nods and places her locket in the inlet in the wall on the left, while Nicolaus places his on the right, and Akari at the bottom.

Casey leaves the room and comes back with a step stool to help Dodge. "Moment of truth." Dodge places his locket at the top. "Well, that was anti-climactic—nothing."

They spend the next thirty minutes attempting different timing, patterns, and placements.

"This is fucking frustrating." María grips onto her locket.

Akari breathes out and closes her eyes. *It has to be a unique combination. Their parents' order differed from theirs. Hers and Nicolaus must be equal, so they should be on the left and right side. And Dodge is the protector, so he represents the base, and that leaves María at the top.* "Let's try again. This time, Nicolaus, you're on the left, I'm on the right, María, you're the top, and Dodge, you're the bottom."

"Who starts?" Nicolaus asks with his locket two inches from the slot.

"You do, and let's go clockwise." *Maybe the order starts from who experienced the Divine burst first. Nicolaus at Shamrock Lake.*

As Dodge places his lockets in the circle inlet, the room glows with a radiant brightness, as if sunlight bathed it. Each locket emits arcs of light, all converging at the center. With a blinding spark, the door makes a loud crunching noise, and a slit opens in the middle.

María fist bumps Akari while Nicolaus helps Dodge up from the ground as he stumbled backwards from the arcs.

Asa points to the door. "It will open after you retrieve your lockets."

When the Four Shadows of Light grab their lockets from the door, a whoosh of air bursts past them as the two sides of the doors flow into the walls.

Asa nods to Casey.

Casey smiles. "I can't go in. See what you can find, review the notes, and I'll go keep watch outside. You'll see an exit route in the sanctuary leading to other tunnels if needed." Casey shakes Nicolaus's hand and gives thumbs up to the rest.

Asa waves his hand out, pointing them to go into the sanctuary. They pace into the square room in awe of its beauty. Akari, María, Nicolaus, and Dodge stand gawking at the room lined with white Austin chopped stones with farmhouse-style black floating shelves. They see the brilliant grayish granite floor that appears to display a bamboo floor pattern through the dust. The ceiling lined with retro glitter emulating a starry nighttime sky.

Directly in front of them, Nicolaus recognizes his dad's handy work in the six-foot round table with the Divinity symbol carved in its center, along with the silhouetted, glowing figure of their visions, Aamirah.

María walks to the left, studying a portion of the wall indented four feet wide, with metal racks displaying eight weapons. The heaviest gun, Little Mamá, rests at the bottom. María's fingertips graze the cold metal of the Valkyrie, positioned at eye height, and lift it off the wall. She knows this was her mom's favorite firearm from her military service. While drumming her feet, she can't help but cackle at herself at the thought that her mom had named the gun after her.

Akari goes to the right. On a wall is a ten-foot-wide corkboard covered in artist drawings of all their moms' visions and sprinkled in between are the pictures of their families together. She sees a photo of her's, Nicolaus's and María's parents at Casey's house and plucks it off the wall with the pin falling onto a small shelf below the corkboard. She gazes at the photo, sees an odd aura around them. Each seems to have a tinge of white shadow, but Nicolaus's dad has a slight orange tone. It has to be the light or reflection from glass or something. She winces. *Nicolaus's dad an Accursed? No, it must be something else.*

Dodge and Nicolaus stroll around the table and stride to an eight-foot-long and three-foot-wide granite pedestal. Nicolaus recognizes it from the visions with a see-through chamber perched on top of it. "This is where the chamber sits." They go around to the left and see a six-foot-high metal arched vault door.

María sets the gun back down and glances to her right. She catches sight of Nicolaus motioning her to come closer. "María, check out this writing. It looks like Cyrillic mixed with lines and dots." She inspects the metal vault door with faint writing.

Akari continues reviewing all the pictures as she moves toward the back of the room, behind the pedestal. Every wall has pictures, shelves, or something, but this wall has a similar metal appearance to the entrance door. While rubbing her hands across the wall, she tries to figure out what's behind it, but gets distracted by a shining light. She glances over at the others surrounding the vault and walks over.

Ancient writing glows and is visible to the four Divinities. Akari reads the symbols at the top of the vault. "A piece of the chamber lies here, and only when it's assembled with the other four sections will the visions become reality."

"How did you decipher the squiggly lines and dots?" Dodge squints at the symbols.

Akari smiles. "The knowledge is in us. Let it be natural. Close your eyes, breath out, and open."

Nicolaus, María, and Dodge follow Akari's instructions, and when they open their eyes, the symbols translate into English.

"My guess is that a locket opens it." Akari points to the middle of the circle.

María takes off her necklace and holds the locket to the vault. With a dazzling glow and a burst of sparks, the door unlocks and swings open. Their eyes widen as they stare at the massive, five-inch-thick cylindrical glass eight feet long.

Nicolaus puts his hand to his temple. It's like a large test tube, or a small grain silo the size of a refrigerator. *Five pieces make up the chamber, two sides and two end-caps. What's the fifth? Is it a control mechanism?* Intrigued, Nicolaus takes a step forward and reaches out to touch the cool, smooth glass. In an instant, an intense halo of silhouettes mold around him. His eyes glow a brilliant emerald green. As he pulls his hand away, the once bright light fades.

The world turns pitch black, and a feeling of plummeting engulfs them. They grip onto walls and slide down, lying on the floor. Asa runs into the room and his body slows to a halt.

ꙨꙨꙨꙨ

They stand in the Divine library with Aamirah holding her iron sword. "Eight lockets and eight Divine Children. Five pieces to the chamber. Once you've found the eight lockets, you can retrieve the chamber pieces." Aamirah draws her sword. "You must do what I couldn't and kill Medium. Sinrye tied his life force to Medium when he created the Accursed. Kill Medium and both fall. If I die, then it breaks the bond, and Sinrye becomes the

Holy Divine. All worlds will become blackened by his fiery touch. It's imperative to go to New York as the next clues are there."

The shadow of Medium casts over them. The Accursed soldiers stand behind Aamirah, ready to strike. She grips the handle with both hands and disappears with a flash of light.

The Four Shadows of Light stand in the middle while the Accursed encircles them. Medium, mutters in a deep tone, and shakes the room with books falling into flames, "Sinrye, your death will be my victory." Medium leaps forward with his staph over the Four Shadows of Light and battles the Accursed.

۞۞۞۞

Nicolaus wakes up first, struggling to get to his feet. Asa helps Akari, and María helps Dodge.

"We need to find four more lockets and four more like us. Fucking seriously?" María stands with a firm stance and a hand on her hip.

Asa waves both arms out. "This is far as your parents got. The four of you and the four lockets. Once they sealed the chambers, they could not get back in, for they didn't know where the rest of the lockets were. You have one piece to the chamber, and you know the location of the second piece." Nicolaus nods, understanding the second piece of the chamber is at Shamrock Lake. "On the back wall, use a locket, which will reveal your parents' visions."

Akari drifts over, takes a deep breath, and places her locket in the circle. A spark emanates around her and the metal door creaks into the walls. The secret panel reveals the timeline of the Divinities from their parents' drawings and visions. The Four Shadows of Light stand in silence.

"You have much to discover. The past two weeks have prepped you for what is coming." Asa bows.

The sound of Nicolaus's phone grabs his attention, and he checks the message. They've got just an hour to reach the airport and start their journey to New York.

"Man, this was just getting fucking good," Dodge replies.

"We have to make a deal with the devil, so let's get this over with," says María.

Akari pulls out the photo, stares at it, and hands it to Nicolaus. He puts his left hand to his mouth. *This can't be right. His dad, Magnar, an Accursed?* His skin turns pale, stomach roils, he sits back down on the ground.

"Nicolaus, what the fuck is wrong?" He hands María the photo.

Akari sits down next to him. "There's got to be more to it." She hugs Nicolaus.

"Hey, I know this is some heavy shit—we have to get going to N-Y-C to go meet the G-R-E-C." Dodge smacks his leg.

Nicolaus nods as María holds out her hand to help him up. Akari stands up and holds his hand.

Asa turns to María and Dodge. "You two really need to clean up your language."

Dodge chuckles. "Are you going to wash out our mouths with soap?"

Asa huffs, and they walk out of the sanctuary. Once the lockets cross the threshold of the room, the metal door shuts. Akari grips Nicolaus's hand tighter. *It's a relay race. Their parents took the first leg and have now handed off the baton.*

Seo-Ah
of
Betrayal

(30)

Present

The Four Shadows of Light arrive in New York from a Kazanowski Moving Forces' private plane at a UFE military airstrip. As they exit the aircraft, wearing their high-tech full-body black suits, an entourage of Global Reform Establishment Coalition operatives with their guns at the ready to greet them.

A familiar face is waiting for them inside the limousine. "What are you doing here? You didn't answer my calls—" Akari asks.

Seok holds up her palm. "I'm here to make sure the deal goes through."

Nicolaus grits her teeth. "You sold us out to the Coalition and Federation."

"I represent DaeChie Pharmaceuticals. You may own it, but I run the company. I've worked my whole life to ensure that DaeChie becomes the leading provider of miracle drugs, and no one, and that means no one, is going to take that away from me."

Nicolaus's eyes narrow and bore into hers. "So—you turned your back on us," he says, his tone dripping. "You betrayed my mom, your supposed best friend?"

"Your mom had limited scope of the possibilities. My goal has always been to see you all complete the Trials of Divinity. I think she suspected—she never trusted me with the important details."

"I can't believe you betrayed us." Seok dismisses Nicolaus's comment and becomes entranced by the view beyond the windowpane.

With every passing minute inside the vehicle, the air seems to thicken, creating an atmosphere of unease as Akari never once takes her eyes off Seok. She is Akari's mentor at DaeChie Pharmaceuticals. *How could she deceive all of them?*

María grabs Dodge's hand with a crushing grip. "Yo, relax fiery lady, my hand is hurting."

As they pull into GREC headquarters and pass through the security checkpoint, the Four Shadows of Light feel a surge of anxious and angry emotions. The car door opens to a view of twenty Federation troops at attention outside the main entrance. Standing in front of them is a South Korean woman in her mid-twenties with a lean and toned figure. She's wearing a sleek, form-fitting uniform of black material with the UFE badge on the left with orange accent strips running down the middle. Her almond-shaped eyes are a deep emerald color, and a subtle smile curves her full lips.

Nicolaus's jaw drops as he stares into a face that's so eerily familiar.

"Hi, welcome to the Global Reform Establishment Coalition headquarters," she greets them. "My name is Seo-ah. I will take you to see Mr. Zhao." Her prominent nose gives her a regal appearance . . . a match for his mom's. *There's no way it's Mi-Cha.*

Akari lets go of his hand, walks to Seo-ah, and stands a foot from her. Seo-ah's pupils fluctuate from green to orange. A UFE officer grabs Akari's arm and she swats his hand away.

Nicolaus intertwines his arm with hers and whispers in her ear, "Do you have one of my lucky glitter bottles with you?" She nods. Nicolaus squints at Seo-ah. She blinks many times, like something in her brain was fighting, her arms twitch, and a subtle aura exudes from her until Carver, the new UFE lead of operations, yells for Seo-ah to move.

"Well, here we go into the belly of the beast," Dodge quips, staring up at the massive GREC headquarters high rise building before the troops part to allow them through the main lobby doors.

María's eyes dart back and forth from Seok to Seo-Ah. She witnesses a younger doppelgänger of Nicolaus's mom, Dae. María clutches Dodge's hand while she leans over and whispers to Akari, "That has to be Mi-Cha. But how? And—"

Akari clears her throat, interrupting María mid speech while they enter the elevator. Akari swings her backpack around, grazing one troop who glares at her. She reaches in, grabs the little plastic container the size of a lipstick and hands it to Nicolaus.

Nicolaus can't take his eyes off Seo-ah or Mi-Cha. His lip quivers. *What did they do to her?*

When the elevator reaches the fourteenth floor, they exit into an extravagant office space. Nicolaus grasps Seo-ah's arm, peers at her eyes, and speaks in Korean. "Are we there yet?" He passes her the glitter bottle. "Mi-Cha, remember—" Before he can finish, Seok pushes her way in the middle, swats the glitter bottle on the ground, separating the two of them.

She glares at Seo-ah. "Go tell Wei Zhao we are here."

Akari seethes. "Our whole life—you lead us to believe that you're part of our family. You are their spy."

"My sister—parents." Nicolaus picks up and squeezes the glitter bottle in his hand. "How could you do this?"

"I'll knock this treacherous bitch out right now." María moves forward, and three UFE pull their guns out.

"How do you think I paid back Pierce Roosevelt Financials? I reached a deal to save your parents' company. I will do what it takes to preserve it." She leans over to Akari's ear before entering the conference room. "Just assemble the chamber before it's too late. That's your focus."

They enter the conference room greeted by Wei Zhao and twenty individuals dressed in formal corporate business attire. He bows. "Let's get to business."

Zhao sits at the head of the table as Dodge mutters to María, "He looks like a Mafia boss." She grips his hand to keep him quiet.

"We'll keep this brief. What do you offer us, so we'll consider a truce?"

Akari glances around the room. She sees orange pupils and a light orange aura flickering throughout the board members while she puts her backpack on the table and grabs the bonded expandable binder. She throws the paperwork onto the table, landing in front of Zhao.

Nicolaus stands up. "Mr. Zhao, please open the binder." Nicolaus's eyes dart at Seo-ah or Mi-Cha out of the corner of his eye. "You will see our proposal for the three pharmaceuticals, the robotic companies, and GREC."

A lawyer moves from the back of the room next to Mr. Zhao, reviewing the high-level sheet of paper. They read the offer for the cure for type one diabetes, type two diabetes, spinal synthesis infusion cure, and robotic heart surgery.

"That won't work unless you double the offer, delivering four more exclusive patents not by next year but in one month, or we will engage." Zhao's cheek muscles twitch.

Nicolaus taps his foot, Dodge scowls, María rolls her eyes, and Akari's muscles tense with a sharp exhale, as if to say, *who do you think you are?* Nicolaus replies. "You have a deal, sir. We will deliver four exclusive licenses to you to distribute to the pharmaceutical and robotic companies."

Mr. Zhao smiles as his orange aura flickers and his voice transforms into a deep tone. "Sign over DaeChie to GREC." Sinrye's voice strangles Zhao's thoughts. *Take them, get their blood, and kill them.*

Seok strikes the chair arm. "That's not part of any deal. DaeChie is mine." She seethes, gripping the armchair. "If you want what is most desired, you will not take DaeChie."

"It's not yours. It's ours." Akari points to María, Dodge, and Nicolaus.

Seo-ah puts her hands on her gun holsters. Medium shouts in her head, *Protect Seok.*

Zhao twitches his neck. "This is my world, not yours!" The orange glow disappears. The board members' eyes flicker to their normal color. "GREC will have all control over the population with or without you, Seok." He pushes the chair out of the way as he stands, using the table to brace him. With a deep exhale, he says, "I would like you all to meet Walter Roosevelt's replacements." He clicks the intercom button. "Send them in."

The conference room door opens. "Meet Buchanan and Genevieve Roosevelt."

The board members chatter. A lady with a Russian accent stands up. "You can't be serious. This is an outrage. They are little children who belong in college, not in the most powerful organization in the world."

"They are more than qualified." Zhao motions his hands outward to quiet the boardroom. "Those two are ten times smarter than Walter himself. I'm confident that their academic accomplishments, business savvy, and not to mention their unwavering loyalty to GREC, will only help our cause." For the past couple of years, Genevieve has overseen Pierce Roosevelt Financials. Zhao enjoyed keeping Walter Roosevelt as the figurehead, but Seok altered his plans.

Buchanan clenches his jaw and strides toward Nicolaus, their faces mere inches apart, "I will avenge my father's death."

"I'm looking forward to the challenge."

Dodge jumps in. "Bring it. You spoiled rich bitch."

Genevieve replies, "Feisty. Maybe he'll be useful to me."

María angrily responds, "Bitch, you come near Dodge, and that pretty blonde head of yours will roll across the ground right next to Parsons's corpse."

Zhao yells, "I've heard enough! Everyone leaves except our four visitors, Seo-ah, and Seok." The chair back bends. "NOW!"

Once the last board member leaves the room, Seo-ah creeps closer to Seok.

María slams her fist on the table. "How can we be in the same room as this asshole and bitch who killed our parents?"

Nicolaus taps the top of the table. "Seok is your lifelong informant?"

"She has been a wonderful partner for many years—"

Seok interrupts Zhao. "I finished the spinal fusion miracle. I completed the diabetes cures. It was me, not your mothers, who did the hard work." She turns her head towards Zhao. "And GREC will not take DaeChie!"

Akari takes a deep breath. "Who is the Iron Scepter?"

Zhao rolls his eyes.

"Answer the fucking question, Zhao!" María yells, unable to control her anger; the glowing Divinity aura emanates around her body, ready to shatter the entire floor. Her knees weaken, and she slumps back into the chair.

Zhao roars while he scrutinizes Akari. His eyes flash to orange, and he presses a button twice on the control panel on the table. Four-foot-thick metal barriers slide downward to cover the conference room. A deafening buzzing sound drops everyone to their knees except Zhao and Seok. "Get their blood samples now!" He pulls out a gun and points it at Seok's head. She pulls out four metal tubes from her coat pocket.

Explosions and gunfire rattle the floor and the metal conference room doors stop and reverse upwards. Seok drops the metal tubes on the floor, trying to keep her balance. The piercing rings dissolve from their heads. The glass shatters and Veda slides into the room underneath the metal shades and shoots Zhao in the head. She turns and lays waste to four more UFE troops. "We have little time!"

Nicolaus and Akari crawl to Seo-ah. Nicolaus clasps her hand and Akari grabs Seo-ah's other hand. The three light up the room in white to orange to green, similar to a light show at a musical concert. The three let out a gasp as a surging pain vibrates their hearts. Through the connection, the details of his parents' death leak out, piece by piece.

Eleven years ago, his body lay on the ground with Mi-Cha in his limp arms. Seok bent down and kissed them on their cheeks. She whispered, "I'm sorry Nicolaus, this was the only way to protect Aamirah, and the eight of you." Veda picked up Mi-Cha and took her body away. The UFE cleaned up the scene and discussed the staging area for the police. Parsons took out a gun, ready to shoot the blacked-out Nicolaus, when Seok stood in the middle. "You can't kill him—we need them." He growled and stomped away.

Mi-Cha opens her eyes in disbelief. The initial shock gives way to overwhelming joy as she smiles ear to ear. "Brother? Akari?" The three of them spring up from the floor and they embrace in a group hug. Tears trickle down their cheeks and Nicolaus's skin prickles with goosebumps. A wave of freedom engulfs Mi-Cha, as if someone has lifted a heavy weight off her shoulders. Akari's heart swelled with the love of her long-lost sister. Questions whirl around them, their time together slipping away in a matter of moments.

Federation troops, and Coalition operatives rush to the floor. Veda throws two automatic handguns to María and Dodge. "I can use your help, otherwise we are all screwed." They take out twenty troops within thirty seconds.

With the silence on the floor, María takes an automatic gun from a fallen troop and points it at Veda. "I'll pull the trigger right now!"

"We're enemies." Veda holds her hands in the air. "But not today."

"Fucking traitor." Dodge spits on the ground.

"Please—if you were in my position, you would understand. Now put the gun down, María, so you all can get out of here alive."

María puts her finger on the trigger. "Why? Spit it out or I'll shoot your ass."

Veda smirks as she walks towards Seok. "There's a chopper heading to the roof to pick the four of you up. You must get to the chamber before Sinrye does." She shoots another bullet into Zhao's head. "He can't die with Sinrye in him—he regenerates thanks to,"—She sneers at Seok—"the triple agent."

Akari asks, "How can we trust you? The helicopter is a trap."

Veda sets down her gun, unsnaps a mini steel backpack, and slides it to Mi-Cha. She opens the case, and an exoskeleton Iron Scepter suite and gun sits inside.

Veda clicks a device the size of a lipstick container. Mi-Cha twitches her head, picks up the gun, and aims at Akari. "Iron Scepter, get Seok out of here."

Nicolaus clasps the glitter bottle in his pocket. Veda picks up her gun and points it at Nicolaus. "Your Divine powers don't work in this building. You felt it, María, didn't you? Mine and Mi-Cha do and that bastard on the floor does, too."

Seok's tone is curt and clipped. "GREC is a week away from locating the three other children of the Divine and the chamber locations. We need to combine forces to stop the Accursed. I need a sample of your blood to help you."

Nicolaus replies, "How do we know you won't kill us once you get what you need?"

"The same reason I didn't kill Mi-Cha or you—to see the Divine unleashed and to be the sole provider of cures. GREC can't and won't have it, along with Sinrye."

Akari, posture stiff, asks, "What about Mi-Cha's locket? We can't get into the chamber locations without it."

"She will be there when you need her with the fifth locket. That's a promise."

Nicolaus pulls out the glitter bottle and throws it towards Mi-Cha. She catches it in midair. "We'll give you the blood samples on one condition. After we assemble the chamber, whatever you've done to my sister, you will reverse."

"Done." Seok sighs. It's getting beyond rough for her to keep Mi-Cha's loyalty. Her love for her family and friends is creating major havoc for herself. She's upped the dosages, and just like any drug at a point, the resistance becomes too much to continue working.

Zhao's wounds are healing, and Veda fires another round into his skull. "Okay, another couple of minutes and this place will crawl with a ton more troops." She winks at María. "Glad you still have mad military skills without the powers. That's going to help you all on this journey."

Seok pokes the Four Shadows of Light with needles and draws four ounces of blood from each.

Dodge huffs, "Yo, this is some shit—steal our blood like a vampire, and then you're going to stab us in our back."

The Iron Scepter puts down her gun, places the exoskeleton suit on her back, and it wraps around her chest. The suit pairs up with the two-seater Federation glider waiting on the roof.

Seok nods to Mi-Cha. "We can go. I've got what I needed."

Veda fires two more rounds into Zhao. "That'll hold him off enough for us to get out of this building." She lowers her gun. "Let's get you all out of here."

They all climb the stairs to the rooftop and see the Kazanowski Moving Forces logo on the side of an advanced military helicopter touching down. The door opens with Mack Irons, rich, dark brown muscular skin, and clean-shaven head, with a few faint scars on his cheek and forehead, waves them to hurry as he sits in a chair mounted with a machine gun. He provides the cover as they bolt and jump into the chopper, except Nicolaus. With ten more UFE troops and GREC operatives returning fire, Nicolaus glows white. Mack Irons yells at Nicolaus over the constant firing of the machine gun to get on the chopper.

Zhao, with Sinrye's spirit, strolls onto the rooftop. He fires from his two automatic sidearms at Akari and Mi-Cha. Nicolaus closes his eyes, ignores the high-pitched whistling sound of the bullets, exhales, and fires from his sidearm. The bullets connect in the air, halting Sinrye's attempt to kill his sister and soulmate. Mack unloads the machine gun at Zhao, whose body flops onto the ground. Nicolaus climbs in and Henry Irons, with his lean toned frame, trimmed beard, and aviator glasses that he never leaves home without, pulls the cyclic control, and the helicopter lifts off. "Hey, hey. It's the amazing four super troopers."

Mi-Cha and Nicolaus peer at each other as she puts on her Iron Scepter helmet. She pulls out the glitter bottle and jiggles it in her hand, and places it back in her exoskeleton suit. She hears Seok screaming to leave and then takes flight off the building. Veda kills the last five troops on the roof with her handguns and then leaps into her solo piloted drone mini-glider. Her mind connects with Nicolaus's. *I will have you by my side.*

Mack Irons pulls his chair back into the helicopter and clicks a device for the camouflage panels to activate. Henry Irons starts the drone flares and blows up six GREC flyers.

Nicolaus shakes off Veda's mind intrusion and watches as the towering GREC headquarters shrink into the distance. His sister is now a speck in the sky. He contemplates the first time he laid eyes on his sister in the hospital. Just a little baby, kissing her on the cheek and saying I love you. He reflects about the EpicBloxx super tower he built recreating the Renaissance Center in Detroit. Her glitter sparkling on every outfit she wore or when she watched him get sacked in a football game, and everyone heard her roaring over the crowd, "That's my brother, I'll kick your ass."

María grabs Dodge's hand. "Hey, after we get the chamber assembled and have some sort of life after this, I wondered if you are ready to move in together?"

"For sure! Excited, smiling, blushing, and rock on emoji."

"Shut up and kiss me."

Akari puts her legs into a meditation pose. *Sinrye, GREC, UFE and the Accursed on one side. Veda, Seok, Mi-Cha, and Veda's UFE loyalists on another side. Aamirah, the Four Shadows of Light, and their friends and family on the third side. What about Medium—What side is he on? Where are the other pieces of the chamber hiding?* Their guess is Melodi is the sixth child of the Divine, but who are the other two? It's now their responsibility to take the baton and dive further to solve what their parents could not.

A chirping sound pierces their ears, and they blank out for a moment as Aamirah delivers a vision. *"You only have a fortnight left before Sinrye and the Accursed gain their full strength."* She hovers inside the sanctuary, her light reflecting off the ceiling.

She points to their parents' vision drawings on the wall. *"It may only be a day or two before Medium's spirit takes human form. Continue the path of the Trials of Divinity."* A light flashes and they stand in the Divine chapel before the condemned war. *"Faith does not make things easy—it serves as a guiding light during the toughest times."*

Check Out the Happenings

Stay ahead of the game and be the first to know about
Robert Andrew Sturm's latest news.

www.evolutionofvision.com

Acknowledgements

I am overwhelmed with gratitude to the many people who have supported me throughout my journey to write this novel. A heartfelt thank you goes out to my family and friends for their constant encouragement. Looking back on my journey, I realize it was the challenges of valleys and mountains that shaped me, and I am grateful for the invaluable presence of all of you in my life.

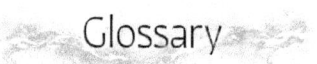
Glossary

Characters In Order of Appearance

Nicolaus Vasili Landowski (ni-KOH-lus vah-SEE-lee lan-DOW-skee)
Intrinsic Inventor, Child of the Divinity, Polish and Korean Heritage,
Expertise in Mechanical Engineering, and Information Technology
Architecture, Works at Pierce Roosevelt Financials & Investments

María Valkyrie Landowski-Jiménez
(mah-REE-ah VAL-kuh-ree lan-DOW-skee hee-MEH-nez)
Lethal Reckoning, Child of the Divinity, Polish and Mexican Heritage,
Expertise in Data Analytics, Works at UFE Contractor

Akari Kanani Iona (ah-KAH-ree kah-NAH-nee ay-OW-nah)
Graceful Assassin, Child of the Divinity, Japanese and Polynesian Heritage,
Expertise in Biological Scientist, Works at DaeChie Pharmaceuticals

Veton 'Dodge' Marku (VEH-ton DAHJ MAR-koo)
Sniping Jokester, Child of the Divinity, Albanian Heritage, Experitise in
User Experience, Graphic Design, Architecture Visual Design, Works at
Pierce Roosevelt Financials & Investments

Veda Devi (VEE-duh DEH-vee)
CEO United Federation of Enforcement, Born in India, Lead Commander on
The Four Shadows of Light Green Beret Operations

Marcin Landowski (MAR-chin lan-DOW-skee)
María's Father, Born in Poland, Owner Julieta & Marcin's Café Texas,
Professional Chef

Chie Iona (CH-iy-EH ay-OW-nah)
Akari's Mother, Divine Child Nativity, Owner DaeChie Pharmaceuticals,
Born in Hawaii

Keanu Iona (kee-AH-noo ay-OW-nah)
Akari's Father, Owner Iona Farms on Oahu, Professional Gardener, Born in
Hawaii

Dae Landowski (day lan-DOW-skee)
Nicolaus's Mother, Divine Child Nativity, Owner DaeChie Pharmaceuticals, Born in South Korea

Magnar Landowski (MAG-nahr lan-DOW-skee)
Nicolaus's Father, Blue Collar Mechanic and Inventor, Born in Poland

Mi-Cha Landowski (mee-chah lan-DOW-skee)
Nicolaus's Sister, Child of the Divinity, Photographic Memory

Julieta Landowski-Jiménez (hoo-lee-EH-tah lan-DOW-skee hee-MEH-nez)
María's Mother, Divine Child Nativity, The Original Divinity on Earth, Born in Mexico

Javier Lopez (hah-VYEH R LOH-pehz)
Cartel Leader, Julieta's Nemesis

Hamilton Parsons (HAE-mihl-tuhn PAHR-suhn-z)
UFE Operations Lead, Former Marine Special Forces, Mercenary

Lawrence Walsh (LAW-ruhns WAWLSH)
Gerald's Son, Former Army Cadet, Paintball Ally

Vincent (V IH n - s AA n t)
Marine Veteran, Paintball Ally

Wei Zhao (way jhao)
CEO Global Reform Establishment Coalition, Elitist, Born in China

Zander (zan-der)
Works at Pierce Roosevelt Financials & Investments

Michele (Mih-SH EH L)
Works at Pierce Roosevelt Financials & Investments

Walter Roosevelt (WAWL-tuhr ROH-zuh-velt)
CEO Pierce Roosevelt Financials & Investments, Elitist, Angel Invest in DaeChie Pharmaceuticals

Asa (AY-suh)
Magus, Magi or Sage, The Children of the Divinity Marital Arts Mentor

Aamirah (ah-MEER-ah)
Baby's Breath, Last Remaining Divinity, Telepathy, Divine Blood Carrier

Seok Quon (suhk kwahn)
Dae Landowski's Best Friend, CFO DaeChie Pharmaceuticals

Raj (rɑːdʒ)
Works at Pierce Roosevelt Financials & Investments

Kaili (K Ay Lee)
Akari's Cat

Casey Kazanowski (KAY-see kah-zah-NOW-skee)
Nicolaus's Godfather, Owner Kazanowski Moving Forces, Magnar's Best
Friend

Wayne Irons (wain ai·urnz)
Henry and Mack Irons Father, Air Force Veteran, Works at Both Pierce
Roosevelt Financials & Investments and Kazanowski Moving Forces

Byung-Ho (B AY AH NG HH OW)
Works at Pierce Roosevelt Financials & Investments

Jasmine (dʒæz.mɪn)
Works at Pierce Roosevelt Financials & Investments

Amber (æm.bər)
Works at Pierce Roosevelt Financials & Investments

Catalina Vargas
(kah-tah-LEE-nah VAR-guhs)
Dodge's Parental Guardians, Manage Julieta & Marcin's Café Texas,
Julieta's Adopted Mom

Herculano Vargas
(eh-RKuw-L AA -Now VAR-guhs)
Dodge's Parental Guardians, Manage Julieta & Marcin's Café Texas,
Julieta's Adopted Dad

Keahi Iona
(kee-AH-noo ay-OW-nah)
Akari's Cousin, Manages Iona Farms on Oahu

Gerald Walsh
(JER-awld WAWLSH)
Navy Seal Veteran, Owner Walsh Country Diner

Medium (mi:.di.əm)
Aamirah's Love, Anti-Divinity

Sinrye (Sin-I-Ree)
Leader of the Accursed, Anti-Divinity

Iron Scepter / Seo-Ah (eye-ern sep-tər / s uh h ah)
Works for GREC and UFE, Bible Reference: Revelations

Ricky (RIK-ee)
Era Texas Sheriff

Johnny (jahn-ee)
Army Ranger Veteran – Sniper

Frankie (frang-kee)
Army Ranger Veteran – Sniper

Andrzej Kowalczyk (AHN-jay Koh-VAWL-chik)
Family and DaeChie Pharmaceuticals Attorney, Owner Kowalczyk Law
Firm

Buchanan Roosevelt (buh-CAN-nən ROH-zuh-velt)
Walter Roosevelt's Son, Works at Pierce Roosevelt Financials &
Investments

Genevieve Roosevelt (JIN-ah-veev ROH-zuh-velt)
Walter Roosevelt's Daughter, Works at Pierce Roosevelt Financials &
Investments

Mack Irons (mak ai·urnz)
Air Force Veteran, Wayne's Son, Works at Kazanowski Moving Forces

Henry Irons (henrı ai·urnz)
Air Force Veteran, Wayne's Son, Works at Kazanowski Moving Forces

Places, Organizations, Corporations, and Extras

DaeChie Pharmaceuticals
Owned by: Akari's Parents, Akari, Nicolaus, and María, Divinity Cures,
Independently Owned Pharmaceutical Company

Julieta & Marcin's Café
Three Locations: Texas, Michigan, Seattle

Global Reform Establishment Coalition (GREC or Coalition)
Manipulates Media Narrative, Influences All Governments, Geopolitics

United Federation of Enforcement (UFE or Federation)
Borderless Troops – Diplomatic Immunity, Soldiers from 112 Countries

Iona Farm
Owned by Akari's Parents, Managed by Akari's Extended Family, Location:
Oahu, Hawaii

Pierce Roosevelt Financials & Investments
CEO: Walter Roosevelt; Shadow Banking, Most Profitable Global Firm,
Government Influence

Kazanowski Moving Forces
Owned by: Casey Kazanowski, Top Rated United States Moving Company,
Michigan Headquarters

The Accursed
Army of the Anti-Divinities

Melodi Marku (meh-LOH-dee MAR-koo)
Dodge's Sister, Runs Kowalczyk Law Firm Michigan

The Ranch
Family Retreat, Divine Location: Era, Texas

The Mountain Cabin
Family Retreat, Divine Location: Snoqualmie, Washington

The Country Walsh Diner
Veteran Hangout, Location: Era, Texas

Ammunition Coffee Café
Veteran Owned Coffee Chain, Pending Iona Farm Coffee Deal

Asa Dojo
Owned by: Asa - Magus, Divine Training Location: Plano, Texas

Warring Combat Zone
Veteran Owned Paintball Field, Holds Battle of the Armed Forces

EpicBloxx
Building Blocks Company, Historic Landmarks & Famous Cities

Gjergj Kastrioti
Historical Reference: Skanderbeg, Led Rebellion Against the Ottoman Empire

Queen Tueta
Historical Reference: Queen Regent of the Ardiaei Tribe in Illyria

About the Author

As a debut author, I've embarked on an ambitious six-part novel series. Throughout its journey, I have drawn inspiration from experiences that left a lasting impact on my soul, shaping the storyline. Woven within the fabric of the pages, I hope you, as a reader, will create a powerful and empathetic connection. I weave fantasy, religion, modern concepts, romance, science fiction, and a dash of conspiracies into my writing.

Armed with 27 years in the creative media industry, you'll catch me grinning ear-to-ear crafting narratives. By designing for users, I have developed a knack for connecting with diverse audiences and what resonates with people on a deeper level. My support for the military, teachers, first responders, and hardworking everyday humans also shapes the characters and themes. Throughout the plot, my unwavering faith and belief in a higher power add a layer of spiritual depth and serve as a source of inspiration and upliftment.

As you delve into the text, I invite you on a storytelling ride with the series' central characters, 'The Four Shadows of Light.' They face their inner demons with divine blessings and fight against evil together, driven by pure hearts and teamwork. This journey, sparked in my imagination, will captivate and inspire you to explore your inner battles, triumphs, laughter, and love.

When not writing or designing, I immerse myself in movies, television shows, reading, jamming to music, exercising, and video games. Like a deep-dish pizza overflowing with cheese, the book series captures the gravity of my life. Inspiration strikes in random places like rodeos, arboretums, museums, cross-country drives, or sipping coffee in a café. Above all else, I'm a proud father cherishing every moment spent with my girls.

Let's embrace our spirits and lose ourselves in the captivating realm of enthralling and evocative fiction.

The
Breadth
of
Família

Book 2

Coming 2025